THE
GRAVEDIGGER

THE
GRAVEDIGGER

a novel

PETER GRANDBOIS

CHRONICLE BOOKS
SAN FRANCISCO

First Chronicle Books LLC paperback edition, published in 2007.

ISBN-10: 0-8118-5818-9
ISBN-13: 978-0-8118-5818-2

The Library of Congress has cataloged the previous edition as follows:
Grandbois, Peter.
The gravedigger : a novel / Peter Grandbois.
      p. cm.
ISBN-13: 978-0-8118-5350-7
ISBN-10: 0-8118-5350-0
1. Spiritualists—Fiction. 2. Gravediggers—Fiction. 3. Spain—Fiction. I. Title.

Manufactured in the United States of America

Cover and interior design by Brooke Johnson
Composition by Janis Reed
Cover photo by Steve Cole/Getty
Cover bird illustration by Getty

Distributed in Canada by
Raincoast Books
9050 Shaughnessy Street
Vancouver, British Columbia V6P 6E5

10 9 8 7 6 5 4 3 2 1

Chronicle Books LLC
680 Second Street
San Francisco, California 94107

www.chroniclebooks.com

For Elena, Olivia, and Santiago

And for Tanya, who opened my eyes

Everywhere else, death is an end. Death comes, and they draw the curtains. Not in Spain. In Spain they open them . . . A dead man in Spain is more alive as a dead man than anyplace else in the world.

—*García Lorca*

We are sunk in a sea of riddles and inscrutables, knowing and understanding neither what is around us nor ourselves.

—*Schopenhauer*

*Because the story of our life
becomes our life . . .*

—*Lisel Mueller*

1

La tierra de la verdad

HIGH IN THE SIERRA DE LA CONTRAVIESA, southeast of the gypsy caves of Granada, a small, whitewashed village, indistinguishable from any other in Andalucia, hangs precipitously from a cliff, overlooking on one side the valley below and the Rio Yátor that waters the valley, and on the other the wild olive and poplars, which cover the hills rolling gently down to the sea. The house of *el enterrador*, the gravedigger, lies a short distance along the cliffs away from the town. Tradition in the Alpujarras says that a gravedigger must live outside a town's walls so that the ghosts who visit him will not bother the town, and the ghosts who visited Juan Rodrigo were many.

Juan Rodrigo was a poor man, his possessions few. The roof of his house leaked when it rained, and though his fence badly needed repair, his burro was too old to try to escape. He lived alone with his daughter, his wife having died shortly after Esperanza's birth thirteen years earlier.

"Bueno, Viejo," Juan Rodrigo said to his burro. "We have work to do today." His callused hand, the fingernails broken and

dirty, caressed the mule's head. "It is the last grave I'm going to dig." And with that, he looked at the many graves about him, most of them people he knew, people he'd had to bury.

As he walked, his burro followed. The sun beat down heavily upon them both. He wiped the sweat away from his eyes, not stopping long enough to let the flies gather. *"Qué calor,"* he said to his burro, as if the burro didn't already know.

The cemetery spread out along the spine of the cliffs overlooking both the valley and the sea, while across the ridge, on the other side of the village, the church stood on a rock outcrop with a view only of the valley. The villagers joked that it was the dead who had the better view. Juan Rodrigo's house leaned into the wind, below the cemetery, below the entire village in fact, so that it seemed as if he was always tired from climbing the pathway through the cliffs to one spot or another.

The burro snorted and brayed when Juan Rodrigo spoke, nuzzling his head against his master's palm. Ursula, the little girl in white, sat in the dirt, waiting for them. Her presence unsettled the mule, and the man's hand once again reassured him. Juan Rodrigo had often wondered if El Viejo was able to see the four-year-old, or at the very least, smell her. Esperanza had never been able to and she'd grown jealous.

"Tiene celos tambien, Viejo," Juan Rodrigo said. "Well, don't. You at least have life. That child brings nothing but sadness." Then he squinted at the sun. "Not an easy day to dig a grave, not even a small one."

The girl in white took his hand, and all three continued on. *"Qué raro,"* the gravedigger said. "All these years and never before did I ask who buried you."

The girl looked at him with round, dark eyes, eyes that until that moment had appeared unnatural. Now they seemed simply the eyes of a child. "Your father," she said.

"Well, it must have been before I was born," the grave-digger replied. "I don't remember it."

He rubbed his crooked nose between his thumb and fore-finger. The mule had heard the story of his crooked nose as often as the old man's daughter, maybe more.

"You know how my nose became crooked?" he would say, a mischievous smile upon his lips. Esperanza would giggle and ask, "How?" Then Juan Rodrigo pushed his nose to the side with his finger, exaggerating the bend. "I stuck it in your mother's ass, and she farted to teach me a lesson!" They erupted in laughter, Esperanza saying, "That's not true!" and he swearing on the grave of his mother that it was. Being in the profession, he was normally not a man to swear upon a grave, but he knew his mother would appreciate the joke. She'd had the dirtiest mind in the village.

They stopped beneath an olive tree whose limbs gave much shade. From the limbs of the tree one could gaze upon both the sea before them and the river running through the valley behind. "She's not going in the stew pot with the rest of the poor," he said to his burro. "I'll tell you that! I'm putting my Esperanza by her mother and *me cago en la leche* of anyone who complains!" With that, he turned to the headstone that marked his wife, Carlota's, grave and said, "I'm glad now that your sister had you buried here with the dandies and the snobs."

With those words he gazed out over the distant sea, attempting to gather his strength for the job ahead. The burro waited patiently, as he had always done. The flies gathered, but the old man no longer cared. Finally he turned, placed his foot upon the shovel and pressed it to the earth, then paused. *"Tengo que decirle algo. Un cuento muy triste,* I have to tell you something. A sad story."* He always addressed his mule in the formal way. It was a sign of respect for one so old. And then breathing a heavy sigh, he pushed the shovel into the earth. He'd grown used to the change that came over him upon first breaking the ground, but this time he seemed to choke on the warm shock of air.

"On the night she was born, the gypsies came out of their caves, smelling jasmine. They followed the scent all the way to our village, and when they saw her beautiful face, they threw a party that lasted seven days and seven nights. Throughout her life, people remarked on the smell of jasmine that surrounded her wherever she went." Juan Rodrigo paused. The mule brayed, as if attempting to coax him to continue with his tale.

"That's not what happened, Papá," a voice from behind him said. He looked at the four-year-old girl, who sat before him, but she only smiled. Afraid to turn around, he began digging again. The mule kicked at the dirt, and Juan Rodrigo patted his head. Still, he would not turn. It was only when he caught the scent of jasmine that he could no longer help himself, and he turned with tears in his eyes to see his Esperanza standing behind him in her green dress, the one he'd bought for her nearly nine months before.

"You never did let me tell a story my way, did you, *mi corazón*," he said. The pain in his heart was strong.

"I thought you said stories should be true, not fanciful," she replied.

"It is true," Juan Rodrigo shouted, the joy at taking part in their old arguments allowing him to forget his grief. "The gypsies did come!"

"Why didn't I smell the jasmine, then?"

"Because your nose was always busy getting in other people's business!"

"That's not true!" Esperanza stomped her foot; the four-year-old girl giggled. Esperanza shot her a look, and Juan Rodrigo noticed that his daughter finally had her wish. She could see where others couldn't.

"So now it's your turn to tell me what is true and what is not," Juan Rodrigo said, smiling and allowing the smile, at least for the moment, to draw the pain from his heart.

"I have a mind of my own, Papá."

"That I know," Juan Rodrigo replied, leaning on his shovel. "That I know."

The four-year-old girl stood, taking his hand in hers. "Tell us the story," she said.

Esperanza was not jealous, as she'd been so many times before. Instead, she waited, watching her father. Juan Rodrigo stood, staring at both the girls. Flowers, the color of peaches, lined the waist of Ursula's white cotton dress, purple and green ribbons hanging from each flower. It was a child's dress, yet it seemed such a short time ago that he'd seen Esperanza in a similar one. And look at her now, he thought. If I'd have known the way that green dress was going to look on her, I would have never let Mercedes convince me to buy it.

But then it was as if Juan Rodrigo was no longer aware of either of them, as if *he* were the one not of this world, for the memories filled his heart and mind until he was lost to the present. Esperanza took his hand as well, and both girls led him to the olive tree, where they sat and listened. Juan Rodrigo told the tale, as he'd so often done in the past, but this time he was not aware of the telling, for to him the events seemed as real as if they were happening at that very moment. So, when he began to speak, he also gazed down the hill that led up to the cemetery and smiled to see his Esperanza coming toward him.

The Story of Sofia and César

"El Romancero viene, Papá!" Esperanza yelled as she ran up the path from the village. "Can we go? Please, let's go see him, Papá!"

"I don't know, *mi corazón*," Juan Rodrigo replied. "Have you finished your schoolwork?"

"No," she said. She thought for a moment that her father wouldn't let her go and began to pout.

"And your chores," Juan Rodrigo continued, feigning seriousness. "The henhouse has not been cleaned."

"But, Papá, I'll do it tomorrow, and you can help me with my schoolwork tonight," she said, realizing her father had almost tricked her into giving in. She would show him. "And El Romancero only comes once a year. Oh, I remember the last time so well. The story of the young Isabel and how she became queen . . ."

"It was poorly told, and not even true," Juan Rodrigo replied. "I could tell you a story, Esperanza, that would—"

"Come, Papá!" She took his hand and began pulling. "Your stories are fine, but this is El Romancero. He brings stories from beyond the village!"

Juan Rodrigo resisted just enough so that she would have to struggle to move him. He liked these exchanges. They reminded him of the flamenco he'd danced in his youth: the give-and-take of the spirit.

"Hurry, Papá!" Esperanza almost pulled her father over. "We'll miss him."

"Good!" Juan Rodrigo said. "His stories are all art and no craft!" But as he spoke, he let his daughter lead him down the hill.

"Venga, Papá!" She pulled him so fast now they were almost running.

"First I must clean my hands," he continued. "And you. You must make yourself presentable. You look as if you've been playing amongst the rocks all afternoon, and I've no doubt that's exactly what you've been doing."

MOST OF THE VILLAGERS had already gathered in La Plaza de Los Naranjos. Being late October, the orange trees were beginning to bloom, and many of the villagers ate the oranges straight off the trees as they waited. The crowd surrounding the colorful wagon in the center of the plaza was already quite large. It seemed the whole village was in attendance, the women dressed in black as usual, their hair pinned with *peinetas*. The men occupied the opposite end of the plaza, many of them adding a bit of color to their dark wardrobe with a red-flannel sash about their waist. The younger women staked out their space in small groups dotting the outskirts of the crowd. Perfumed and dressed to dazzle, they stood like statues before the tiled walls, only moving to fan themselves or to conveniently cover their face whenever a man looked in their direction. The young men smoked together behind the gypsy wagon, each daring the other to walk past and tip his hat at a select group of ladies. The only reward for this act of courage: If one of the ladies should glance at the man as he passed, he knew he might have a chance and then might dare to walk by her window that night to see if she had put out a pot of sweet basil. And if he finds himself so lucky, he will creep through the shadows beneath her window to steal a leaf and press it to his lips. There, he must wait. If a neighbor or family member catches him, he will have given up his chance forever. But if he remains concealed until his chosen approaches the window, he can then break the leaf and stick his hand through the iron grate, placing the other piece upon her lips. The next day, they will announce their betrothal.

Juan Rodrigo arrived at the plaza and paused, taking in the wondrous olfactory concoction of oranges combined with the great variety of women's perfumes. He wondered where his friend Pedro was, then eyed him laughing with José and Enrique in the back of the crowd. He joined them just as Esperanza spied her friends Anna and Eugenio in the front row. She ran from her father, squeezing her way through the crowd to kneel beside them.

"*Mis amigos,* you won't believe what Juan Rodrigo's burro did the other day," Pedro remarked.

"I swear that burro has a mind all his own," Juan Rodrigo chimed in, already laughing.

"We'd loaded El Viejo up with the cheap northern wine to take to Pepe's party, but the old fart wouldn't move," Pedro continued.

"He just looked at us." Juan Rodrigo was all smiles, waiting for the rest of the story. Pedro always knew how to tell a funny story, and Juan Rodrigo appreciated that.

"Yes," Pedro went on. "He looked at us as if to say that the northern wine was not worthy of him. I told Juan Rodrigo that his burro had become a connoisseur."

"I suggested that we try the sweet Malaga wine," Juan Rodrigo said, "since El Viejo has such an exquisite palate. But—"

"And sure enough," Pedro interrupted, "as soon as we loaded the old fart up with the barrels, he took off straight for Pepe's house!" The men burst out in laughter, José doubling over in a fit of coughing after.

El Romancero had a flair for the dramatic and, being a veteran of the stage, knew the value of a delayed entrance. Waiting behind the curtain, guitar in hand, he watched the crowd reach just the right level of agitation, and as soon as a couple of older women in the back began to walk away, he emerged, flamboyantly tossing his cape over his shoulder. The younger children were at first shocked by the fact that he appeared much older than they'd expected. The others, having seen El Romancero in previous years, knew better. He spoke slowly at first, and softly, knowing that the best way to grab the crowd's attention was to make them strain to hear him. When he knew he had them, he let forth with the full tremor of his voice.

"Illustrious citizens," he boomed so that even his own thin body shook. "I come from beyond the mountains, from lands beyond time, from worlds even the gypsies have not seen, to tell you a tale of love more tragic than any you have heard told before." He surveyed the crowd, noting the wide eyes of the children, the hopeful stares of the women, and the veiled attention of the men, and he knew they would believe whatever he chose to say. Slowly, he walked across the small stage that unfolded from his wagon and sat gazing at the clouds, as if their very shape would dictate the form of his story.

He struck the strings so loud the children in the front row jumped back. "A great lord there was in Aragon by the name of Juan Carlos, who loved to hunt, spending his days roaming the woods about his kingdom." Having gotten their attention, he plucked the strings more softly, bringing forth music that was in reality quite accomplished. "He was a fine man," he continued. "Well esteemed by his people for his generosity of spirit. A noble man and handsome. One day, while out walking, he spotted the lovely Maia, washing her golden hair in a nearby pond. Fairies flitted about the maiden, bringing her a comb of silver, a washbasin of pearl, and encircling her with beautiful colored scarves. Her arms were as white as the snow, her feet as slender as the ocean's foam." Here, the music flowed like water over the rapt audience. "Juan Carlos fell in love instantly. And he could see by the shimmer in her eyes that she, too, loved him. Against the will of the fairies, he took Maia back to his castle and made her his wife."

"You see how he has to embellish everything," Juan Rodrigo said to his friends. "He covers up the truth with his 'feet like the ocean's foam.' Whoever heard of such nonsense?"

"You have a point there," Enrique replied. "Of course, we know that no one can compete with your ability, Juan Rodrigo." Enrique nudged Pedro with his elbow.

"At least my storytelling is a far cry better than your cooking!" Juan Rodrigo replied, clearly pleased with his quick retort.

"It so happened that Juan Carlos had a brother named Esteban, different from him in every respect," El Romancero continued. "Lazy and greedy, he was always looking to take what was not his. When Esteban came to visit, he took one look at Maia and fell deep into a love sickness. Then he retired to a cottage at the edge of Juan Carlos's land, where he concocted his plans to win the beautiful Maia, telling his brother only that he'd fallen ill and needed rest."

"*Brujas y diablos!*" an old woman with wild hair screamed. "You're all witches and devils, cursed to rot in your foul holes, all of you!" The old woman pushed her way through the crowd, interrupting El Romancero's tale. Some of the villagers grabbed their children and covered their ears; others crossed themselves, making way for her as she marched toward the stage. "And you," the old woman continued, pointing her finger at El Romancero. "You call yourself a storyteller, when you know nothing of the despair in people's hearts."

"Good lady," El Romancero responded, visibly flustered. "If you don't mind . . ."

"You are no better than a worm!" she screamed, the sound of her voice driving El Romancero back against the curtain. "A worm making his living by distorting other people's lives."

"Do I know you?" El Romancero asked, and there was a glimmer of understanding in his eyes.

"I curse you with the vilest of curses!" the old woman ranted. "May your tongue shrivel up, and your heart grow empty as mine has done!" And with that, she stormed away, cursing the villagers as she passed them. Poor Matilde actually fainted when the old woman grabbed her by the cheek and called her a whore!

El Romancero had grown pale as a result of the disturbance, and with the appropriate theatrical flourish begged to be given a brief respite during which he could gather himself to continue with the tragic tale.

Esperanza ran to her father, while the villagers gossiped wildly about the appearance of the old woman. "Is that the one I've heard about?" she asked her father. "The witch who cursed the birds so that they don't come around anymore?" And, not receiving an answer, she continued talking to herself. "Her eyes were flecked with gold, like Mamá's."

Juan Rodrigo looked at his daughter, the light in her own eyes reminding him more of her mother than anything else. "Really," he replied. "I hadn't noticed."

"Yes. Yes. They were just like you told me Mamá's were," Esperanza continued. "You said that the gold came from the Berber blood, and that Mamá must have had some."

"And you as well."

"Maybe she's a Berber sorceress from Africa!" Esperanza clapped her hands together. "Or maybe she's an escaped slave of the Caliphate."

"I'm sure she's none of that, *mi corazón*."

"Is she from this village?" Esperanza asked, not really wanting to hear the answer, as it would mean an end to her fantasies.

"Yes," he replied. "She has lived on the outskirts for a long time. But she rarely makes herself known."

Just then El Romancero returned to the stage with an alacrity that belied his age and the fact that he had recently appeared so shaken. "Good people," he called out. "I do not want to deprive you of my tale's end."

"No, we wouldn't want that," Juan Rodrigo said. Normally, Esperanza would have given him a pinch or a kick for such a comment, but this time she didn't hear him, as she was still thinking of the old woman's golden eyes.

"If you'll grant me your indulgence, I shall continue," El Romancero said, sitting now on the edge of the stage itself, gently plucking the strings of his guitar. He waited until all was silent, then began. "Learned in the art of sorcery, Esteban bewitched poor Maia." The children in the audience leaned forward. "And she gave herself to him, though her heart was aware of her body's betrayal."

The music increased in tempo. "Juan Carlos knew nothing of his brother's treachery, but the fairies sensed that their beloved Maia was heartsick." And now, as it would until the end of the tale, the music moved like a heavy march, building the tension. "Planning to take his treasure far from his brother's kingdom, he sat his prize atop his horse and then mounted another, taking only a few possessions and riding through the fairies' woods. But Maia reined her horse in as they entered the woods, her broken heart exerting itself to return to her beloved Juan Carlos. The fairies took advantage of the moment and unleashed their magic. Maia's snow-white neck grew long, her arms extending into wings as she flew from her horse. She flew high above the treetops only to settle in the same pond she'd visited so often before. Esteban's face grew flat, his skin turned green, and his body elongated. He slithered off his horse and snaked his way into the woods, never to be heard from again. Juan Carlos, of course, searched high and low for his beloved, often visiting the pond where he'd first espied her, but seeing there only a beautiful swan. He swore that if ever he found her, he would take her to the land of eternal youth."

El Romancero strummed his guitar to a crescendo. Then, all in one grand movement, he rose, flipped his cape around him, and bowed deeply. "Thank you, my gracious people. Thank you for allowing an artist to unburden his heart!"

"Now I've heard everything," Juan Rodrigo said.

"As you all know," El Romancero continued, "the work of an artist is difficult, the monetary rewards few. So, if you would be so kind, my hat awaits your generous thanks." He twirled the cap from his head and walked through the audience, bowing graciously to each villager who tossed in a coin.

"It's a wonder he can get up after such bows," Juan Rodrigo said, winking at his friends.

"Papá," Esperanza implored. "You're not being fair. He's a good man, and his story was beautiful."

"*Mi corazón* . . ." Juan Rodrigo replied.

"And she turned into a swan. How lovely!" Esperanza went on. "I'll bet Juan Carlos found Maia and then hired a sorcerer to change him into a swan as well so he could be with his beloved forever."

"It would serve him right to be turned into a bird!" Juan Rodrigo said, laughing.

Juan Rodrigo and his friends said their good-byes, and as he and Esperanza made their way down the path through the olive trees to their home, Esperanza clung to her father's arm, talking dreamily of the lovers' tale. The afternoon sun filtered through the olive branches, creating a shadow play of light and dark on the pathway before her, fueling her imagination; the sound of the wind whistling through the cliffs made the perfect accompaniment to her fantasies.

"That manipulator of truth knows better," Juan Rodrigo told her. "The way he carts himself from town to town, peddling those theatrical clichés he calls stories! He knows the truth as well as I."

"You know the story of Juan Carlos and Maia?" Esperanza asked. "Papá, tell it to me again."

"I'm sure you wouldn't like the way I tell it, Esperanza," Juan Rodrigo said, pulling his daughter close. He enjoyed walking with her. It seemed these moments came seldom lately. "You see, the real Juan Carlos was no Aragonese lord, he was a flower shop owner named César, who lived in the village on the other side of the valley, and Maia was a sickly girl named Sofia who had hardly any friends."

"Papá, you're not even talking about the same people."

"Yes, they are the same," Juan Rodrigo replied. "Their story has been forgotten over time, distorted by traveling charlatans, but it remains their story nonetheless."

The setting sun was behind them now, and the first stars appeared before them. Esperanza shivered, and Juan Rodrigo took off the tattered brown suit jacket he wore whenever he went into the village and placed it around her shoulders. "Not every star in the night sky represents the life of a king or hero," he said. "There are a few reserved for the common folk." Juan Rodrigo stopped and pointed at the sky. "I have it on good authority, for example, that the bright one just over the horizon there is reserved for you," he said, winking at his daughter. "Though I would not begin to say that you are common, and I think it will be many years before that star will have your willful spirit to fire its light."

"Which stars hold the spirits of Sofia and César, Papá?"

"None, yet," he replied. "For their story is not over. César's supposedly evil brother, whose name was Nacho, died a long time ago, and no one knows what happened to Sofia or César."

"How do you know about them, Papá?" Esperanza sat on a nearby rock, hoping to hear more.

"Nacho told me after he died," Juan Rodrigo replied, sitting down next to his daughter. "It is a beautiful night, is it not?"

"Yes, Papá, but tell me more," she said, squeezing his hand.

"Well," Juan Rodrigo said, looking to the trees and rocks, as if for approval. "Shortly after your mother died, a ghost came to visit me. Very strange, as this ghost was from the village across the valley." The wind picked up, and Juan Rodrigo stopped to listen to its mournful moan. Satisfied with what the wind said, he nodded his head, knowing it was all right to continue the story. "Across the valley they don't have a gravedigger anymore," he said. "It seems they don't believe in them. They've gone modern, even offering cremations!" Juan Rodrigo stopped and chuckled to himself.

"What are cremations, Papá?"

"You don't want to know, *mi corazón,*" Juan Rodrigo replied. "For in a cremation the body does not get the time to adjust to its new situation. No time to greet the earth, to return to it slowly." He shook his head. "That is why the ghost traveled across the valley to me, for a living being to whom he could tell his story."

"That was Nacho, the evil brother, right?"

"He was not evil," Juan Rodrigo said, turning to her. "Life is rarely so simple as good and evil, though the church and the politicians would like us to believe that way!"

"Tell me," Esperanza demanded, "did Nacho put a spell on her?"

"No," Juan Rodrigo replied. "Nothing like that. But, to understand what happened, you must hear the story from the beginning."

Esperanza listened, wide-eyed. He began the story the way he always began his stories: "On the day she was born the lizards came to the village by the hundreds and settled upon the outer walls and porches of the houses. Upon seeing the ugliness of her face, they stayed for seven days and seven nights, covering the village in their *mierda*. It took them a month to wash all that shit away."

"No, Papá," Esperanza interrupted. "She was not ugly. She was beautiful, with snow-white skin like a swan."

"I'm sorry to say it, but she was ugly," Juan Rodrigo replied, looking into his daughter's eyes, wishing he could tell the story the way she wanted it but knowing that would not be right. "She fought constantly at school, as the kids made fun of her."

"No!" Esperanza screamed, pulling away from her father, standing before him. "If you're not going to tell it right, then I don't want to hear it."

Juan Rodrigo rose, wiping off his hands on his trousers. "It's your choice, *mi corazón*," he said. "I can only tell stories that have truth."

"But how do you know that *your* story is the true one?"

Juan Rodrigo paused, frowning at his daughter. He hated when she did this. Then he gazed at the stars, searching for an answer. Finding none, he cocked his head, listening to the wind, but since no answer was forthcoming there either, he decided to rely on his paternal authority. "I just know, that's all!"

"Well, I'm not going to listen," Esperanza replied, turning from him.

They walked the rest of the way home under the moonlight, Esperanza desperately wanting to hear the rest of the story but not wanting to concede on so important a point, and Juan Rodrigo wishing he could give in to his daughter's desire but knowing he was unable.

THROUGHOUT THE REMAINDER of the week, Esperanza found herself dreaming day and night about the lovers; she'd also not forgotten the fact that the old woman's eyes were so much like her mother's. She'd thought she knew everyone in the village, and the fact that her father and the other adults had kept the woman's presence a secret intrigued her, at least just enough that on the following Saturday, after going to the Oliveiras' for milk and fresh baked bread, Esperanza took the long route home, passing close to the area where she'd heard the old woman lived. She'd dropped subtle questions around the village all week, picking up bits of information, mostly rumors about the spells the old woman had supposedly cast on various villagers over the years, but she also got a sort of general agreement as to the location of the old woman's cottage.

The way wound through the cliffs across the village from Esperanza's house. It was arduous going at first, as the cliffs on the western end dropped steeply, leveling out only after seventy meters or so and finally opening to a pine-and-fir forest with cork oak and poplars interspersed throughout. The rocks kept Esperanza entertained, as she loved climbing, and, once in the forest, she imagined herself to be the beautiful Maia, with fairies as her servants. Her daydreams kept her fear at bay, for in truth she was afraid; these woods were unfamiliar to her. The trees seemed closer together, and the red rocks took on a darker shade, as if bruised by the little sunlight that made it through the trees.

Esperanza walked warily, not really wanting to meet the old woman, but rather hoping for a glance again of those eyes so that she could imagine what her mother must have looked like, if only for a moment. And besides, she could tell her friends that she'd found the old woman's house. They wouldn't believe her, and she'd have the added pleasure of leading an expedition there.

The stone cottage sat next to a small pond, whose waters reached nearly to the garden that wrapped around the house. The entire area was overgrown with scrub oak that pricked Esperanza's legs as she walked. She couldn't see the old woman, but she could hear her singing, her voice scratched and broken, like one who has eaten her way up from beneath the earth.

When Esperanza stepped forward, the singing stopped. She turned to run, but the woman was before her.

"What do you want?" the old woman asked, her voice even more rough than when she sang.

Esperanza's legs urged her homeward. But, instead, much to her surprise, she kept her head low and answered, "I am Esperanza Rodrigo. My father is the gravedigger." I will be polite, she thought. And then I will tell her I must go to help my father. Her mind attempted to convince her that she remained of her own free will, when in reality, while she was afraid to stay, she was even more afraid to run. The old woman might take offense and turn her to stone.

"An ancient profession," the old woman said. "I didn't know they existed anymore." And saying that, she leaned in close, as if she couldn't see well and wished to study the girl before her.

The skin of the woman's face appeared dark and deeply wrinkled, like rock chiseled away by wind and time. The front teeth in both the top and bottom of her mouth were missing, and her breath smelled of garlic and rotten apples.

"Are you a little imp sent by the witches of the village?" the old woman asked, her face hovering inches from Esperanza's. The stench of sour milk could now be added to the other foul odors on her breath.

Esperanza raised her gaze, willing herself to focus on the old woman's eyes, which, though they were tired and red, were flecked with gold. Leaves rested in the woman's hair as if they'd simply fallen from the trees and landed there.

"No," she answered. "I told you. I'm the daughter of Juan Rodrigo, the gravedigger."

"Does your father talk to ghosts?"

"Yes." Esperanza stepped backward, again thinking of escape. The old woman moved closer.

"Good!" The old woman cackled. "Maybe I'll talk to him once I'm dead. I have been alone for far too long."

"My father needs me to help him."

"Nonsense!" The old woman grabbed Esperanza by the arm before she had a chance to get away. "You will sit with me and tell me what you know of the village. I bet you've never tasted anything like my apple cider." With that, the old woman let go of Esperanza and turned for the door. "Come," she said. "Tell me, is Matilde still the gossip she always was? And Isabel's garden, is it still the most beautiful in the village?" She didn't wait for an answer but rather walked to her back door, farting with each step. Esperanza let slip a giggle, then covered her mouth, afraid she would anger the woman. But the old woman simply waved her hand back through the door, signaling for Esperanza to enter.

Halfway through her mug, Esperanza decided the old woman's cider was the best she'd ever tasted. Little did she know it was made with alcohol! The old woman talked to herself most of the time, occasionally asking Esperanza a question about some person or other in the village.

The woman lived with an old goat and an assortment of hens, all of which had free rein in her house. Esperanza watched as she talked to each of them, asking what mischief they'd been into while she'd been out. The old woman had names for each one, grand names that sounded foreign to Esperanza. The goat's name was Balthasar; Esperanza liked him, though he kept nuzzling his face under her arm, attempting to drink her cider.

"I've told you my name," Esperanza said, finishing her mug, "but you haven't told me yours. That's not good manners." The cider had erased all trace of fear in her now.

At first the woman didn't hear her, she was so busy feeding her chickens. She threw the feed over her floor, and the chickens scampered around, creating quite a riot. Esperanza tried again, but to no avail. Then she noticed one of the chickens had a bad leg. It hobbled across the floor trying to get the feed but was always beaten out by another hen. Esperanza reached into the bag of feed and brought it to the hen, who immediately started eating out of her hand.

"My name is Sofia," the old woman said.

Esperanza turned too quickly, and the hen bit her finger. "Hey," she said, dropping the feed.

She didn't really believe it; the old woman didn't fit her conception of the Sofia her father had mentioned. For one thing, she still believed that the Sofia in the story had been beautiful, no matter what her father had said; for another, she couldn't conceive of the ancient woman before her as ever having been young. And besides, she thought, that other Sofia had lived across the valley; it's not possible that she could have come so far. But the real reason was that at some level she'd already begun to think of the woman as her mother. Of course, she imagined her mother as much more beautiful, but it was not beauty she was thinking of, rather it was the feeling of being cared for.

On her way home that afternoon, she found herself wondering about the life of the old woman, trying to relate it to what she knew of her mother's life. Was the old woman from a good family, as her mother had been? Had she ever been in love? And if so, was it to a poor man like her father? She had so many questions by the time she was home that when her father arrived from his Saturday afternoon checkers match with José and Enrique, she asked him if he could tell her the story of Sofia and César.

"Oh, so now you're ready to hear the truth," Juan Rodrigo said as they ate their *habichuelas*—a special gift from Leti, a female admirer whom Juan Rodrigo tried to avoid, except when she brought him a pot of her fine *habichuelas*. "Got tired of the foolish 'sea foam feet' of that simpering impostor?"

"How did they meet?" Esperanza asked. "Was it romantic? Did he sing to her from the courtyard beneath her window?"

"You tell the story your way, since you are so set on how it should go," he said, smiling.

"No, Papá!" Esperanza didn't like giving in, and once she had, she certainly didn't like being made fun of. "Tell me the story!"

"Now you're making demands, I see." He gathered the bowls, clearly enjoying the reaction he was getting from his daughter. "I think you'll have to calm down, and then we'll see if I can tell a story to your liking."

"Papá!" Esperanza stormed out of the house and sat on the porch.

After taking his time, not only cleaning the dishes but making sure all the clothes were nicely folded, Juan Rodrigo sat at the kitchen table and picked at his teeth. He could see Esperanza on the porch, the way she would turn her head just slightly to see if he was coming, then pretend to notice something new in the stars. It wasn't that Juan Rodrigo loved torturing his daughter, but rather that he knew she was headstrong. He wished his wife, Carlota, were with him now. She'd had more subtle means of dealing with people. Juan Rodrigo remembered how she'd dealt with him that first time in the plaza, making him feel as if he directed the dance of courtship, when it was she all along. My methods may be crude, he said to himself, but they are all I have! And he went out to see his daughter.

"Where was I the other day? I've forgotten," he said.

"The kids made fun of Sofia at school."

"Yes, yes," he said, sitting next to his daughter. The porch looked out over the stable and beyond that to a grove of pine that disappeared in the darkness. "Sofia became a loner, spending much of her time hiding in the woods, acting out the lives of ancestors she never had who lived across the sea."

"Like me," Esperanza said. "That's what I do."

"Yes," Juan Rodrigo replied. "In that way, she was very much like you." He put his arm around his daughter and continued. "And then sometime after her eighteenth birthday, a man in the village, a flower shop owner, named César, who must have been half-blind, began to court her."

"That's not nice, Papá."

"And do you think she was like the ugly duckling turned into a swan?" he replied. "Is that how all stories must go?"

"No, but she couldn't have been that ugly, or why else would César fall in love with her?"

"In truth, she looked like the back end of El Viejo."

"Papá! How do you know that's the truth? You said yourself that César's brother, Nacho, told you the story after he died. If he was mean and evil, he probably lied."

"He was not evil, *mi corazón*," Juan Rodrigo replied. "And it is true that I only have his word for all of this. It could be wrong in some details."

"But you always said you knew when a ghost was telling you the truth and when it was not."

"Yes, I can generally tell, but that is because the ghosts I talk with are normally those of this village. I knew them all as living beings and grew to understand them. Nacho sought me out across the valley; I didn't know him while he lived. Still, I believe he told the truth, at least as it appeared to him."

"How do you know?"

"He was very distressed about what he'd done," Juan Rodrigo replied. "I think he hoped to redeem himself by confessing it to me. Now, do you want me to tell you the story or are you going to question me all night?"

Esperanza answered by nodding her head, letting her father know with her eyes that she wanted to hear more.

"They were both terribly shy, so their courtship was nothing fiery. Still, when César waited each day in the plaza during the heat of the sun just to catch a glimpse of her, or when he recited his poetry beneath her window, under the moonlight, they achieved something like the beauty of lovers."

"See!" Esperanza yelled. "I knew he would call to her from beneath her window."

"Yes, it was all very nice. Though no one in the village was quite sure what César saw in Sofia. *He must have lost his mind,* they said. *César understands the beauty of flowers. What could he see in her?*"

"How did the brother steal her away? Did he cast a spell or use a potion?"

"Nothing of the kind," Juan Rodrigo replied. "The brother was opposite from César in every way. Where César was thin and elegant of movement, always concerned with appearances, Nacho was round and rough. He'd been working the pig farms outside of Almeria and had returned to the village to show off his wealth. Sofia and César had been married for three years. It was not the marriage either had hoped for. They fought over everything. It turned out that César was not very good with money, and though his business was successful, he'd saved little. Sofia had been raised to be frugal, and so did not understand his extravagant ways, the fact that he liked nice clothes, soft linen for the bed. They both wanted children, and not bearing the fruit they desired, they began attacking each other. Nacho was living with them at the time, and seeing Sofia crying one morning in her room, he felt sorry for her. Of course, she'd stopped the moment she was aware of his presence, but the image stayed with him. Though he admitted he wasn't attracted to her, at least not at first, there was something about the earthly solidity of her face. When she cried, he said, it was like the cracking of a great rock, and he felt compelled to heal the wound.

"At first it was only out of compassion that he sat talking with her mornings while César was at work. But then his feelings changed. It was the weakness in a woman who appeared so strong that drew him. For her part, being inexperienced and not used to attention from other men, she became drawn to Nacho as well. After all, he was handsome and rough and so different from her husband."

Esperanza broke away from her father. "But she would never leave her husband if it were not for an evil enchantment. How could she do that?"

"Perhaps you are too young for this story," Juan Rodrigo replied. "I may have misjudged."

"I'm old enough," she said. "I just don't believe that she fell for Nacho like that."

"Sometimes a person willing to listen to another is more enchanting than any spell," Juan Rodrigo said. "That is enough for tonight, I think. I will tell you more if you still want to hear tomorrow."

"Papá?"

"Yes."

"How did you court Mamá?"

"It is late, *mi corazón*," Juan Rodrigo replied, rising to enter the house.

"You always tell me the stories of others, but why don't you tell me anything of how you and Mamá met?"

He stopped, breathing deeply. "You remember which star is your mother's?" he asked, tilting his head to the night sky.

"Of course, the bright one that sits in the shoulder of the lion—there." Esperanza pointed the star out as she spoke. "But that doesn't tell me anything about her. You say she was sweet like candy, and more beautiful than the birds, but that sounds more like El Romancero."

Juan Rodrigo flushed. "That's not fair, my child."

"Then tell me more. I want to know."

He turned to her, searching for the right words, but as usual, when it came to describing his feelings for Carlota, his abilities as a teller of tales left him.

THAT MONDAY AFTER HER CHORES, Esperanza returned to Sofia's house. She knew the old woman was far too old to be her mother, and she'd certainly never thought of her own mother as crazy, yet she'd found herself playacting conversations with her mother in her mind the night before as she lay in bed and then again during Doña Villada's boring lessons in school that day, and each time she imagined the conversations, the image she saw in her mind was that of the old woman with her mysterious eyes.

As she neared the cottage, she heard yelling. At first she thought that the old woman was simply talking to herself again, but then she heard the voice of a man, a familiar voice arguing back.

"You cannot make me leave now," the man's voice said. "I've wandered for thirty-five years, hoping to see you."

"Romantic babble!" the old woman yelled back. "You've been listening to your own stories for too long."

"But this is not one of my stories. This is our life!"

"We were never good for each other. Now get out before I cast one of my spells on you."

"You're no witch!"

"Just wait around and you'll find out!" the old woman screamed, and she must have thrown something because there was a loud crash.

"I will not leave. Not after I've found you again."

"You'll leave or I'll kill you."

"You wouldn't," the man's voice said defiantly. Esperanza wasn't so sure. The old woman sounded like she meant it. "I'm declaring my love for you," the man continued. "Let us fly away to the land of youth and begin—"

"Declare this!" There was another loud crash. The man ran from the house holding his bleeding forehead in his hands. A few of the chickens flew out behind him, clucking wildly.

"It's El Romancero," Esperanza said under her breath. At the edge of the woods, he stopped, looked at the blood in his hands, then back at the cottage, his face distorted by something more than physical pain. Esperanza wondered if her father looked like that when he'd heard her mother was to marry another. For her mother had been married before, as had her father—she'd gathered that much from Mercedes on her visits to the dress shop.

El Romancero ran into the woods. Esperanza waited in the rocks above the cottage, deciding whether or not she had the courage to see the old woman.

She didn't have to wait long. The old woman emerged, kicking at her chickens, then grabbing one, holding it to her, and apologizing, *"Lo siento mi pobrecita.* I'm nothing but an old and crazy woman. I'm sorry."

"Don't cry," Esperanza said, sitting beside the old woman, putting her arm around her the way her father had so often done with her. "I'll tell you the story of another Sofia, a Sofia with such a sad life, it will make you forget about your own troubles." Esperanza liked playacting. She felt as if her father's skill and knowledge might pass on to her. But as soon as she started the story, mentioning the names of César and Nacho, the old woman flew into a rage.

"Who told you such lies?" the old woman screamed, throwing the hen off of her lap and pacing the pathway before Esperanza.

"My father had it on authority from the ghost of Nacho himself," Esperanza said, growing worried for her own safety and thinking of where she might run if the woman began throwing things at her as well.

"I was not so ugly as that," the old woman said. "How dare Nacho say such a thing!" She picked up a watering can and threw it against the house. "And César. I grant you he was a romantic, but his poetry was awful, and when he serenaded me from the plaza, the police arrested him. I doubt he's ever gotten over the shame!" As she talked, she picked up gardening instruments—a spade, a shovel—throwing them in all directions, until she pushed herself into a fury. *"Brujas y diablos!"* she screamed. "They are all witches and devils! They destroyed me with their spells!"

Esperanza backed out of the reach of the flying objects and was looking for the quickest path of escape when the old woman called to her with a voice as calm as the still pond whose waters reflected the old woman's garden and house. At first Esperanza thought she was talking to her chickens again: *"Lo siento pobrecita."* But then the woman called her by the same name her own mother called to her in her dreams. *"Esperancita reinita*, please sit with me and have some cider."

As she sat drinking the mug of cider, Esperanza watched the old woman talking to herself, pacing, again farting with nearly every step. It was impossible for her to imagine that El Romancero had once been in love with her.

"Your father thinks he knows the truth, does he?" the old woman asked. Then without waiting for an answer, she sat beside Esperanza, drinking her own mug of cider. "There are many truths, *mi reinita.*"

As she listened to the old woman's story, Esperanza found that she couldn't look her in the eye. If she did, she would only think of her own mother. Nor could she stare at the mouth that quivered as the woman spoke. So she concentrated on the leaves tangled in the old woman's hair.

"You can't explain anything by reason," the old woman said. "Anything!" Then she found a spot of grease on the wall to focus on, and she told her story. "I was so young. I didn't know that you could hate someone and yet love them at the same time, that you could fight with them over everything and still miss them once they were gone. And César didn't win me over with his god-awful poetry. No, he won me with the sincerity of his heart."

"That's still romantic," Esperanza said.

"Yes, my child, it is romantic," the old woman replied, massaging the fingers of her hand. "But too much sincerity can also suffocate. César was a man who loved appearances. And though I was not the prettiest flower in the village, I was certainly not ugly. That *hijo de puta* Nacho!"

"I think you must have been a princess," Esperanza replied, her eyes lighting up.

"César and I were foolish. We fought over many things. But what broke us was our desire for a child. For three years we tried, and for three years I was barren." The old woman paused for a moment, rubbing the bony joints of her hand. "Your story was correct at least in that Nacho saw me crying one day and actually stopped to listen to me. César tried to listen, but his head twisted everything in its attempts to make life more elegant or desperate than it really was." The old woman took a long sip from her cider.

"But how could you leave your husband like that?" Esperanza asked.

The old woman rose and absentmindedly picked up rags and chicken feathers, anything that was lying about.

"I mean, you loved César, didn't you?" Esperanza continued.

The old woman began sweeping, then stopped and leaned on her broom. "Yes, I loved him. Though I couldn't tell you why. We fought with such rage. And I don't know why I left him. If I had to do it over again, I wouldn't have. I suppose it was because I thought I was miserable. I was so concerned with what I didn't have, I forgot what I had. I didn't know that things could get so much worse."

"How?" Esperanza asked. "How could it get any worse?"

The old woman smiled and Esperanza saw a hint of what she might have looked like as a child, with pigtails and a pretty dress, running through the countryside. She'd often imagined her own mother the same way.

"You are perhaps too young to hear any more of this story," the old woman said.

"That's what my father says," Esperanza replied, crossing her arms for the fight. "But I'm nearly a woman."

"Yes, you are." The old woman studied Esperanza, then spoke. "For that reason alone maybe it's good you hear the rest of the tale." The old woman sat beside her again.

"I've heard many things," Esperanza said, "and seen them, too! Once Margarita and Doña Villada's Miguel were in the woods, and I saw them. . . ."

"We didn't run to the woods," the old woman went on, smiling. "But we did do what I think you were going to say. And soon I was pregnant."

"From Nacho!"

"I was shocked, having given up hope of a child. But there it was. Nacho convinced me to run away with him, but first he wanted to tell César. I've never forgotten the way César's face withered, like a flower that has gone without water. César did nothing to stop us; he didn't even leave his room. I remember that I was afraid he would do himself harm. I wanted to stay, but events had been put into action. Sometimes we realize we've passed the point where choices can be made. I didn't know how I felt about Nacho, but there we were on the road like two gypsies."

"So where is your child now?" Esperanza asked. "He must be full grown."

"My daughter died shortly after Nacho left." The old woman began sweeping as she related the last part of the story. "Once Angelina was born, Nacho became despondent. By then he was out of money, being more reckless than his brother. He said he had to return to Almeria to earn more. But I knew he wouldn't come back. He was afraid and not prepared for the responsibilities of fatherhood."

"What did you do?"

"I returned to César." The old woman's voice faltered. "But in his pride, he threw me back on the street. The villagers had talked to him by then, casting their witches' spells and convincing him that to take me back, to accept the child of his own brother, would be a crime. César's need to maintain appearances won out. My milk went dry, and I wandered the alleys of the village by night, looking for trash to eat. Mornings, I stole goat's milk from the neighbors to feed my hungry Angelina. But it was not enough." The old woman threw her broom across the dirt floor.

Esperanza reached out to her, grabbed the woman's hands, swollen with arthritis, and rubbed them in her own. "I'm sorry," she said.

"They can all go to the devil," the old woman said softly.

"But César has come back for you," Esperanza said, guessing now at El Romancero's identity.

"He is many years too late." The old woman sat once again beside Esperanza. "May he rot for what he has done."

The old woman stared at the spot of grease on the wall to which she had originally begun telling her story. Esperanza took a blanket from the bed and wrapped the woman in it. "My father is a storyteller, like El Romancero. I think my mother must have loved that about him."

The old woman looked at the child before her. "Do not be too sure," she said. "Storytellers live in a world of lies. Sometimes they have difficulty understanding the truth."

"Not my father," Esperanza replied, but the old woman was no longer listening to her.

SITTING WITH HER FATHER on the porch that night, Esperanza pointed out a cluster of stars that resembled a swan and said it was the soul of Sofia.

"Why do you say that, *mi corazón?*" Juan Rodrigo replied. "We don't know if Sofia is dead yet."

"She's had a hard life, Papá, and she deserves to be beautiful in death."

Juan Rodrigo studied his daughter. "What do you know of her life?"

"Just what you've told me," Esperanza replied. "It must be very difficult to leave the husband you love." She liked playing this trick on her father, feigning ignorance. And she was curious to see how her father might render the rest of the story.

"Well, her life was difficult," he said. "She and Nacho ran off together, for she was with child."

"You skipped over a part, Papá," Esperanza goaded him.

"Not anything fit for your ears," Juan Rodrigo replied. "Now, where was I? Nacho left because he felt guilty over the poverty to which he'd led Sofia and their daughter. He wished to make things right, to earn enough money to keep her in style."

"No, he left because he was afraid of the responsibility."

Juan Rodrigo gave his daughter another look. "Where did you hear that?"

"Nowhere."

"You certainly are a Rodrigo," he said, studying his daughter with a questioning eye.

EVERY MONDAY AT SCHOOL, Doña Villada gave a lesson from the Bible explaining Father Joaquín's sermon from the day before. Doña Villada was old, but she still carried the same haughty expression and ruled the school with the harsh discipline one expected from a woman who rode her burro through the gully to the schoolhouse every day. She had no tolerance for alternative points of view, and so, when Esperanza questioned her interpretation of Christ's words in the Sermon on the Mount, she did not take it well: *If a man looks at a woman with a lustful eye, he has already committed adultery with her in his heart. If your right eye causes your downfall, tear it out and fling it away; it is better for you to lose one part of your body than for the whole of it to be thrown into hell.* Doña Villada was a literalist and she made it perfectly clear that if any of the children so much as had one bad thought, they would go to hell.

"What if a person commits adultery but then feels horrible about it after?" Esperanza asked. She sat in the back of the room because Doña Villada made her sit there as an example to other students. Esperanza hated it there because during the spring, snakes slithered in through the back window, occasionally dropping from the ceiling. "What if they know what they did was wrong? They won't still go to hell, will they?" she continued.

The corners of Doña Villada's mouth tightened, and she raised her head, surveying the classroom to see which of the children nodded along with the blasphemer. "The Lord is very clear on that point, Esperanza. If your eyes were open, you would see. Once the act has been committed, the soul is lost."

"But that doesn't seem fair." Esperanza stood behind her desk. "What about forgiveness?"

Doña Villada began to shake, her face turning red, then purple. The children knew her explosive temper and they lowered their heads, all except Esperanza. Storming down the aisle, Doña Villada grabbed Esperanza by the ear and pulled her to the front of the room near the chalkboard. She made Esperanza stick her arms out to the side and then placed a Bible in each hand. "You will stay that way for the rest of the class, then you will understand about the Lord's forgiveness."

Esperanza didn't cry; in fact, she didn't utter a word, but just stood there, with her arms weakening, dropping inch by inch at her sides. With what seemed like a sixth sense, Doña Villada knew whenever Esperanza's arms began to droop, and she would stop her lecture, turn to Esperanza, and say, "The Lord has not forgiven you yet. Arms up!" Esperanza forced her arms up, her face locked in a grimace; she felt sure her arms would break. She didn't know that her friend Eugenio sat at his desk near the front, watching her, trying to take her pain inside him.

When class let out, Esperanza ran home, crying so hard that it wasn't until nightfall that Juan Rodrigo could get her to speak. Once she did, he took her hand and marched right to Doña Villada's door. Never had a teacher in that village, or any village for that matter, received such a talking-to. Juan Rodrigo's curses rumbled through the alleyways, crashing through the cliffs, so that the entire village knew of the teacher's humiliation.

"Me cago en la leche del burro que la lleva a la escuela!" I shit in the milk of the burro who brings you to school! he said. And "I shit in the milk of the education that teaches a person to treat another so!" At first the corners of Doña Villada's mouth tightened, as they so often did, but Juan Rodrigo's barrage was so intense that quickly her jaw dropped and even began to quiver. However, it wasn't until Juan Rodrigo said, *"Coño!* If you try anything like that again, I'll sick the ghosts on you!" that Doña Villada turned pale.

Father and daughter walked home arm in arm as they always did, Esperanza giggling all the way as she recounted her father's curses.

"It's a good thing your grandmother had the foulest mouth in the village," Juan Rodrigo said to his daughter, laughing. "I learned my vulgarities from her. Poor María, she had a good heart but a rotten mouth. May she rest in peace."

Two days later, while Esperanza was at school, Juan Rodrigo helped out in Pedro Martinez's bar, a side job he'd had since his marriage to Carlota, when the bar was owned by her brother-in-law, Tesifón. Juan Rodrigo spent a few mornings a week there, cleaning, preparing for the afternoon and evening crowds, and chatting with Pedro, the owner. Juan Rodrigo enjoyed Pedro's company, which was probably why he helped out in the first place. He didn't need the money, not that he was rich—far from it—but rather, he had few wants. He provided for Esperanza, and beyond that he didn't think to desire. Pedro was one of the few men in the village whom Juan Rodrigo trusted completely, always ready to listen and generous with his infectious laugh. He was also one of the few who didn't seem to mind Juan Rodrigo's occupation.

"Have you heard?" Pedro poured Juan Rodrigo a glass of wine as they took a break from cleaning. "El Romancero is dying."

"That old charlatan will never die," Juan Rodrigo retorted, sitting back in his chair, thrusting his feet out before him. "He's probably already begging his way through the next village."

"No," Pedro went on, sitting next to his friend, the old chair creaking under his bulk. "It's true. Enrique found him lying in his cart out beyond *la iglesia*."

"Probably just trying to find a way to steal the wine from the church cellars!" Juan Rodrigo laughed, but Pedro remained serious.

"It's not good to joke about a man's dying, my friend," Pedro said. "You of all people should know that."

"You're right, Pedro," Juan Rodrigo said. "I couldn't help myself. El Romancero's arrogance gets under my skin."

In reply, Pedro patted his friend on the back. "Enrique brought him home," he said at last. "Says he has a horrible cut on his head, that it's infected. His fever is very high."

"I'm sorry to have made light of the situation, then," Juan Rodrigo replied.

"You'll have to prepare the grave right away." Pedro downed his wine in one gulp, visibly shaken by the subject of their talk. "Enrique says he could go at any time."

"I will visit him. If it's as you say, I better get to work."

Doña Villada had not been of a pleasant humor since she'd endured Juan Rodrigo's tirade. Each day since the incident, she'd forced the students to stand and recite passages of the Bible for the first half of class. They spent the second half discussing the opening chapters of *Don Quijote*.

"Cervantes was clearly showing us the danger of books," Doña Villada lectured as she marched up and down the aisles. "Señor Quijote reads too much, and he goes mad. Sancho is presented to guide us, to point out the error of his master's ways."

Esperanza observed the other students writing down each word the teacher said. She couldn't stand it. The story of Don Quijote was one of her favorites. Her father had told it to her often, when he wasn't recounting the lives of the ghosts. And she didn't think Quijote was mad; like her father, he saw things other people couldn't. At last, unable to take any more, she called out: "Why *can't* the windmills be giants?" The class turned their attention to her. Doña Villada stopped lecturing but continued her march, as if the blasphemous words had reached her mouth but not her feet. "Who is to say Don Quijote was wrong?" Esperanza continued.

One would have thought it was impossible, but Doña Villada stopped mid-stride, her foot suspended in air, as if she held it there ready to crush beneath it the child who challenged her. She didn't look at Esperanza, but everyone knew her attention was fixed on her. "Cervantes meant Quijote as a warning to all not to listen to fanciful stories."

"But who is to say that Sancho saw things truly and Don Quijote did not?" Esperanza replied. "Especially when, in the end, Sancho agreed with his master." Eugenio gave her a warning look from the front of the room, signaling her to be quiet, before he slid low in his chair.

Doña Villada turned then to face her challenger, no question now about the direction of her gorgon's gaze. For a moment everything was silent; the children waited. Then Doña Villada shot across the classroom faster than any child had ever done. "He never agreed."

"He did so agree." Esperanza glared at Doña Villada, strengthened by her father's tirade from two days before and the effect she'd seen it have on her teacher.

"How dare you openly defy me!" Doña Villada screamed. The children looked on in horror, sure that they were seeing the last of Esperanza. "You are an insolent little beast!" And with that Doña Villada raised her hand to strike Esperanza, but then, remembering Juan Rodrigo's last words, she checked her hand, backing away.

Esperanza rose from her desk and stood, defiant, knowing she need not unleash her power by saying the words Doña Villada feared. It was the first time in her young life that she realized there were advantages to being the daughter of the gravedigger.

Juan Rodrigo found El Romancero lying in Enrique's own bed, deep in fever. Enrique was cleaning the wound, singing to the old storyteller, when Juan Rodrigo entered the room. Enrique's home was similar to Juan Rodrigo's, only smaller. Where Enrique existed simply in one room with a stove in an alcove off to the side, Juan Rodrigo had built an extra bedroom: the result of Carlota's nesting instincts and a gift of funds from her sister, Consuela. Still, the whitewashed walls of both houses made the small spaces feel a little bigger. And Juan Rodrigo's porch—also built under Carlota's influence—gave his house a particular welcoming feeling, rare in a place of that size. Red clay tiles on the roof kept out the rain and occasional snowfall. But here Enrique had his friend beat, for his roof was sound, and Juan Rodrigo hadn't worked on his roof in years.

At first Juan Rodrigo didn't say a word. He watched his old friend tending to the dying man. Enrique was a short man, almost dwarfish, who'd always taken pains to portray himself as tough, in winter wearing a raccoon-skin coat. He'd never married, and the villagers used to say, *What woman could marry such a man? He's meaner than a goat that's just been sheared. And not much bigger.* But Juan Rodrigo had noticed the sadness with which his friend watched the young couples in Pedro's bar, and the way in which Enrique would bluster about if asked for a favor, inevitably always lending a hand, and so he stood by his friend.

"You sing almost as badly as he tells a story," Juan Rodrigo said.

Enrique stood, cleared his throat. "I was just practicing for the village choir. I'm thinking of joining."

"God help them if they let you in," Juan Rodrigo replied, putting his arm around his friend. "He doesn't look good, does he?"

"No," Enrique replied. "Don Alfonso has seen him and given him something for the fever, but he says there is nothing he can do." Enrique turned to his friend, eyes downcast. "I liked his stories, Juan Rodrigo, though I know you didn't approve. I looked forward to the time of year when he might arrive."

"So did my daughter," Juan Rodrigo said, gazing at the thin and pallid man on the bed. "He brought much joy to this village. That's more than I've done."

Enrique gazed up at his friend but did not speak.

Juan Rodrigo sat beside El Romancero and took his hand. "We are kin, I suppose," he began. "Please forgive a fellow weaver of tales for his selfish behavior."

El Romancero opened his eyes, trying to focus. When he finally spoke, it was as if he was looking past the gravedigger. "Your name is not unknown beyond this village," he said. "And I have heard other towns exclaim: If only we had a gravedigger who healed wounds like the one they have in the village along the cliffs."

Juan Rodrigo squeezed the man's hand. "Death is a foul thing, my friend," he said. "I wish it had not come for you, and I'm sorry that I must always be part of it."

El Romancero smiled weakly. "Our lives are only loaned to us," he said.

"Yes, and we don't even make any interest!" Juan Rodrigo said, and then all three men laughed, El Romancero choking on the laughter in the end.

Enrique and Juan Rodrigo attempted to ease the dying man's coughing fit, bringing water and arranging the pillows. At last, when it was over, El Romancero pulled Juan Rodrigo close, saying, "Our world is passing, my friend. You and I are a dying breed. And there is nothing to be done. How can one lie, or at least embellish, when people can talk to the next town over wires and find out the truth, or visit them in a motor car!" Then he turned to Enrique and said, "At least I found my love. It is too much to ask forgiveness." And with that he drifted off into sleep.

Not understanding those last words, Juan Rodrigo returned home to carry the burden of his pick and shovel.

Esperanza had finished her chores early, excited to tell him about her victory over Doña Villada. But she knew her father well. Upon seeing his slow gait and empty face—the face of one who has resigned himself to his duty—she understood that someone had died, or was dying.

She approached slowly, taking his hand, walking silently with him to the cemetery. She sat in the dirt beside him as he thrust his shovel into the earth, knowing that soon the ghost would appear. She couldn't see the ghosts, though she'd tried so hard in the past. But she'd learned to notice the way her father stopped often just before the ghost arrived to warm his hands between his legs, and the way in which he wiped his forehead, whether there was sweat or not, as if he felt ill. None of these things happened, however, and Esperanza knew that the person had not yet died.

"Who is going to die, Papá?"

Her father looked to her with a mournful countenance, for he knew that she loved the stories of El Romancero perhaps better than his own. He did not have the heart to tell her. "Someone not of this village," he said.

"Then why are you digging the grave?"

"Because he will die here."

"Who, Papá?" she asked. "Why are you so secretive?"

Juan Rodrigo leaned upon his shovel. "I'm sorry, *mi corazón*, but it's El Romancero."

"No, Papá," she said. "How is that possible?" But in her heart she knew; she'd seen the blood, and she'd seen the despair in his face.

"I don't know," Juan Rodrigo replied, digging the shovel into the earth once again, unable to face his daughter. "But he lies in Enrique's house sick with fever and will not last long."

Esperanza jumped to her feet. "I must go, Papá." And with that she turned and ran down the hill.

Juan Rodrigo watched her go, overwhelmed by the certain knowledge that he could not hold on to her forever.

THE OLD WOMAN was tending to her garden, talking to herself as she so often did. Esperanza bounded so fast down the slope and across the edge of the pond that this time it was she who scared the old woman, not the other way around.

"Por la Virgen!" the old woman screamed. "I thought you were a witch flying down the mountain to cast a spell on me!"

"He's dying!" Esperanza shouted through panting breaths.

"If someone is dying, that is their own business," the old woman said. "What can I do about it?"

"You can forgive him," Esperanza said, grabbing the old woman's callused hand.

The old woman looked at Esperanza for a long time, as if waiting for the truth of what she said to arrive from somewhere far away.

"Quick! There's not much time."

"César is dead to me," the old woman said.

"No!" Esperanza screamed, tugging at the old woman, almost yanking her over. "He's not dead yet!"

The old woman stared at Esperanza, breathing deeply, then shook her hand away, cursing Esperanza. "Get out of here!" she screamed. "Leave me in peace!"

"But there's still hope," Esperanza entreated. "How can you do this? I pray every night that one day my mother will return, even when I know she will not."

The old woman looked for a moment with clear eyes, though there was madness brewing behind them now. She took Esperanza's hand in both of hers. "I'm sorry, my child," she said at last.

"No, you're not!" Esperanza tore her hand away. "I never knew what it was like to have the love of a mother. At least you had something!"

"You have your father," the old woman said, her eyes watery with age and remorse.

"Yes, and I love him," she said, and then she paused, searching for the right words, not so the old woman would understand, but so that she, herself, would. "But sometimes late at night, when he thinks I'm sleeping, he talks to my mother, and I see the pain on his face that she does not answer. And the way he walks when he returns from digging a grave, or from the bar where he must watch the young couples. I see the sadness that is forever about him, and I wish that my mother were here. I wish God would take me and give my mother back."

"What are you saying, child?" The old woman stepped close, reaching for Esperanza.

"He told me once how happy they were before I was born, that they were the happiest years of his life. He caught himself, and he's never repeated it, but I know it's true."

"I've seen your father, Esperancita," the old woman said. "No one could love a daughter more."

"I know he does. But it doesn't bring my mother back." Esperanza kicked at the dirt, trying to figure out what to do next. "Come with me," she said.

The old woman gazed at her, and Esperanza saw the fear mixed with bitterness in her eyes. "I want to tend my garden," the old woman said, turning away.

"No," Esperanza begged. "You must come!"

"Leave me in peace!" the old woman screamed, mumbling curses to herself as she walked away.

"Not until you come with me." Esperanza moved to block her.

"Is this some devilry? Are you a witch?" And with that the old woman picked up the spade, pointing it at Esperanza. The action dislodged one of the leaves in the old woman's hair, and it floated slowly to the ground.

AFTER SCHOOL the following day, Esperanza rushed once again to the old woman's home, but she was not there. She then ran to Enrique's, hoping that El Romancero would agree to come with her to find the old woman, but when she arrived at the house,

Enrique was sitting upon the big rock that marked the front of his porch. "El Romancero is gone," he said. "Your father buried him while you were at school. The old woman is inside. She must have known him."

"Her name is Sofia," Esperanza replied. Enrique simply nodded his head.

The old woman knelt before Enrique's bed, weeping. "I dreamt last night that you were alive," she was saying to the bed. "That you returned to me even after what I did to you. How was I to know that you loved me?"

Esperanza kneeled beside her. "I'm sorry," she whispered.

"It all seemed so real," the old woman said. "I thought it was real, but I don't know the difference between the dream world and the real anymore. That's what happens when you live alone long enough."

"Maybe there is no difference," Esperanza said.

"Yes, you are right," the old woman said. "For I am alone in both."

They sat for a time together on the bed, and then Esperanza took the old woman by the hand and led her to her own house, where her father sat waiting for them on the porch.

"Once César told me his story, I thought you might come," he said. "But I didn't know my own daughter would bring you!"

They made her *Manzanilla* tea and a delicious *tortilla*, Juan Rodrigo waiting for the time when he would sense she was ready to hear César's story. But the old woman seemed too far gone. There had always been something of the earth in her, and now she resembled a volcano in her cycles of torment: mumbling to herself at first, then flying into a rage, only to calm down after a few moments and sink into complete silence. Juan Rodrigo was a patient man, and he waited a very long time, but as the sky darkened, he wondered if she would ever be fit to hear his story.

"César would like to speak to you, Sofia," he finally said. "Would you like to hear what he has to say?"

"Our lives have held nothing but grief," she said. "Why would I want to relive that?"

"He asks your forgiveness," Juan Rodrigo said.

"My forgiveness? Why should he need my forgiveness?"

"He says he was too proud. He tried to make you something that you were not," Juan Rodrigo went on. "And he says he will never forgive himself for turning you and the child away."

The old woman sat so still that for a moment Juan Rodrigo thought she had died as well. Esperanza sat beside her, squeezing her hand. Finally the old woman spoke. "César, you had a right to be proud," she said. "You were a good man. Maybe too good. Maybe that's why I went with Nacho. How could I measure up?"

"He says he never stopped loving you," Juan Rodrigo said. "That he died the day he turned you out, and that is why he became El Romancero."

"Why do you ask my forgiveness, César, when it is you who should forgive me? How can a man be expected to do right when his wife runs off with his brother?"

"You reacted from your heart. I reacted out of stubborn pride," Juan Rodrigo said. Esperanza studied her father, intrigued by the rare occasions when he spoke as if he were the ghost.

The old woman raised her head, her gaze falling upon Juan Rodrigo. "We, neither of us, understood a thing. We ran from it. Instead of forgiving the other's faults, we ran. That's not love."

"Do you forgive me now?" Juan Rodrigo stepped closer, kneeling before Sofia.

Tears rolled down the old woman's face. At first she said nothing. Her hand shook so that Esperanza was sure there would be another violent episode. But there was none. The old woman nodded her head at last, whispering, "Yes."

A MONTH PASSED, during which the village saw its first cold nights of the year; there was even a dusting of snow. Esperanza didn't visit the old woman every day, but she visited often, bringing a loaf of bread or some eggs. The old woman was glad to see her, but Esperanza marked a change in her countenance: Though she'd always seemed to be just barely on the side of the living, there had at least been a fire about her; now that fire was going out.

Many afternoons they sat together drinking cider and watching the ice form on the edges of the pond, the way it spread like fingers reaching across, desperate to embrace the ice straining from the other side. They occasionally threw bread crumbs out upon the water and watched the fish swim to the surface, greedily gulping down the morsels. The old woman talked to the fish and swore that they talked back, the brown and rainbow trout, the carp and barbel speaking of life in the pond, and how they hoped that she would someday join them there.

The pond rarely froze over completely, and the old woman was glad of that, for the closing of it would be a shutting out of life. What would the fish do? she asked, and Esperanza had no answer.

THE OLD WOMAN DIED just before winter while Esperanza was at school. That afternoon, she watched her father struggle as he dug through the frozen earth. Enrique came to see the old woman laid to rest, but no one else from the village was in attendance, not even Father Joaquín, who'd excused himself on the grounds that the woman had incited the devil on numerous occasions and thus had obviously been in consort with him or his minions.

Esperanza stood by the graveside, once again thinking of her own mother. If she were alive, would she love her the way her father did? She felt sure she would. But what of her mother and father's relationship? Her father had said they never fought, but Esperanza had seen enough of the other couples in the village to know better. Married people always fought about something.

On the way home from the burial, she and her father talked as they so often did. "Is it strange that I miss Mamá, even though I never knew her?" she asked.

"Of course not, *mi corazón*," Juan Rodrigo replied. "Though, I tell you, she is with us every day. You feel her in your heart, but you don't see her, and you can't hold her, and worse, she can't hold you. It's that physical presence that you miss, that we miss."

"When you talk to her at night, can you see her?"

Juan Rodrigo looked at his daughter and gave a wry smile. "You are a trickster like your father," he said. "And I always thought you were asleep."

"But can you see her?"

"No, *mi corazón*. I'm afraid I can't. But I see her in you, and that is more than enough for me. The two of you together make a force I can barely deal with." They laughed together as they walked.

But a few moments later, Esperanza spoke, "I saw her in the old woman, Sofia. Was that wrong?"

"Why would that be wrong?" Juan Rodrigo stopped and turned to her. "Death is a funny thing," he said, taking her in his arms. "That's one thing I've learned as a gravedigger. It teaches us to let go, and at the same time it reminds us that the dead are never far away—they exist with us still, in memory, yes, but also in the many quiet movements of the world around us."

Esperanza smiled and let her father hold her, imagining that somewhere, perhaps from the rocks and trees around them, her mother looked on, watching over her.

The old woman's ghost had not appeared, the way the ghosts normally did, as Juan Rodrigo was digging the grave. But that night, while Juan Rodrigo and his daughter were eating dinner, a fight broke out around them. Not being able to see the ghosts or hear the words, Esperanza could only guess at the nature of the spat until her father told her later. But she did enjoy watching the dishes fly about, crashing into the walls, and the way the wind kept blowing open the shutters and extinguishing their lamplight. Juan Rodrigo was not so pleased. He stomped about the house, relighting the lamp, and screaming at César and Sofia, as if he, too, had joined their feud.

It seemed that the two lovers were together again after so many years, but that, as before, their relationship was a stormy one. César berated Sofia for having not kept up her appearance—after all, she had leaves in her hair, and her clothes were ratty, not to mention the fact that she hadn't bathed in months. Sofia, for her part, didn't like the changes that had taken place in her husband.

"You've been an actor for nearly four decades," she said, "and now you can't help but act all the time. The stories have become your existence! If you want to be a character in your own play, that's fine, but don't imagine for a moment that you'll make me your Ophelia!"

Juan Rodrigo laughed in recounting this to Esperanza. "I was so happy to hear her refute her husband's pomposity like that. He discredits life when he tells such inflated stories!" Then, tucking his daughter in bed, he added, "It's funny that after so long, after enduring so much, they have returned to their old ways."

"You can't explain anything by reason, Papá," Esperanza answered. And Juan Rodrigo studied his daughter yet another time, wondering by what manner she was growing up so quickly.

"Very true," Juan Rodrigo replied. "And no one should dare question the rhythms of love."

The day after the burial, Esperanza visited the old woman's cottage and sat at the edge of the pond. The villagers had already come for the chickens and the goat. Her father demanded they send the goat to Señora Herrera, who, having recently given birth, was desperately in need of milk. Esperanza smiled, knowing Sofia would approve.

Two swans floated upon the water, dipping their long white necks in search of food, seemingly unaware of the encroaching ice. She rose to tell her father of the beautiful birds, then stopped and sat once again. He wouldn't believe her. After all, there weren't supposed to be any birds in this village; he'd told her so many times. Then she remembered El Romancero's story. She didn't really believe in his imaginative tales, not anymore, but maybe there had been a glimmer of truth after all. She stayed by the pond, dreaming of what was to come in her own life—not fanciful dreams, but musings upon the truths and half-truths that make up one's life story. She still believed in her father's stories, though not in the same way that she once did. And she knew enough about the world to understand that the old woman had had her reasons for telling her story the way she did. So what was she to believe? And what would be said of her own life once it became time to tell the tale? As she watched the swans circling about, she decided that she desperately wanted to know.

Entre los dos mundos

"You tell so many stories, Papá," Esperanza said as she sat under the olive tree with her father.

"So many people have died," Juan Rodrigo replied, wiping the sweat from his brow with his dirty handkerchief.

The four-year-old girl rose. "I leave you to tell the rest of the tale," she said.

"I will not need you again," Juan Rodrigo replied.

"Who is to say when need arises?" the girl said, twirling her hair with her finger. "The story of your life is not finished." Then, looking to Esperanza: "Nor do I think is hers."

Juan Rodrigo rose, puzzled, wanting to ask more, but the girl in white was gone, El Viejo giving her a wide berth. Again he wiped his brow, dropping his handkerchief as he tried to stuff it back into his pocket. "I'm too old to bury one so young," he said to his daughter. "You see, I can barely bend to pick up my rags." And he groaned as he bent over.

"You work too hard, Papá," Esperanza said. "That's why you can never catch me in the cliffs!" And with that she was gone, down the path and through the outcropping of red rock that marked the entrance to the cemetery.

Did his daughter really run before him, or was it all in his mind? He decided it didn't matter and followed her down from the hilltop and into the cliffs.

"Papá!" Esperanza called to him from behind a pine growing out of a crevice a few meters below. "You can't find me. I'm hiding with the birds."

Juan Rodrigo searched among the rocks and, laughing, said, "Just like your mother, always with the birds!" He rounded the pine and lowered himself down into the crevice, hoping to surprise his daughter, but she wasn't there. "I don't think they ever would have forgiven me if it wasn't for your mother," he yelled. "The birds have longer memories than a scorned woman!" He joked, but inside he felt panic rising. The arms of the olive trees writhed before him. "Esperanza!" he yelled. "You know you're supposed to stay close to me. *Cabezona!* Why are you so willful?"

A giggle from somewhere among the red rocks to his right was the only reply. "Esperanza!" But there was only silence. "Esperanza!" He moved as quickly as a man his age could, no longer hoping simply to surprise her in the rocks, but desperately needing to find her. Mistakenly thinking that he could hold her in his arms, that he could feel the quick beat of her heart, that he could stop from happening what had already happened, he lunged around a boulder, but she was gone. Then he caught sight of her green dress darting behind a finger-shaped outcrop near the top of the cliff. It was then he thought he saw her fall, even though he hadn't been there the first time. He'd arrived too late, finding only her mangled body. "Esperanza!" he yelled. "Come here this minute!"

Again, the giggle.

"I'm loosening my belt, Esperanza," he said, searching behind the boulder and the pines for a glimpse of her. "If I don't see your face before me by the time I count to ten, there'll be hell to pay! *Válgame Dios!*" He counted, taking off his belt as he did so, but when he reached nine and she still hadn't appeared, he stopped himself. He would not make the mistake he'd made the last time. He would not force her to choose between her own life and obedience to his will. He began to retie his belt, when Esperanza lunged out from the rocks behind him, making him jump and drop his belt. She'd been there all along, he realized, relief at not having lost her again nearly overwhelming him. To combat the emotion, he played the part of the angry father, blustering about, picking up his belt and slapping it on the rocks and telling his daughter how much more the spanking would hurt him than it would her. Esperanza wasn't taken in; she'd seen his act too many times before.

"Papá, men don't beat women," she said, lowering her head to look at him, practicing with her father the techniques of flirting she would never use.

"I don't care how old you are," Juan Rodrigo said, knowing full well that he would not be able to maintain his anger much longer. "You are still my daughter, and as long as you are, you will listen to your father."

"Yes, Papá, I will always be your daughter."

Juan Rodrigo gave up all pretense of anger at this point. He hugged his daughter to him but felt not the racing of her heart, only a strange absence, as one feels upon entering the room or holding a possession of the recently deceased. *"Válgame Dios!"*

he screamed to the rocks and the trees. The rocks stood silent, but the poplars and pines, having a greater understanding of the sorrow of loss, groaned with the effort of bending their great trunks, if only to be a bit nearer to the man kneeling upon the cliff face.

Here is a tree whose leaves have fallen too soon, said one poplar to the other. *Yes, he has carried the burden of an early snow.*

4

The Story of José Pérez

THE FLU EPIDEMIC that had been devastating Spain throughout the early twenties swept again through the village during the year that followed, and the gravedigger was kept busy. It was a time when the flu moved through Spain like the plague had done in centuries past. Sometimes the outbursts were mild and only a few of the older villagers died, but other times the villagers were sure the sickness was sent by the devil himself and many suffered and died. Each time, after digging the grave, when the body still lay in the living room, watched over by the family, Juan Rodrigo went to the grieving family's house, accompanied by his daughter, gathered the family together, and told them the story of the deceased. He told the truth, for the most part, the stories coming to him directly from the recently departed ghost. But as Juan Rodrigo knew all too well, sometimes people didn't tell the truth about their lives: They either didn't want it to be known, or they'd fooled themselves into believing their own story for so long that they could no longer distinguish the truth. Juan Rodrigo had been a gravedigger for a long time, and it was a very small village. He knew when a ghost was telling him the truth or not. He also knew that these misrepresentations and falsehoods rarely did anyone any good, particularly the ghost. Sometimes he let it slide, if the falsehood didn't hurt anyone, and especially if it helped the story. But other times he contradicted the ghost, telling the truth as he knew it, or even bending the truth a bit for the purposes of his art. For Juan Rodrigo had a high opinion of his role, considering himself much more than simply a gravedigger. Anyone can dig a grave, he would say, but who can tell a story the way I can? Needless to say, his versions of the lives of the dearly departed often disturbed the families of the deceased. But the gravedigger didn't take his job lightly; he revealed the secrets hidden in the dark corners of rooms only when he was sure the truth should be told. Occasionally, when he looked about the living room at the people in mourning and saw the light of remembrance in their eyes, he would get carried away and embellish the story where it brought joy or where it clearly worked like a broom, sweeping away the dust of old memories. This was not a bad thing, he told himself at night before going to sleep. Our memories become the lives and deeds of the departed. Why not rework them a bit to help the living? The ghosts themselves rarely minded when he invoked the liberties of his storytelling art because it often meant he was exaggerating in their favor, but even when it didn't, they could see, too, the faces of their loved ones, and how the story weaved its way in and out of memory, purging it when needed, arranging and ordering it where necessary.

Occasionally, the ghost of Ursula, the four-year-old girl, would meet Juan Rodrigo at his house and take him by the hand to the home of the newly deceased. Juan Rodrigo noticed that this only happened when the deceased was someone he knew particularly well, a friend, of which there were many in the village, or a family member, of which there were a few remaining cousins. He didn't know why it happened that way, as Ursula had never had any special connection to him or his family, as far as he knew. She'd said his father had buried her. Maybe his father had secrets even Juan Rodrigo did not know. Still, somehow her presence eased Juan Rodrigo's pain, allowing him, in turn, to ease that of the family of the deceased. They spoke little to each other, as on one occasion during the recent flu epidemic, when she appeared, saying simply, "Come, *Viejo*, your friend José Pérez, with whom you have so often played checkers in the plaza, has died." And he grabbed his pick and shovel, slung them over his shoulder, and said, "*Ay, por Dios*, you weigh more than a forced marriage." Then he took the wintry hand of the girl and called to his daughter, Esperanza, to accompany them.

Often, when the little girl appeared, Esperanza refused to take her father's hand, for though she couldn't see little Ursula, she knew the girl walked beside her father. There was a time when she hadn't minded the little girl so much. When she was little as well, it had been a game to try to discover some trace of the ghost—footprints, the moving of a curtain or door, a subtle change in the air around her—but she could find nothing. Yet her father persisted in talking to the little girl, finding out what she knew about the recently deceased, gathering information he could use for his story. It was the fact that she was left out of these conversations that bothered Esperanza. At first she'd walk behind her father and try to piece together the entire conversation based on what he was saying, but later she grew bored with that and found herself only thinking of ways to hurt the little girl.

On this day, Juan Rodrigo climbed the hill to the cemetery but found it difficult to dig the grave.

"Venga, Viejo," the four-year-old girl said. "The family waits for you."

"I knew he would die soon," Juan Rodrigo replied. "It had been a long time coming. We could scarcely finish a game of checkers with all of his coughing." And with that, Juan Rodrigo smiled and pushed the shovel into the dirt. "You were a funny man, José, with your straight face and dry wit. Enrique could never tell when you were joking with him!"

Esperanza marked the direction of Juan Rodrigo's gaze when he'd spoken with Ursula, then waited until he was engaged with José's ghost. Her father was halfway through digging the grave before José appeared.

"You must be sure to get my story right, *mi amigo,*" said a voice from within the grave. José Pérez climbed out of the hole and sat beside the feet of his friend. "I was a faithful husband," he said. "You must forget those conversations in the plaza."

"Leave me be to tell the story as I see fit, old friend," Juan Rodrigo replied, setting down his shovel.

Esperanza took advantage of the situation by picking up rocks and throwing them in the direction where she thought the little girl was sitting.

"You must think of Pilar and the children," José continued. "They must have a good image of their father."

"You think an image is what a child needs?" Juan Rodrigo turned to his old friend with a sterner look than any he'd given over the checkerboard. "And what about those children you haven't recognized?" he said, taking his hat from his head. He gazed in the direction of José's house. "Trust in your family to recognize you for the good man you were," Juan Rodrigo went on. "You took care of them well. You were as loving a father and husband as ever I've seen."

"But I should have never had those indiscretions. What a fool!" José now rose and paced back and forth before his own grave.

"Yes, you were very foolish also," Juan Rodrigo said, picking up his shovel and continuing to dig. "But who hasn't been? There are many types of indiscretions, José. Not all of them are so easy to spot."

José stopped his pacing. "What was that saying you told me once?"

"*Un bicho malo nunca muere.*"

"*Sí, eso.*" José looked worried. "A bad bug never dies. I think a man should be allowed to die. Who wants their deeds to live on after them?"

"That depends upon the nature of the deed," Juan Rodrigo replied. "When I spoke of bad bugs, I was talking about Father Ramon. There have been few in this village worse than him. His deeds, I think, needed to be revealed so no one would forget."

"Is that what you're trying to do to me?"

"You know me better than that, old friend," Juan Rodrigo replied. "And I know Pilar. She'll understand. We don't want her thinking you were too perfect!"

"That she will never do," José replied, looking relieved for the first time since he'd appeared. Both men laughed and soon moved on to other matters.

Esperanza sat, glaring at the space where she thought Ursula was, occasionally throwing handfuls of dirt, but mostly trying to concentrate her energy on making the four-year-old feel her hatred. Little did she know that Ursula had vanished soon after José had appeared.

Once in the Pérez household, Esperanza played in the back of the living room, behind the line of mourners sitting in their chairs. Those who were unaccustomed to seeing a child playing freely without attempting to imitate the sad countenances of the adults labeled her behavior as unnatural, when in reality her indifference to the customs and trappings surrounding death made her behavior the most natural of all. It is not that she didn't feel sadness—she often did, particularly when it was a member of a family she knew well—but she accepted the sadness as part of the moment and incorporated it into her play.

José stood in the corner of the room, waiting for Juan Rodrigo to begin his tale. But Juan Rodrigo was taking his time, talking first with the family and friends, patiently greeting everyone until the moment was right. José had hoped that he'd be sorely missed, but now, seeing the grief that washed over the room, he wished for a way to lessen the pain. The coffin lay in the center, draped in velvet. It seemed short to José, but he knew Jorge, the carpenter, well, and knew that Jorge would let no detail slip. The room was filled with flowers: jasmine, lilies, and magnolias. It all made José feel a little silly. The only time he could remember giving Pilar flowers was before they were married. The men stood smoking and conversing on one side of the room; the women sat praying, crying, and holding one another's hands on the other. José picked out his wife sitting with Rosalia and Mercedes. Rosalia had lost her husband the year before to a stroke, and José could see in her eyes how his own funeral rekindled the loss. But he also noticed how Rosalia sat beside Pilar, holding her hand, whispering in her ear, occasionally making her laugh. He knew Rosalia stood guard over his wife, and he was glad for it. Rosalia was a good friend.

José couldn't find his children and wondered where they were. He checked the kitchen and the bedrooms, but they were not there. However, as he stood beside his bed, remembering the times he and Pilar talked through the night, holding each other to keep back the winter chill, he heard their voices from outside, beneath the window.

He found them, together with their spouses, sitting on the back patio, talking about the brevity of life, and how they wanted to leave the village someday so that their children would know more of the outside world. Elena, the eldest, had been married for three years and already had a child of her own. Iago, his son, had just married last year. José felt fortunate that he liked both their spouses. He'd known many other parents who were not so lucky.

"Life is suffocating me here," Iago said. "Look around. After the war, the old people are all that's left. Sure, there are a few children, but they'll be gone as soon as they're old enough. Why do we hang around?"

Didn't you have a good life here? José wanted to ask. *Your mother and I gave you everything.* And, as if she heard him, Elena said, "Still, we have family here. Much more can be learned from dealing with Uncle Jesús' temper than could ever be learned in the city!"

José laughed along with his children. He wanted to tell them to stay, to remain in the village for their mother. But he didn't. He had a feeling they would, anyway. There had been much love in their household.

He made his way around the side of the house, wanting to look at it one last time, to run his hand along the whitewash—he'd painted many of the houses in the village and was proud of it—and to see the fence he'd built and the roof he'd spent so many hours repairing, the roof that protected his family. But as he rounded the corner he saw Teresa and Agustín, his illegitimate children, standing on a barrel, trying to peek through the window into the living room. They were just reaching adolescence and looked awkward to José with their long legs and gangly arms. Forgetting himself, he called to them, but, of course, they couldn't hear him. Then he realized that even if they could hear him, it wouldn't matter. They didn't know who he was, or, rather, they knew him as José the owner of the *estanco* where they bought candy, not as their father. Part of the bargain he'd made with their mothers was that he would support the children financially if they kept his identity secret. So he found himself watching them. They whispered to each other and giggled like siblings, though they were only half brother and sister.

As he watched, tears formed in his eyes. These were his children, yet because they were bastards, the rest of the village would treat them horribly. Teresa may not even be able to marry, he thought. And will Agustín be allowed to prove himself, whatever work he chooses? How strange that while I was alive I didn't think more about them, he said to himself. I should have at least been thinking about them when I lay with those women. But then he smiled to himself. No, I was thinking with another part of the body at that time.

The two children sat on the barrel and talked of Paquita's big rooster. Was it the biggest in the village? they wondered.

They did not appear sad. Why should they be? José thought. They do not yet know the difficulties in store for them, though they must have had a taste. I'm sorry, he said then. I'm sorry I brought you into this world because of my own desire but then didn't have the strength of will to see it through. He approached them, hesitantly, wanting now to kiss them on the forehead.

A cry broke from the house, an inhuman howl that José at first didn't recognize. Then he heard Elena scream, "Mother!" and he forgot about the children on the barrel and ran inside.

The line of mourners viewing the body had stopped. Pilar had thrown herself over the coffin, wailing, trying to tear at her hair, her face. Rosalia was beside her, not attempting to stop her, only holding her hands so that she wouldn't hurt herself. The children ran to their mother's side now. Elena stopped before the body, then crumpled to the floor. José had not realized that she'd been afraid to view the corpse. Pilar cried out, "Take me with him! My children are grown and no longer need me. Take me!" Rosalia finally pulled her away and forced her to look where Elena was now being tended to on the couch. "Silly woman!" Rosalia said. "You don't think your children need you. Children always need their mother." And Pilar rushed to her daughter's side, shoving the mourners out of the way. "My dear Elenita," she said, running her hand over her head. "I'm sorry, my daughter."

José noticed a long tear in his wife's black stockings. On any other day she would have been appalled to go out like that, he thought. And then he, too, was overcome with grief. He ran to his wife and daughter, trying to hold them, to whisper in his wife's ear that she must be strong, that to care about little things like stockings would help Elena and Iago through their own troubles. "Don't just stand there, you good-for-nothing men!" Pilar turned to the group of men in the corner. "One of you run and get Don Alfonso, now!"

That's my wife, José Pérez thought. Even today she is capable of taking charge of a household.

Juan Rodrigo watched, still waiting for the moment when his services would be of use. Often, he had to wait all day until the rising tide of grief began to ebb, not that it disappeared, but there always came a moment when the mourners let go, if only for an instant, wanting, needing to travel back through memory and nod along with the familiar details Juan Rodrigo brought back, or sit up in surprise when he told them something they did not know. The time for his story came slowly, for José Pérez was much beloved, but as the afternoon wore on, some of the distant cousins made coffee and brought out cakes, and the mourners made their way to the various couches and chairs about the room. Only a few older women still knelt beside the coffin, their rosaries in hand.

The pharmacist, Don Alfonso, had arrived, and Elena had much improved. Many of the men still stood smoking in the back, but Juan Rodrigo could see their ears turned toward him, despite their attempts to appear disinterested. He moved to the center of the room and stood beside the coffin. Two of the old women who still prayed shot him a look, then crossed themselves and moved away. But José's half sister, Juanita, remained. She'd always been given to show.

"It's not Christian to listen to this man," she said, standing. "You should all be praying, as I plan to do throughout the night for my beloved brother."

Pilar stepped forward, clearly in possession of herself again after having to care for her daughter. "I invited the gravedigger here because it was my husband's wish," she said. "We know you enjoy being sad and making a spectacle of yourself—the ritual and pretense suits you—and you are welcome to spend the night praying, but now get out of the way!" With that, Pilar sat down. Juanita turned with wide eyes and quivering lip to the others in the room, but they avoided her gaze.

Juan Rodrigo waited for the room to settle once again, looked Pilar in the eye, and began his story.

He knew not all the members of the family would want to hear his particular version of the story, but he also knew that Pilar needed to hear it and that his friend José Pérez should hear it. He told how his friend had slipped out of the house after midnight to spend time with the whores in Pepita's house. How he'd fathered children from two other widows in the village. Children he'd supported financially for as long as he could, even though he didn't acknowledge them. The mourners stirred in their chairs. Fans fluttered about the room. Pilar's eyes remained fixed on Juan Rodrigo. Rosalia stood watching both her friend and the storyteller, ready to intervene if necessary.

Finally, Juanita stood. "That man is of the devil!" she shouted. "He is all filth and lies. My brother never did such a thing." Elena's husband jumped to his feet, pointing at Juan Rodrigo. "That's slander, pure and simple!" he yelled. "Elena, I told you the gravedigger should not be allowed in the house. Why, he told my mother that Father had hidden money from us." Pilar's sister and her husband also rose in anger, demanding that Juan Rodrigo amend his story.

Juan Rodrigo looked to his friend, who stood behind his wife. José Pérez appeared nervous, but he nodded his head, acknowledging that Juan Rodrigo could continue. Pilar stood then, her stone gaze hushing the room. "Silence!" she screamed. "I said I invited Señor Rodrigo here because my husband wished it, but I also invited him because I wanted to know. I've had my doubts for a long time, and I wanted to know everything. It is time I understood."

"But, Mother!" Elena's husband protested.

"Enough, I say!" Pilar yelled, turning to face her son-in-law. Then, to Juan Rodrigo: "Please continue."

Juanita made a loud "Hmmph" and left the room.

A murmuring wave rolled across the mourners, but soon they hushed again and Juan Rodrigo continued his story.

He told of José Pérez's prayers when he was alone in the fields, where no one could see. How he asked God's forgiveness for being a weak man. How he spoke every day to God of his love for his wife and all of his children. "She is the only light that shines in my life," he said of Pilar. "I would be nowhere without her strength. May God forgive me for betraying her, and let her know that she was the only woman ever in my heart." And at that moment, Pilar stood, smiling through her tears, and nodded her head at Juan Rodrigo. "That's right!" she yelled to the heavens. "You were a weak man! But I loved you!"

It was then she noticed the faces of Teresa and Agustín peering through the window. She hesitated, and the entire room followed her gaze. The children, realizing they were the center of attention, ducked beneath the window.

"Grab them!" Pilar shouted. "Before they get away." And her boy, Iago, was out the door.

The crowd erupted immediately into gossip, for although it had never been formally acknowledged that these were José's children, many suspected. Iago returned, holding each child roughly by the scruff of the neck. Juanita had also returned, and she approached the children, waving her finger at them. "The children of whores should not be allowed in a Christian house and, once more, a house grieved by death." She crossed herself, gazing about the room triumphantly.

"Shut up!" Pilar screamed, standing now between Juanita and the children. "I've put up with you for thirty-two years, and I'm sick to death of it!"

Juanita looked about the room for support, but if anyone supported her, they didn't dare show themselves in the face of Pilar's wrath. Juanita put on her best face, as she was so good at doing, saying, "I thought I was family, but I can see you always thought otherwise. I know when I'm not wanted." And with that, she turned her head proudly, as if posing for a picture, flipped open her fan, and left the house.

Pilar turned to her own son. "You can let them go," she said. "They are part of this family now."

Iago held on a moment longer, unsure how to take what was happening, but in the end he did what his mother asked.

"You have two homes now, children," she said. Then, gazing about the room as if looking for challengers, she said sternly, "These children belong to their mothers, and they belong to me, to this family. Do you understand?" The women nodded; the men puffed on their cigarettes silently.

After, José hugged his friend Juan Rodrigo one last time. A tear appeared in each man's eyes as they held each other. Both knew there was no more need for words.

Juan Rodrigo and Esperanza left José with his family. Though Juan Rodrigo could not relieve the family's sadness at the passing of his friend, he was pleased that his story had had such an effect.

5

❧·❦ ❧·❦

El muerto al hoyo, y el vivo al bollo

THOUGH HE HAD HELPED the family in their grief, Juan Rodrigo felt the weight of his friend's death as a particular burden on that night, and he asked his daughter if she would accompany him to Pedro's bar. Esperanza jumped in delight, as her father rarely went out, and when he did, it was alone. She recalled the only other time she'd been allowed in the bar, two years earlier. She'd spent the entire evening hidden under one of the tables in the balcony, watching the roaming hands and searching lips of the young couples.

Juan Rodrigo sat his daughter atop the wine barrels behind the bar, then brought her a drink from the soda fountain. "Stay here," he told her. "I'm going to sit with Pedro for a bit. I'm very tired tonight."

Esperanza nodded her head, but as soon as he'd left for the back room, where Pedro and a few of his select friends chatted and passed the time, she crawled up the narrow stairs to the balcony. She was soon disappointed, however, as there was only one couple in the corner, and they didn't look very promising.

The young man was so busy talking about himself that he didn't notice the way the woman clearly rested her hand on his side of the table, and how she occasionally brushed her foot against his shin. From her vantage beneath a table in the opposite corner, Esperanza could see all.

"Welcome, *amigo*," Pedro exclaimed when he saw his friend enter. "You look worse than many that you bury!"

"*Pues sí*," he said with a nod. "Now pour me a drink."

"A glass of my finest cognac for you!" Pedro said, pulling out a bottle and two glasses.

"That's not your finest," Juan Rodrigo remarked, smiling wryly.

"It is the finest we have," Pedro replied. "Don Anselmo bought the last of the good stuff yesterday."

"So it is only second best for gravediggers and bar owners, eh?" Juan Rodrigo sat down at one of two tables in the back room. "Slow night. Everyone's at home."

"Yes," Pedro replied, pulling up a chair and sitting next to his friend. "Though I think we'll get more business as people leave the Pérezes' house. Poor José. He was a good man."

"Yes, he was," Juan Rodrigo said, gazing into his glass. "A toast to José. *Un bicho malo nunca muere!*" he said, causing both men to burst into laughter, a laughter that just as quickly turned silent as each man gazed into his drink. "I'm too old for this work," Juan Rodrigo went on. "Too tired of my part." He took a piece of stale bread from a basket in the center of the table.

"You are another bad bug," Pedro said, but there was love in his voice. The two men had grown very close over the years.

"You've got a job. You make a living. You have the most beautiful daughter in the village."

"And the most strong willed!"

"Yes, and the most strong willed," Pedro replied. "And yet you complain."

"You call burying friends a good job, Pedro Martinez?"

"One man's death is another man's bread," Pedro said, taking a piece of stale bread himself. "I see many men come into this place, few of them as fortunate as you, *mi amigo*."

"I never thought of myself as fortunate." Juan Rodrigo chuckled to himself. "If I am, then where is my fortune?"

"Truthfully, Juan Rodrigo, it's often the people who appear to have much who inside have nothing," Pedro said, stuffing the rest of the piece of bread into his mouth.

"And those who have nothing inside have much?" Juan Rodrigo raised his glass to his lips. "I need another drink to think about this one."

"It's not always the case," Pedro said. "What I'm trying to say is that people make themselves appear one way. But in here . . . In here, I see something else."

Both men sat quietly sipping their cognac.

"And what about you, Pedro?" Juan Rodrigo offered the basket of bread to his friend. "You look like a happy man to me. You have this bar. You have three strong sons. You have a wife, though I admit she is a bit of a shrew. Are you happy?"

A silence slipped between them greater than any Juan Rodrigo had known in all his experience of waiting for the ghosts to talk. It was surprising how difficult it was to get many of the ghosts started telling their stories. Juan Rodrigo didn't push things but sat sipping his cognac, refilling both their glasses when they were empty. "Well, *mi amigo*," he finally said.

"It is not an easy question," Pedro said, gazing at his friend now with all seriousness.

"What do you mean, not an easy question?" Juan Rodrigo replied. "Either you are happy or you're not. One or the other."

"I'm as happy as a man who owns a bar can be." And with that Pedro smiled and took a long drink.

"Spoken like a true bartender," Juan Rodrigo said. "Ambiguous, yet with a trace of the appropriate sadness."

Just then a group of men recently arrived from José's funeral entered the back room. The lead man, Jaime, stared at Juan Rodrigo as if the gravedigger had done him some personal injury. Juan Rodrigo ignored him, continuing to sip his drink. He'd grown used to the stares over the years. The man spoke quietly to the other men in his group, then called to Pedro. "You're lucky this is the only bar in town," he said. "Otherwise we'd go where they don't let devils in."

"My friend is no devil," Pedro replied. "He's an honest man, doing honest work."

"If that is honest work, then why must he live on the edge of town? Don't insult my honest work by comparing it with a gravedigger's."

"You don't need to stay here, Jaime, if the presence of my friend bothers you."

"We stay because we want a drink," Jaime replied. "But we'll sit out here. We wouldn't want to take a chair from any of Juan Rodrigo's ghosts." The men broke into laughter, one of the men slapping Jaime on the back, the other nodding his approval as they were leaving.

"Pigs!" Pedro exclaimed.

"Still, those pigs are your business," Juan Rodrigo replied. "And there are not so many people in this town that you can afford to make enemies."

"But, Juan Rodrigo!"

"Serve them, Pedro. I've been doing this a long time. It comes with the pick and shovel. I'm used to it."

"I'll not serve them."

"Serve them," Juan Rodrigo said again. He stood and took his glass and the basket of stale bread to the counter. "Serve them and smile. It's getting late, and Esperanza is no doubt watching the couples in the balcony. I'd better get her home before she gets any ideas!"

Juan Rodrigo was nothing if not thick skinned, and so, despite the comments of the men, the visit to Pedro's bar lifted his spirits. As a result, on the way home, he told his daughter many stories, whether she wanted to hear them or not. In fact, she did want to hear them. He told her the story of the olive trees that grew along the path—how the ghosts reside in them, and how the crooked one in front of the church came to be. It had not always been crooked, but when Father Ramon passed away, the tree became hunched and bent, and all the village knew that his soul had been black and that the stories were true. He told his daughter the story of the mountains and how they speak to the animals and the people who will listen through the voices of the rivers and the cliffs, and of the moon and how it shines on them because of the love of two young gypsies, Luciano and Rosalinda, who died among the cliffs many years ago. The walk reminded him of other walks, the nights when he'd carried his daughter, a babe in his arms, then, later, a young girl upon his shoulders.

Halfway through the story of the gypsy lovers, Esperanza screamed, *"Por Dios,* Papá, I'm dying!"

Thinking instantly of the flu that had already devastated the village, Juan Rodrigo put his hand to her head for signs of fever, but there was none.

"I'm bleeding, Papá," she said, then hid her face in shame, having remembered what her friend Anna had told her about when a girl begins to bleed. "It's nothing, Papá." She walked ahead.

Juan Rodrigo stared at the moon, seeming to ask it what he should do. Then he grabbed his handkerchief from his pocket and ran to his daughter. He kneeled before her, happy for his quick thinking. "Here, *mi corazón,* put this between your legs. It will stop the bleeding."

"Papá, no!" Esperanza screamed, covering her face.

"Corazón," he pleaded. "There's no need to be embarrassed. It means you are a woman."

Esperanza gazed at her father as the meaning of his words slowly dawned upon her. "Papá, no!" she said again, quietly under her breath as if ashamed. Then she ran from him, crying.

"Esperanza!" he called after her. "I'm sorry. I only want to help." But she was gone. Juan Rodrigo sat in the dirt beneath the glow of the moon and wished, not for the first time, that his wife were alive. "It's a hard road, Carlota," he said to his wife. "And I think it will only get harder." She didn't answer him.

He searched the stars as if trying to decide which one he should address. "You were married young, Carlota. You know what it's like to have womanhood thrust upon you. But at least you had a sister, both older and wiser than you." He laughed at that thought. "Your sister, Consuela, was the youngest monarch of the village!" He slapped his knee and bellowed. "How she married the richest, most prominent man in the village at the age of fourteen could only be the work of *el diablo!*"

The wind shook the branches of the olive trees, knocking several olives to the ground, and what sounded like the call of a nightingale echoed through the cliffs. "There are no birds here anymore," he said, as if he had to convince himself.

"Carlota!" he yelled to the stars. "It's been twelve years. When are you going to speak to me?"

He was aware of the futility of his request, yet still he wanted so much to talk with her. As if also aware of the impossibility, but wanting nevertheless to hear what the gravedigger had to say, the wind stopped, the olive branches stilled. A lone olive dropped next to Juan Rodrigo, and he picked it up, rubbing it between his thumb and forefinger. "I would have married you first if I'd had the courage. Saved you from El Capitán," he said, and sat down against the trunk of the olive tree. "But Consuela had big ideas for you, and I . . . I was too poor and foolish." Again the nightingale's voice haunted the mountains. The sound carried him with it through the cliffs, back to a time when he rose from bed without pain, when he danced through the plaza, a trickster full of himself and of life.

6

The Story of Carlota

JUAN RODRIGO WAITED OUTSIDE the pharmacy for a glimpse of Carlota as she returned from buying her mother's medicine. She wore a simple cotton dress, the sleeves embroidered with flowers. He loved her warm, round face, the way she wore her hair up, but not too tight like the rest of the women in the village. And to him, her thin lips seemed just right, giving her face the appearance of the birds she so loved.

She stopped as usual in the plaza, sitting on the bench by the fountain to talk with the doves that lived in the orange trees. Her smile was like the song of the birds themselves as she sat, happily, in the shade of the trees. And, standing near, Juan Rodrigo could almost hear the words beneath the cooing of the doves: *Fly with us, and we will sing to you always!* Later, when she rose to leave, he almost believed she would fly, but instead she walked across the plaza.

Juan Rodrigo stepped in front of her, but she walked around him without even a glance, picking up her pace. "Carlota, *mi paloma,* I have a special gift for you," he whispered in her ear as he followed her. "I found it yesterday, while burying Señora López."

Carlota slowed her step. Juan Rodrigo took advantage and attempted to press the crystal into her hand. She pushed it away.

"Aren't you taking my gifts anymore?"

"I cannot be seen with you," she said, increasing her pace. "It's not right." There were tears in her eyes, but for Juan Rodrigo those tears were like the crystals themselves—full of hope and magic.

"You don't love him," he said, again stepping in front of her, and this time taking her hand, placing the rose-colored crystal in her palm and closing her fingers about it. "El Capitán is not right for you," he said. "It's because you are afraid to stand up to your sister. *La virgen salvenos!* Consuela is going to smother the village with her ideas of what is proper! She's barely a woman and she runs the lives of everyone!"

At that moment Jorge and Matilde emerged from Ana's bakery, Jorge stuffing a chocolate-filled roll into his mouth. They were dressed in their Sunday best, though it was Monday.

Juan Rodrigo nodded in greeting, then whispered to Carlota, who had started walking again, "The town's full of them, like your sister with her feather hat. Well, at least their black suits fit their sour faces."

Carlota laughed, and glanced back at the other couple. They glared at her, and she felt the shame of a woman of the street, no better than one of Pepita's whores, which was what she was if she continued to talk to Juan Rodrigo when she was to be married in less than a week. Their acquaintance must end now if she was to maintain any respectability. She stopped, and Juan Rodrigo collided with her. It was then, when she felt his breath upon her face, the dirt smell of him so close, that she almost lost her nerve.

"Juan Rodrigo." She forced herself to look at the ground as she spoke; she had to if she was to have any hope of finishing. "I can't deny that you make me laugh. But I am a decent woman, and I am to be married. I will no longer speak to you. Please be a gentleman and leave me." Her voice trembled at the last. "I give you back your crystal, and I will accept no more of them." With that, she grabbed Juan Rodrigo's hand and placed the crystal inside. Her own clammy hand lingered a moment in his, feeling the roughness, the dirt dried and crusted to the skin. Then she turned and walked away.

Juan Rodrigo was left staring at Jorge and Matilde, who continued their prying gaze. "The lady requires my services," he said to them with a bow. "But she knows we gravediggers don't come cheap!"

Jorge and Matilde hurried away for fear the gravedigger would come too close, and Juan Rodrigo went on his way, scratching his head with his dirty hand and wondering if it would be his lot never to be married again.

He'd always wanted children, but his first wife, Josefina, may she rest in peace, died before she'd ever become pregnant. She'd eaten bad cheese and was dead three days later. They'd only been married two years, and they'd tried to have a baby, but it was not meant to be. She was young, a dozen years younger than Juan Rodrigo's thirty, and hers was the second grave he'd had to dig, having inherited the position of village *enterrador* from his father, but having as yet not exercised his occupation, as his father had died only six months before. That had been a difficult year for Juan Rodrigo, and perhaps that was why he'd not yet heard the voices of the ghosts talking to him. Josefina would surely have comforted him during the night with stories of what their lives might have been and the great things their children would have done. He expected to hear from her, as his father and grandfather before had heard from the ghosts of the village. It was part of being a gravedigger.

But he'd heard nothing, and it was perhaps the silence more than anything that drove the grief deep inside him, so that he consoled himself with Pepita and her whores late at night, after he'd given up trying to sleep. If he had been younger, then perhaps he would have weathered the deaths of his father and Josefina better, but now, two years later, he still had not heard the voices of the ghosts. He wondered if perhaps the line of gravediggers had ended with his father, and the thought gave fuel to his ideas of venturing to the city and starting a business. He didn't know what he would do, but he had many thoughts. He liked the idea of driving those new machines, the burro-less carts they called cars. There were no cars as yet in his village, but he'd heard stories about them, how they roared through the city, spewing smoke, and every once in a while he'd seen one of the big ones climbing the narrow mountain road meant only for burros, to deliver tobacco or canned goods to José's *estanco*. He'd thought maybe he could drive one, too, and maybe, though this was something he scarcely allowed himself to entertain, he could own a few of them and hire other men to drive goods to and fro, from town to town. He'd told Carlota of his idea before she became engaged, and she didn't laugh. That's when he was sure he loved her.

Juan Rodrigo did not see Carlota again before the marriage, but on the wedding day, he hiked from his house up the winding road that led to the top of the mountain, where the church sat at the cliff's edge overlooking the sea. And it was here he saw his *paloma* standing in the garden beside the church, surrounded by the doves she loved, and wearing the long gown that had practically broken her mother to buy. The sunlight on the sequins illuminated her, such that the flowing folds of her gown appeared as glittering wings. Juan Rodrigo once again felt that at any moment she would rise into the sky and fly away.

El Capitán played his part well. Ever concerned with appearances, he stood erect, dressed in the blue, decorated, and creaseless uniform of the Spanish navy. The captain's name was Manolo Manuel Carranza, but he was known simply as El Capitán because he was the only man in the village of recent memory to have served in the armed forces. Nobody in the village was actually sure that he was indeed a captain, and they never bothered to ask; for them it was good enough that he'd served their king in the military. Truth be told, they were also a bit afraid of him. Though he was a slight man, he was tall, and his stern face tolerated nothing less than perfect decorum in all interactions. Juan Rodrigo couldn't help but feel sadness when he thought of his dove, Carlota, subjected to such a cold and demanding husband. The man was more suited to Consuela. They would be perfect together, Juan Rodrigo thought.

Consuela stood behind her sister, alongside her husband, Tesifón, the huge plumes of Consuela's feather hat practically blocking all view of the bride. And a stray feather seemed to be falling across Tesifón's face, causing him to wrinkle up his nose and sneeze just as the priest brought out the sacrament. This caused Tesifón no small embarrassment because, though he was the most prominent man in the village, he'd always been very sensitive. That is perhaps why he'd spent so much time alone, working out his theories and inventions. They say he spent little time with his first wife, not like he did now. Consuela demanded that he accompany her wherever she went. But, years before, he would spend day after day working in his shed, sometimes even at night by candlelight. And then one night, if anyone had bothered to look through the window of the shed, they would have noticed a strange yellow-green glow emanating from within. Tesifón no longer worked by the light of the candle. He had discovered electricity. That's not to say he'd invented it—everyone knew an American had done that. The cities and larger villages already had electricity, but no one had bothered to bring it up to the poor mountain towns. Tesifón had read the books and studied the diagrams until he'd discovered electricity for the village, then he went about wiring, first his own house, then the doctor's office, then the bar (which at that time he owned), and finally the mayor's house, which he eventually occupied.

Consuela couldn't have been more proud, though she was only ten at the time; the villagers figured she'd already set her sights on him. At first she visited Tesifón's family in their big house at the end of the plaza because she said she was curious to see the electricity. The odd thing was that when she said "see," she meant she wanted to understand how this miracle worked. Tesifón took to her immediately; none of his own children were curious to understand, and his wife had never fully recovered from the birth of their last child. Over the next four years, Consuela became a fixture in the house, visiting every day. She began taking care of the children, who were scarcely younger than she, and managing the household, as it was clear Tesifón's wife wouldn't last much longer. When his wife finally died, it seemed the most natural thing in the world that Tesifón marry Consuela, though he was forty and she barely fourteen. He genuinely loved her, and she managed the household better than his previous wife ever had. Consuela was a strong woman, and soon she not only dominated Tesifón but also began to run the affairs in the village. No one was sure how it happened, but by the time she was twenty, even the mayor, Don Anselmo, consulted her whenever an important decision had to be made. On her twenty-second birthday, Tesifón became mayor, and from then on, when they strolled down the main street, people bowed their heads to them. Consuela never had children of her own, seemingly content to raise Tesifón's. Perhaps that is why she had so much time to devote to other people's affairs, particularly her sister, Carlota's. Desiring to see the rest of her family rise as she had, Consuela conspired with her mother to arrange a suitable marriage for Carlota. Being younger, and of a submissive disposition (at least at that time), Carlota yielded, though she loved Juan Rodrigo.

But now we must turn to Carlota's story, for her marriage was an unhappy one, and it began the first night of the honeymoon, in their hotel along the Ramblas of Barcelona. After a fine dinner and a stroll along the seashore, Carlota and El Capitán returned to their hotel. Carlota had been terrified all evening. Though her sister had instructed her in the ways of love, wanting to be sure that Carlota did nothing to displease her husband and ruin the perfect match, Carlota was fearful of her husband's strict demeanor. Would he beat her if she failed in her wifely duty? She wanted to love him, believed in love, but he seemed so distant. She hoped it was his own fear that made him so.

"Your room is to the right," El Capitán said, kissing her on the cheek and turning down the hallway.

"But where are you staying?" Carlota asked, reaching out yet afraid to touch him. "Aren't we going to spend the night together?"

"Mine is next door," he said sternly. "There is a door that joins them. But we will not use it. Is that understood, Carlota?" he asked, avoiding her gaze. Carlota thought she noticed his hand straining to meet hers. "Good night," he said, and walked down the hall.

Carlota hardly slept, crying into her pillow, wondering what she'd done wrong. He hated her, she thought. And when later in the night her hand drifted between her legs, satiating the desire her mind attempted to deny, she hated herself, thinking that he'd seen through her weakness.

Each day during their two-week honeymoon, El Capitán was polite and considerate but cold in his dealings with Carlota. He made conversation but never broached anything too delicate. Carlota tried to ask him about his days in the navy, but he refused to speak of them, saying they were not fit to discuss with women. And each night was the same. He would take her to her room, kiss her on the cheek, and say good night. But Carlota grew sensitive to her husband's emotions. She saw clearly now the regret in his eyes as he pulled his hand from hers; she noticed the slight delay in his step as he started to go, as if unsure of his actions— something he never seemed to be, and she couldn't help but think that he loved her, and that his actions were the result of shyness on his part. Perhaps through all his bravado he's never been with a woman, she thought. Maybe he's as frightened as I.

On the last night of their honeymoon, Carlota lay in bed, again touching herself, and again feeling ashamed. Her own mother had told her she should never do such a thing. Father Ramon had told her it was a sin against God, though he made her explain everything in detail at confession. But the burning feeling inside of her wouldn't go away. And Consuela had told her it was her right just as much as it was her husband's.

She tossed and turned throughout the night, fighting with herself and the fears her mother had instilled in her that kept her from going to her husband and taking the lead, showing him what to do. Surely, once she touched him and placed his hand on her, the rest would happen as nature commanded. Twice she rose from her bed and marched to the door, both times falling short of opening it. She sat on the edge of the bed, again wondering if she'd done something wrong. She knew she was attractive—many men had told her so, including Juan Rodrigo. What would he do if he were with her now? She smiled at the thought. He would have to clean his dirty hands first of all! She imagined looking into those eyes, which seemed buried by the weight of the earth yet somehow shined like a rough gemstone first exposed to the sun whenever they gazed upon her. El Capitán didn't look at her that way, even when he kissed her good night. She grabbed the pillow, threw it against the wall. Maybe he would if he was given the chance. Maybe he felt trapped like she did. Finally she rose from the bed, put on her robe, and opened the door adjoining the two rooms.

She heard him breathing, long, deep breaths. He was asleep. As she glided through the room, a ghost in the darkness, she felt almost giddy. She couldn't believe she was breaking so many unspoken rules. Well, if my sister can do it, so can I, she thought, and slipped into the bed beside El Capitán. He lay on his back and didn't stir. She lay next to him, afraid to move, listening to his breathing. The sound of it, deep, trusting, encouraged her. Perhaps her theory of his shyness was true. She let herself inhale deeply, taking in his scent. The smell of the cologne he wore throughout the day was strong, but now there was something else mixed with it, a scent she couldn't place because it was not of the earth, but rather, a smell like the cry of gulls over a rime-covered sea. What mysteries does he keep from me? she wondered. And with that she placed her hand softly on his chest. She let it lie there awhile, feeling his breathing and gathering courage to carry out her plan. Again the thought flashed through her mind that she was going against all propriety. What if he told her she was nothing but a simple woman of the street? She pulled her hand back, then heard her sister's voice: *He will expect you to give him pleasure. It is your duty as his wife.* Surely he wouldn't be angry, and her hand dropped as if of its own accord onto his stomach and moved slowly downward.

She reached between his legs. Her fingers felt the coarse pubic hair, but below that the skin felt rough and flat. She searched further, grabbing and pinching the skin in her attempt to find what Consuela had described to her. She realized now her first impression was wrong. Instead of being flat, there was a small flap of skin and an indentation next to it that felt as if there was a tiny hole inside. She thought maybe she'd entered the wrong room and pulled her hand back. But she knew there was only one adjoining door. A thought far worse crept into her head: What if he'd left her, and she was now in some stranger's bed?

"What devil's work is this?" El Capitán yelled, springing from the bed. "Who is here?" And before Carlota could answer, he'd turned on the light on the bedside table, grabbed the pistol from within the table drawer, and pointed it at Carlota's head.

"It is Carlota, your wife," she said, staring alternately at the gun and at her husband's face. "I'm sorry if I've startled you. I didn't mean to. I just thought. . ." She didn't finish her sentence, but rather waited, scarcely breathing, expecting him to put away the pistol. He did not.

"What did you see?" he asked, and his dark eyes showed no sign of love. "What did you see?" he repeated.

"Nothing. It was dark. I couldn't see anything," she said, shaking now. "What are you doing, Manolo? Please put away the gun. It is your wife." She reached out her hands to him, grasping the hand that held the gun, holding it tightly. *"Por favor, Manolo, soy tu esposa,"* she said. But her pleading only hardened him.

"If you ever speak a word of this to anyone, I'll kill you. Do you understand?" he asked, placing the gun directly against her forehead. "If I so much as hear a snicker from a neighbor or see a condescending glance from a stranger in the street, I'll shoot you."

The gun shook against Carlota's head. "I understand," she whispered, stroking the hand that held the gun with both of hers. "I won't tell a soul," she said, gazing directly into his eyes, pressing her forehead against the barrel of the gun, softly.

El Capitán dropped the pistol onto the bed and sank to his knees, resting his head against Carlota's breasts, weeping quietly. Carlota stroked his hair and repeated, "I'll never tell a soul."

The years passed one after another and Carlota kept her promise. Juan Rodrigo resigned himself to the fact that he would not marry again, contenting himself with a weekly visit to Pepita's whores. The ghosts still had not visited him, and he'd buried many people in the years that followed Carlota's marriage. The first of the many flu epidemics that swept through Spain took countless lives, including that of Carlota's mother. With each coming spring, Juan Rodrigo planned to leave for the city, forsaking his job as gravedigger, telling himself the silence of the ghosts was a message. Yet each spring he remained in the village, passing by Carlota's house whenever he was in town and wondering what kept him there.

Carlota rarely left the house, and when she did, she appeared pale, stricken by a grief no one could understand. Juan Rodrigo heard the whispers of the townspeople: *That girl has everything, yet she looks like a cow that doesn't give milk. She's married El Capitán but it's not enough. She wants to be better than her sister. She's too proud. And why does she have no children? Five years married and no children. Her pride makes her sterile. Poor Capitán!*

Indeed, Carlota was miserable. El Capitán was a hard man, expecting his wife to present herself with distinction even inside his own house. Carlota could have handled that if there had been some sign of warmth, but since the honeymoon any hint of that had disappeared. Supplied with a stipend from the navy, El Capitán had no need to work. At sunrise he donned his suit, walked to José's *estanco* for tobacco and a newspaper, then returned home to read throughout the morning. After lunch he took his siesta, and in the evening he walked alone along the cliffs, staring out toward the distant sea. Carlota lived for the slightest hint of attention from him, sure that his disfavor was her own fault, stemming back from her impropriety on that night. But she still longed for relief from her own burning desires, and more, to be desired. After the first year of her marriage, thinking she could take no more, she'd tried to talk to her sister. Not knowing how to broach the subject and wanting to be true to her promise to her husband not to speak of his deformity, she tried to bring up the topic in roundabout fashion by first asking if her sister thought touching oneself was wrong. She'd meant to explain that she had yet to make love to her husband and leave it at that, but Consuela's response was so strong that Carlota couldn't bring herself to continue. *Masturbation is an abomination before God. Your husband should be enough for you, Carlota. Do not speak to me of this again!*

However, Consuela was an astute woman. She would not have become the first lady of the village otherwise, and she'd noticed for a long time the misery that sat on her sister's face. She'd noted that Carlota rarely left the house, and when she did, she completed her errand and returned immediately, never stopping in the plaza to speak with the doves as she was once so fond of doing. Though she could be a harsh woman, Consuela was not without love for her sister, and over the years the fact that her sister appeared without hope, and that it was she herself who'd arranged her sister's marriage, plagued her with guilt. And then there was the fact that her sister had no children. Maybe that's where her unhappiness was coming from, she thought.

One evening she decided to visit her sister during the time she knew El Capitán to be out on a stroll. The decision had taken her five years to reach, but as Consuela later said, it had been five years too long.

"Carlota, there has been a secret between us," she said the moment she entered the house. Carlota stopped plucking the chicken she was preparing for dinner, and turned, fearing her sister's words. "I know you are unhappy in your marriage, and that fact alone has bothered me, since arranging the marriage was largely my doing, but there is something deeper, and it is time you told me what it was."

Carlota wiped her hands clean and moved slowly to the kitchen table. "I cannot speak of it. I've sworn I would not," she said before sitting down and covering her face in her hands.

"Does he hurt you?" Consuela stepped forward, an imposing presence, and in that moment Carlota felt afraid for anyone who crossed her sister.

"No. Maybe that would be something," Carlota said. "At least he would notice me. It's as if I don't exist for him. As his wife, I'm one of his medals that he wears so proudly on his chest. I mean nothing more to him." And with that she began crying in earnest.

Consuela sat at the table, taking her sister's hand. "Do you take care of him?"

Carlota looked at her sister, fearing to answer the question she hinted at. She pretended not to understand.

"In bed, I mean," Consuela continued. "Oftentimes a man can become resentful if he is not satisfied. I learned this earlier than many, as Tesifón's hunger was like an animal's." She smiled, though, and Carlota knew it had not been unpleasant.

For a moment, it looked as though Carlota would speak, but then she burst into a fit of sobbing. "I can't," she said, and rose to busy herself again with the chicken.

Consuela followed her, grabbing her by the arm. "Tell me," she demanded. "Tell me or I'll confront him myself when he gets home. I'm not leaving until you tell me."

Unable to withstand Consuela's fortitude, Carlota collapsed in her arms, crying softly now, trying to gather her strength. Consuela carried her to the living room couch and laid her down. "Tell me, my sister," she said, lightly stroking Carlota's forehead. "The time for secrets is over."

"We have not consummated our marriage," Carlota said.

"What!" Consuela looked in disbelief. "That's impossible. Are you saying he is one of those, like poor Francisco, one of those who like men?"

"No, no." Carlota pushed herself up on the couch and looked her sister in the eye, grief and despair making her momentarily forget her promise to her husband. "He has no penis."

The bluntness of the statement caused Consuela to burst into laughter. Carlota remained serious; then, suddenly, a small giggle escaped her mouth, like the first bubble from the fountain at the soda shop. Her sister gazed at her, surprised by the realization that she had not seen Carlota laugh in a very long time. Consuela took her sister's hand across the table. "Oh, my dear," she said, thinking she was going to say something serious, when what she said was, "How on earth does he go pee?" Carlota sat thinking in all earnestness. "I don't know," she said. "He never lets me see him. But I'm sure the doctors must have thought of that." She rushed the last few words as if she had to get them out, for in truth she did, as the words were in danger of being overrun by the laughter that raced up from deep inside, laughter that had been stifled for too long. Consuela smiled at the sight of a side of her sister that had almost been lost, then she, too, joined in. It wasn't until Carlota nearly fell out of her seat that she thought about her broken promise to her husband. If he heard their laughter, he would know, and she'd never forgotten what he said that night she made her discovery. "He told me that if I told anyone he would kill me," she said to her sister, and immediately the realization that she'd broken her promise and that he would undoubtedly kill her fully entered her mind.

Consuela stifled her own laughter instantly. "Over my dead body and that of La Virgen Santa, he'll kill you," she exclaimed, already picking Carlota up off the couch and gathering up her things. "It's not natural living under fear like that, and without sex!"

"What are you doing?" Carlota asked as she watched her sister enter her bedroom and gather her clothes from the armoire. Once again she was afraid of the answer.

"You're leaving!" Consuela exclaimed. "You're not staying here another second. I'll tell him myself!" She threw Carlota's clothes along with a few photos and the candlesticks their mother had given her as a wedding present into the suitcase Carlota had used on her honeymoon. "I'm taking you to Father Joaquín. He will annul the marriage. It never existed if it wasn't consummated."

At that moment, El Capitán entered the bedroom. "What is the meaning of this?" he said with as much dignity as he could muster, standing in the brown suit he saved for his evening strolls.

"I'm taking Carlota," Consuela said, moving directly before El Capitán. "She's leaving you, and you are not going to stop her, nor will you carry out your threat to kill her, Manolo Carranza!" Then she moved in close and whispered in El Capitán's ear. Carlota couldn't hear what she said, but she understood her sister's threat by the way her husband's eyes grew wide, and afterward how those same eyes seemed lost, as if he were looking at her from beneath the sea, and how his head hung low as he stood in the corner of the room, watching them pack and biting his lip as if he wanted to say more, perhaps to say he didn't mean for it to be this way.

As Consuela dragged her sister from the house, Carlota couldn't bring herself to look at her husband, ashamed of her broken promise and fearful of his wrath. But El Capitán didn't try to kill her as he'd said, nor did he appear much different. He went about his life with little break in his routine, greeting José each morning at his *estanco* and nodding pleasantly at those he passed on his evening walks, though many returned his greeting with stifled giggles and concealed smiles.

The combined power of Consuela and Tesifón was too much for Father Joaquín, and besides, he reasoned, God meant for his children to multiply; a marriage without children was a sin against God. He did not express this rationalization to the childless Consuela and Tesifón, but he did perform the rites of annulment and Carlota was soon free.

Her freedom was bittersweet, as she often saw El Capitán in the plaza and was reminded of her broken promise. The fact that he nodded to her, smiling politely, again made her feel that somehow the failure of their marriage was her fault. Still, she actually enjoyed living with her sister and over time she began talking again to the doves in the plaza, knowing full well that Juan Rodrigo observed her from the outskirts. This also made her smile.

Consuela did not learn the lesson of her misguided match-making well. Within a month of the annulment, she brought the dandy, Fulgencio, home for dinner. She pretended it was in order for him and Tesifón to discuss the possibility of turning the bar into a millinery. The bar had always bothered her; it wasn't a proper possession for a respectable family. But Carlota divined the real motive immediately.

"Fulgencio is a man of means," Consuela said over dinner. Fulgencio nodded his head and adjusted his bright blue and yellow tie.

"Yes, I already own one dress shop, and I hope to open another in Montefrío."

Carlota studied the way he delicately placed the fork in his mouth, taking the pork with his teeth, careful not to let his lips touch the meat. Afterward he dabbed at his mouth with the napkin, meticulously brushing at his mustache in case any food may have been caught there.

"He's thinking of buying one of those auto cars, aren't you, Fulgencio?" Consuela placed a second helping of pork on his plate without asking him, then commanded, "Eat, eat, you need some fat on you, you skinny boy!"

Fulgencio quickly downed more wine and shakily proceeded to cut his pork.

As Fulgencio was leaving, Consuela and Tesifón disappeared into the kitchen and Carlota was left to see him to the door.

"It has been a great pleasure to dine with you," he said, his mustache twitching as if a fly had landed there. "I would very much like to have another opportunity to become better acquainted. I shall talk to your sister about arranging another meeting." And with that he took her hand, slowly drawing it to his face and kissing it. The hairs of his mustache tickled, and Carlota drew her hand away.

That night, Carlota and her sister fought for the first time, but it proved not to be the last.

"You're practically a soiled woman, Carlota," Consuela said, preening the feathers in her hat for the following morning. "You need to be married as soon as possible."

"But how can you say that, when we never consummated the marriage? And besides, it was annulled. That's supposed to mean it never was."

"It doesn't matter what it means," Consuela responded. "It's what people think, and the people see you as a fallen woman."

"That's ridiculous."

"Well, that's how it is."

"And I don't like Fulgencio. Every time his mustache twitches, I feel like I need to scratch. He makes me nervous."

"And you'd rather marry the gravedigger!" It was the first time Consuela had mentioned Juan Rodrigo. Carlota thought her sister hadn't noticed his attentions in the plaza. She berated herself for her foolishness. Of course, her sister knew everything that went on in the town. "Why do you flush, Carlota? Is it because there's truth in what I say?"

Carlota felt the heat in her face and was almost as astonished as her sister. Did she really have feelings for the gravedigger?

Of course, she'd thought about him, but weren't those just fancies?

"I know you're not foolish enough to consider that dirt pusher seriously, but be careful. People do talk if you give them reason." She placed the hat on her head and turned to Carlota. "There. It looks much more festive, don't you think?"

The next morning, Carlota lingered in the plaza, enjoying the shade of the orange trees, and finding the language of the doves the only thing that put her spirit at peace. She knew Juan Rodrigo was watching, and she dared to whisper, asking the doves what they thought of the gravedigger. One of them said that he was a lonely man, living in his cottage by himself. Another added, under her cooing, that she thought him handsome, though he was dirty all the time. And yet another, who didn't seem to understand that not all humans can soar above the trees like Carlota, added that he seemed to lack belief in other worlds, but then feeling bad for criticizing, said that she shouldn't think poorly of him for that, as he'd never hurt a bird, and that was rare among men.

As she stood to leave the plaza, Juan Rodrigo pulled her into a clump of orange trees, causing the birds there to fly off in quite a commotion.

"I see you've washed yourself today, Juan Rodrigo," Carlota said with a wry smile.

"Yes," he answered, fumbling for the words. "*Mi paloma*, I wanted to tell you . . ." He paused.

"What?" She reached for an orange and held it between them as if it were a crystal ball they could peer into and divine their futures.

"I wanted to tell you that I'm going to leave this village, and I hoped you would come with me."

His dark eyes pierced, making Carlota nervous. Yet she held his gaze, wondering at the intensity of it and feeling that she could yield to the strength of that gaze. "But you are the gravedigger, like your father and his father before."

"No, I'm not cut out for it," he answered. "I don't have the feeling."

"You lack belief in other worlds," Carlota said with a giggle.

Juan Rodrigo studied her, wondering what she knew of his profession. "I want to go to the city and start a business. I'm going to drive a truck."

"You want me to go with you and live in sin?" she asked, feeling a thrill run through her, not unlike the thrill she felt when she talked with the doves.

"Of course not," he said, and then, slightly encouraged, dared to say, "I want to marry you right away."

Carlota dropped the orange and stepped back. "It's not right that people should see us here together," she said. "They might talk."

"You sound like your sister."

"I speak my own feelings."

"Carlota," he pleaded, "we've already lost five years. All that time wasted with no one to savor your beauty, except from afar. You deserve better."

"And you think you'd be better," she replied, but her voice trembled. Sensing her own weakness, she rushed away across the plaza.

Juan Rodrigo watched her go, feeling hope again for the first time in many years.

The following Sunday evening, Fulgencio made his way through the village, dressed in his best white suit, with the bright purple tie his cousin in the city had sent him. He was on his way to Consuela's house, having been invited for dinner. Being that it was Sunday, Arturo's flower shop was closed, so he picked the flowers from Isabel's garden, knowing she took a late siesta.

Juan Rodrigo had heard of Fulgencio's invitation to dinner and was determined to put up a fight this time, or at least to fight in the only way he knew how. The day before, he'd bought some fine tissue paper and a beautiful pink box from Martina's stationery store, then went home and waited for his burro to unburden himself. He carefully wrapped the offending pile in the tissue paper and placed it in the box, dousing it with his own cologne to hide the smell. The next evening, as Fulgencio crossed the plaza and was about to reach Consuela's house, Juan Rodrigo sent a boy to give Fulgencio his present, with the instructions that the boy simply say the package was from an admirer.

Upon seeing the package, Fulgencio clapped his hands together, as if in anticipation of a great meal, his mustache twitching as the boy told him the present was from an admirer. Fulgencio dug in his silk-lined pockets and tipped the boy quite generously, then grabbed the box and held it up to the sun. However, much to Juan Rodrigo's horror, he did not open the box then and there. Instead, Fulgencio tucked it under his arm and continued on to Consuela's. Juan Rodrigo followed, fearing he'd made a grave mistake, but at the same time giddy that he now had a wider audience for his joke.

Standing behind the Lady of the Night that grew so thickly around Consuela's porch, Juan Rodrigo heard her greeting and

Fulgencio's comment that "I received a gift from an admirer, who I believe resides in your house!" She ushered him in quickly, both of them exclaiming and gesticulating about the secret gift. Juan Rodrigo crept along the house, until he sat crouched under the open living room window, listening to the excited conversation.

"Carlota, Tesifón, come here at once!" Consuela's voice rang through the house. "Fulgencio has a gift he says comes from an admirer. Who could that possibly be?"

Juan Rodrigo heard steps but only Tesifón's voice: "What a lovely box! Whoever picked it certainly had Fulgencio in mind." And Juan Rodrigo hoped he was not mistaken in recognizing distaste in Tesifón's words.

"Well, open it. Open it!" Consuela demanded.

But where is *mi paloma?* Juan Rodrigo wondered. He wanted her to be near so he could imagine she stood in the air above him as he crouched below the window, but he was also desperately afraid that she would not appreciate his joke. She is too much like her sister, he thought. And I fear that the longer she lives with her, the more like her she'll become.

"Carlota, you see Fulgencio has other admirers. Unless, of course, you sent this to him." Consuela didn't bother to disguise her obvious insinuation.

"I sent nothing, sister."

So she was there. Juan Rodrigo crept closer, pressing his body against the wall, hoping to feel her presence.

There was a loud scream followed by a thud, as of a body hitting the floor. Was it Consuela or Carlota? Then a shout from Tesifón. "*Que diablo tenemos aqui!* How dare you bring such filth into my house!"

"*Pero, señor,* I had no idea," Fulgencio stammered. "I swear *por La Virgen* that a boy gave me this package in the street."

"And now you dare to swear in my house? Get out!"

"*Por favor, señor,* you must believe me. I'm very sorry."

"I'm sure you are, but nevertheless you must leave at once and take that 'present' with you! And don't come back until you can think of a good reason why you would bring such a stinking pestilence inside a lady's house."

Juan Rodrigo heard the front door open and shut with a bang, followed by Fulgencio's quick steps. He thought of pursuing him. Watching Fulgencio fume over the incident, talking to himself as he was prone to do, would be so much fun, but Juan Rodrigo didn't dare move. What if Tesifón saw him leave his spot beneath the window? He would wait until darkness, then creep away. Besides, he wished to be near his *paloma.* If it was she who fainted, he would never forgive himself.

"Carlota, your sister is coming to now, and it won't do to be smiling like a monkey," Tesifón said, allowing himself a stifled laugh at the end. *Gracías a Dios,* Juan Rodrigo thought. But did she find my joke amusing? Does she suspect me?

"What's so funny?" Consuela's voice sounded weak but quickly regained its strength. "That man is perverse!"

Tesifón and Carlota burst into laughter, and Juan Rodrigo heard Consuela's voice rising above all: "Desist at once! I do not find it amusing."

Late that night, Carlota took a red silk scarf from her armoire and crept downstairs to the kitchen. Quietly, she took out a bowl and poured olive oil into it, then grabbed an egg from the basket they kept on the table and cracked the egg, allowing the yolk to fall into the bowl. She waited, glancing nervously behind her for fear her sister may have heard something and was coming to investigate. Her sister would not appreciate her superstitious ways, though the last time she had done this had been years ago, when she and her sister were both children, and it was Consuela who'd had a crush on Jesús, an older boy at school. Back then Consuela had believed in the powers of divination contained in the egg.

Carlota took a deep breath and placed the scarf over the bowl. She waited, afraid to peer in and see her future. But she needed to know. She did not want to make the same mistake again. She remembered Juan Rodrigo's words in the plaza: *All that time wasted with no one to savor your beauty.* She longed to feel his lips upon her skin. But what if the egg showed Fulgencio's face? With trepidation, she forced herself to look into the bowl. It was difficult to see through the scarf. She should have picked a lighter color, she thought. Did Juan Rodrigo's eyes stare back at her from within the yolk? Was that his crooked nose? She leaned closer. Or was it Fulgencio's mustache? The yolk seemed to be changing, shifting in the oil. She waited. But the longer she waited, the more she feared the outcome, until it felt as if she were inhaling the scarf, suffocating on it. She tore the scarf away, flinging it to the floor, and dumped the egg out the kitchen window. "I can't do it," she said as she sat at the table, breathing heavily. "I'll die if I go through another marriage like the last."

The next week, Fulgencio followed Consuela around so much that people started asking if she had adopted a new puppy. He didn't seem to mind their insults, nor the new humiliation he was bringing on himself, desperate as he was to erase the horror of his humiliation from the previous Sunday. Finally, while shopping in Fulgencio's shop, surrounded by the shimmering dresses and glittering purses, Consuela consented to give him another chance.

"You would be a good husband for Carlota," she said. "And so you may come to our house for dinner this Sunday. But be on your best behavior, for I cannot vouch for the forgiveness of Tesifón and Carlota."

"I will dress in splendor," Fulgencio said, following her out the door of his own store. "I will arrive like Apollo on his chariot, with the sun's rays upon me."

Consuela raised her eyebrow, took him by the crook of the arm, yanked him close, and said, "Just don't act the fool!" And with that she walked away, the feathers of her hat lightly bouncing with each step.

Carlota and Juan Rodrigo met each day in the plaza. At first she pretended to be angry with him for the trick he played on Fulgencio, telling him the joke was very low. She made him swear not to do anything like that again, and he promised so earnestly that she gave him a quick kiss on the cheek when no one, except the birds, was looking. For, in truth, meeting him here in the plaza eased her worries. Perhaps Juan Rodrigo would charm her sister after all, and she needn't fear a second mistake. But then she pictured her sister's imposing face, the grimace that was sure to come at even the mention of the gravedigger.

To keep her mind off her fears, she talked hopefully with Juan Rodrigo of their lives together, and when they might move to the city. How he would bring gifts home to her every day, just as he did now. But unlike the crystals, these gifts would be taken from whatever he was hauling in his truck that day. If he carried fine necklaces for the jewelers of the city, he would save the most beautiful necklace for her. If his cargo was flowers, then he would save the freshest.

"And what if you carry chickens?" Carlota said with a smile.

"Then you will have the biggest chicken to pluck for dinner!"

SUNDAY CAME AGAIN TOO SOON, and Juan Rodrigo, knowing that Fulgencio was scheduled for another visit with his beloved, paced under the orange trees in the plaza.

"I know Consuela!" he shouted to the birds in the trees. "She'll marry her sister to any idiot who has money! All the fool has to do is show up and not fart during dinner, and she'll have them engaged by morning!"

The doves stirred in the trees, flapping their wings wildly.

"So you understand the problem, too, *mis palomas*," he said. The doves cooed back at him. "What are we going to do?" he asked, and then thought, Look at me, now I'm talking with the birds. Wouldn't Carlota smile to see me!

"You know me, *palomas*. I am not a wealthy man, nor well bred. But I love her, I tell you. I see her fly with you when she talks. I see the way her body rises off the ground, as if she's one of you, and I love her for it. I have nothing to offer her, except that I promise I would never hold back that spirit that wishes to fly!"

The leaves shook in the orange trees as the birds excitedly flapped their wings, cooing and talking with one another. "He sees more than we thought," said one, with brown feathers streaking its wing. "Yes, he may not believe yet, but he can see," said another. And then a young one with a black-spotted chest, whom the others sometimes thought to be headstrong because he often wouldn't leave the trees when the dogs entered the plaza, said, "Why don't we help him?" and the other birds had to admit it was a good idea.

Fulgencio marched through the village as if he truly were Apollo, holding his head high, his great nose pointing to the sky as if it were Olympus itself. He nodded to those he passed, granting them the favor of his gaze. His hair, slicked back with brilliantine, shimmered beneath the setting sun. The light blue suit he had accented with an uncharacteristically conservative gold tie, not wanting to risk offending Tesifón on this night. The large box of chocolates under his arm was wrapped in a blue ribbon to match his suit. All in all, he was a truly spectacular sight. Unfortunately, his glory was not to be, for as he crossed the plaza, a dark cloud appeared over the horizon, moving rapidly toward him. The doves from the plaza had gathered other birds: magpies and starlings from the cliffs, larks, hoopoes, little bustards, and blue chaffinches from the great olive groves, and even a few of the beautiful green and yellow bee-eaters and Bearded Tits from beyond the mountains. Leading them were a Red Kite and a rare Siberian Blue Robin that everyone thought had become extinct. The great cloud moved in on the plaza, and on the as yet unaware Fulgencio, circling once, then swooping down, suddenly.

It happened so fast, Fulgencio was not entirely sure what had occurred. For a few minutes, he stood in the plaza, alternating between staring at the mess of his clothes and attempting to wipe off the thick white coat. But very quickly he gave up, throwing the box of chocolates into the street and storming back the way he had come.

Juan Rodrigo, who'd been tailing Fulgencio, was in a sort of giddy shock. He'd never imagined the birds would come to his aid, and since he hadn't heard their talking, he'd been as unaware of their plans as Fulgencio. But what happened next surprised him even more. Without thinking, he went to Isabel's garden, picked the most beautiful flowers, and marched to Consuela's door. He hadn't even cleaned himself properly!

When Consuela answered the door, he presented her with the flowers and stepped in. At first she tried to give the flowers back and shoo him out the door, but as he wouldn't budge, she attempted to gather herself by looking for a vase while she thought of a strategy to politely get rid of him before Fulgencio should arrive. Fortunately, Carlota had seen Juan Rodrigo's approach from her window, and she ran downstairs to meet him.

"I regret to inform you that Fulgencio will not be coming tonight," Juan Rodrigo said with a playful smile. "He sent me in his place, hoping you would understand."

"How delightful!" Carlota exclaimed, pressing her hands together as if in prayer. However, Consuela had returned by then, her wits fully restored.

"How odd that Fulgencio wouldn't tell us himself," she said. "He is a well-bred gentleman." And with this she looked directly at Juan Rodrigo. "It is unlikely that he would send a gravedigger as a replacement."

"A gravedigger is a very old and respected profession, my dear Consuela," Tesifón said, entering the room from the parlor. "Juan Rodrigo's father, Fernando, gave much of himself to ease the grief of this village. His son is welcome in our house." And with that he shook Juan Rodrigo's hand and led him back to the parlor. Consuela immediately crossed herself.

As they drank brandy they could hear Consuela storming about the house, taking out her anger on the cook, a poor peasant girl who'd arrived only last month after her parents had been killed, hit as they were walking home along the dirt path they'd walked nearly every day of their lives, by the first truck to carry goods into the Alpujarras. Occasionally, Carlota found an excuse to pass by the parlor, lingering at the entrance, and lowering her eyes when Juan Rodrigo raised his.

The dinner felt almost like a birth: moments of calm punctuated by Consuela's screaming at the cook, and finally elation that it was all over. Still, Tesifón appeared to enjoy Juan Rodrigo's company, both being older men, and having many stories to tell about life in the village. And Carlota had made it clear that she was pleased with Juan Rodrigo's performance by letting her arm brush up against his as they walked to the door.

Their courtship was quick. Tesifón, who seemed to submit to his wife's will in so many things, stood up to her in the matter of the gravedigger, seeing clearly that Carlota had never been happier, and he proved to be quite nimble at keeping his wife in check. When, after a month, Carlota and Juan Rodrigo announced their intent to be married, Consuela flew into a rage, tearing out the feathers in her beloved hat. But, once again, with Tesifón's quick intervention, she calmed down, consenting after a week to the idea and agreeing to plan the wedding, thinking that at least the disgrace of her sister's unmarried status would be over and being impressed by Juan Rodrigo's plan to start a business in the city. God forbid her own blood should be involved with ghosts, she thought.

The wedding was extremely tasteful, as everyone expected it to be. All of the upstanding citizens in the village were there, and a few of the lesser in standing as well, as Juan Rodrigo had invited his few cousins and even more friends. They were married in the courtyard of the church, overlooking the sea, the doves once again perched in the surrounding trees, providing the music. El Capitán sat in the back row, dignified, with legs crossed, wearing the same decorated uniform he'd worn five years before when he married Carlota. His stoic face betrayed nothing of the despair and humiliation that tore at his heart, and everyone said he behaved quite the gentleman.

Fulgencio, on the other hand, took a seat near the front and, dressed almost more dazzlingly than the bride, wept throughout the ceremony, at one point even stopping the service until Tesifón escorted him out.

They didn't take a honeymoon, preferring to use their money to fix up Juan Rodrigo's house, which until then had been in great disrepair. Carlota's touch transformed the main room into a place that could at the very least welcome the guests they now received. Urged on by his wife, Juan Rodrigo built an extra bedroom for the baby they hoped to have one day. Then, inspired by his results, he fixed the leaky roof and repaired the fence. Even the burro looked happier.

They planned their move to the city but decided to wait until after they had a child, as Carlota had heard stories of the horrors that occurred in the city hospital and did not want to give birth there. Her aunt Martina had said they made the women unconscious and then cut the baby out. They also needed to save money, as they knew it would cost a fortune to buy a truck, so

Juan Rodrigo dug graves, still not hearing the voices of the dead, and during the mornings and evenings he worked in Tesifón's bar, serving wine and brandy to the wealthier merchants. And though he would return home exhausted, he and Carlota made love. They blocked out everything but the smell and feel of each other during those times, their intertwining bodies renewing their bond, the sharing of their breath forming the silent repetition of their vows. Afterward, lying in each other's arms, when the nightingale's song woke them to the world, each wondered how they could have been so fortunate.

A year came and went, and still Carlota was not pregnant. They talked again of moving to the city, thinking perhaps the change would help, but as they made their plans to move, the first of the flu epidemics swept through the village. It was a mild outbreak, though Juan Rodrigo's shovel was busy enough. And one day, returning late from working at the bar, he noticed Carlota was pale.

"You are burning, *mi paloma*. You need to sleep," he said, taking her in his arms and laying her on the bed.

"It's nothing," she said. "I feel tired, that's all." And she repeated those words each night, even as Juan Rodrigo grew more and more concerned.

She never fully recovered from that first bout with the flu, and from then on the villagers blamed her want of child on the effects of the flu, forgetting that she had not been pregnant for a year before being sick. Her physical condition prevented her and Juan Rodrigo from acting on their plans to move to the city. Always, it was next month or next year when Carlota would be feeling better. And, strangely, she found that this relieved her, for she had begun to prefer the country. Once she was better, she spent whole mornings walking about the countryside gathering red poppies, crown daisies, wild gladiolas, sea lavender, and honeysuckle, then decorating their house, so that Juan Rodrigo would come home and complain of the smell, joking that he preferred the stench of his burro.

One night, a little over three years after her bout with the flu, Carlota came to see Juan Rodrigo at the bar. When she entered, the men silenced their conversations to look at her, not only because women did not usually walk through the doors, but also because she appeared so radiant. She'd remained pale during the three years since the flu, but now her skin seemed luminous, as if warmed by an inner light. "A pearl," one of the gentlemen said aloud. "She's the pearl of the village."

Juan Rodrigo escorted her behind the bar and sat her on a barrel. "*Mi paloma,* you worry me with this visit," he said. "Are you feeling well?"

"I've never felt better," she said, unable to hold back a smile. "We are with child."

"What?"

"I'm pregnant. You're going to have a boy, or so says Doña Isabel."

"What does she know?"

"I am the one who knows I'm pregnant," she said with a laugh. "Women know these things, but Doña Isabel has divined that it will be a boy. I wanted to wait until I knew for sure to tell you."

Juan Rodrigo hugged her so hard that she almost fell off the barrel. Never had a man been so happy over the news that his wife was with child. Yet over time his excitement turned to worry as he watched the effect the pregnancy had on Carlota's already weak constitution. He helped her as much as he could, but he often felt impotent. She stubbornly refused to let him help with the household chores, saying the exercise was good for her. Finally, during the last three months of the pregnancy, *el medico,* Dr. Gonzalez, confined her to bed. At least, Juan Rodrigo thought, I can be of use to her more now, though the bed Dr. Gonzalez was talking about was in the house of Consuela and Tesifón. They moved in temporarily so that Consuela could nurse her sister. Juan Rodrigo sat uncomfortably in the house, powerless but hopeful.

No one in the village noticed the fact that El Capitán no longer took his evening walks, until a few weeks before Carlota gave birth, when Jorge said to his wife, Matilde, over dinner: "*Qué raro,* my dear, that El Capitán has not passed by our house on his way to the cliffs. He was so precise, but I think it has been quite some time."

"Well, he's an odd man," Matilde said, and pretending that they were unaccustomed to delving into people's affairs, for the moment they left it at that.

As the rest of the town could not have been privy to their conversation, nobody's curiosity was sparked. At least not until two days before Carlota gave birth. Juan Rodrigo was cleaning the bar that morning as usual, when he heard what sounded like a gunshot coming from the other side of the village. Somebody was always shooting something in the cliffs around the town: a bird or a squirrel, or occasionally a deer.

So Juan Rodrigo didn't pay any attention, nor did any of the other villagers, until Jorge, unable to forget about the fact that he hadn't seen El Capitán, decided to pay the captain a visit that evening. After receiving no response from knocking on his door, Jorge decided something was not quite right and climbed in the house through the open kitchen window—barely able to fit and tearing his new trousers on the nail sticking out of the windowsill.

El Capitán sat in his favorite chair in the living room, his navy-issue pistol having fallen in the pool of blood on the floor beside him. Jorge screamed at the sight, then paced frantically about the room, wondering what he should do. That was when he noticed a picture lying in El Capitán's lap. Careful not to touch any of the blood, he leaned over the body and picked up the picture as one might pick up an object that is hot, with only his thumb and forefinger. Looking at it for a moment, Jorge decided it would be better if no one knew, so he placed the wedding photo on the shelf where the other photos sat and left the house.

They notified Juan Rodrigo of the death at once. And, the next day, after sitting with Carlota through breakfast, he made his way to the cemetery to dig the grave, stopping first to pay his respects to El Capitán, who was lying peacefully now in his living room, all traces of blood having been cleaned. The few people who counted him as a friend—mostly because of his position— were gathered there. He had no relatives. Jorge was there as well, keeping quiet, almost as if he were guarding El Capitán's secret.

Juan Rodrigo climbed the hill to the cemetery and, before he began working, sat in the hot midday sun. He wiped his brow and thought that he felt sorry for El Capitán. No one should die alone. But then he thought, You should know better than anyone else, Juan Rodrigo—we all die alone. He worried for his wife, and the death of El Capitán only made his worry more intense. She was overdue, and the pregnancy had not been good for her. He wished it was all over, so that they could get on with their lives. And with that, he grabbed his shovel and plunged it into the earth.

As he dug deeper, he felt the coolness of the ground, almost as if it passed through the shovel into his hands. Soon he stopped and rubbed his hands together. He didn't like the feeling, yet he pushed himself to continue; he wanted to get back to Carlota. The dark, rich dirt piled higher and higher, until he had to climb into the grave to dig it out properly. It was then that the earth whispered to him, *Give me* . . . , but he could hear nothing more, the whisper fading as if suffocated by the surrounding weight of dirt and rock. At first he was frightened, but then he decided it was nothing, his mind playing tricks, and he continued digging. Each time he dug at the earth, the whisper came again, searching for a voice. Is this what my father and grandfather talked about? he wondered. Is it the voice of the dead? He did not want to hear it, in any case, and dug faster, hoping to finish the job and escape before the whisper found its voice. He reached a difficult spot, where the dirt wouldn't give way. *"Válgame Dios!"* he exclaimed. "The earth is hard here!" He jumped on the shovel, sweat dripping over his brow. *"Venga!"* He jumped again and again, pushing downward with all his strength. "Another foot or so and this cursed grave is finished." His shovel broke through, and a shock of warm breath blew over him. The coldness of his own body faded. A voice from behind him spoke. *Give me back my dignity,* it said. And Juan Rodrigo turned to meet the ghost.

"I do not want to see you, El Capitán," Juan Rodrigo said. "I'm moving to the city after Carlota gives birth. You bode nothing good for me."

"You are the gravedigger, no?" El Capitán replied, and as he spoke he began to take on a corporeal existence, or at least it seemed that way to Juan Rodrigo. The details of the many decorations upon El Capitán's navy uniform were clear. "Given the choice, I would rather tell my story to someone else, someone who hadn't stolen my bride, but perhaps it is best. There is reason in all things."

"You don't understand," Juan Rodrigo continued. "I'm not the gravedigger."

"Then why are you standing in my grave?"

"It is a technicality. I'm not digging any more graves. Consider this a favor."

As if El Capitán did not hear him, he sat down on a rock and began telling his story. "My father was in the navy, and so it was expected that I would follow. . . ."

"No, no!" Juan Rodrigo threw down his shovel. "This is no longer my life. My father spent more time with ghosts than with me. I have a son coming soon, and I'm taking him to the city!" And with that he leaped from the grave and made his way down the mountain to the village.

He arrived home at sunset, visibly shaken. "What's wrong, my dear?" Carlota asked.

"Nothing. Nothing," he said, gulping down a glass of Tesifón's brandy. "I want to leave this place. After the baby is born, when you are well, we shall leave this village behind us."

"Of course. That's what we planned," Carlota said, bringing her hand to his cheek. "You will be a great businessman, and your son will follow in your footsteps."

"No! No son should be expected to follow in his father's footsteps!" Juan Rodrigo shouted, and was immediately sorry for losing his temper. He hugged Carlota close, feeling her full belly press against him. "I'm sorry. Our son will be free to choose his own life," he said.

"Of course."

Juan Rodrigo tossed and turned throughout the night. Caressing Carlota's head, running his fingers through her hair as she slept, he thought that she was looking healthier than she'd looked in a long time. *The baby will come soon, and this will all be over.* He lay on his back and stared at the ceiling, thinking of names for his son. But the voice of El Capitán, carried on the wind from the mountain, blew in through the window: *Give me back my dignity!* Juan Rodrigo shut the window so hard he almost woke his wife, but even as he got back into bed, the floorboards creaked as the wind pushed through their cracks, and the groans of the boards spoke the same anguished words: *Give me back my dignity!*

Just before dawn, Juan Rodrigo left the house and made his way to the cemetery to confront the ghost.

"You're late," El Capitán said, checking his pocket watch. "I expect punctuality in those who meet with me."

"Meet with you!" Juan Rodrigo blared, throwing his hands in the air. "You are forcing yourself upon me! I have no interest in meeting with you!"

"Either way, you are here, and for these few moments we are joined, teller and listener. Let's do make the best of it, shall we?"

Juan Rodrigo said nothing, simply sitting on the edge of the grave, dangling his legs within.

"Suffice it to say, my father was a hard man," El Capitán went on. "He expected excellence in everything."

"At least I know where you get it from," Juan Rodrigo exclaimed.

"Please allow me to tell my story," El Capitán said, continuing, "I entered the navy to please him. For some reason, I'd never gained his approval, and I was sure the blame was mine. No matter what I did, he found fault in it. I remember, once, when I was fifteen, we'd had a few friends over for dinner, including a girl, Mercedes, whom I had a particular crush on. We all sat at the long dinner table, and as I was cutting my steak, the knife slipped from my hand and knocked some peas off my plate. I remember the hushed silence as I watched the green peas roll across the polished marble floor. My father called to the cook. 'María,' he said. 'Please bring the large tin tub for my son.' A moment later María brought the tub, and he said, 'Place it on his lap and put his plate inside; he can eat his food in there like the pig he is.'"

"Your father was the pig!" Juan Rodrigo said. "To humiliate a son like that in front of his friends, and his girl!"

"Do not speak of my father in that tone of voice!" El Capitán's own voice filled the air around Juan Rodrigo, and for a moment he grew cold again. "You do not know his story. Please allow me to tell you mine."

And El Capitán talked of his childhood, the romance with Mercedes, for all had not been lost on that night. He talked of the time his father gave him a shotgun, and the time when his mother died and she told him to be a good man, to strive to be better than his own father. At the time he didn't understand the meaning of the words, the hope that lay beneath them. He grew angry with his mother for disparaging his father, and she died with the memory of that anger on his face. El Capitán talked throughout the morning, Juan Rodrigo trying to push him along, but to no avail. It wasn't until past midday that he reached the point of his naval career.

"As I said, the navy was my final attempt to gain my father's approval," El Capitán continued with his story. "I distinguished myself early on, rising to the rank of captain."

"So we were right about your being a captain!" Juan Rodrigo laughed. "I'd thought we had it all wrong, and that you had been a lowly ensign or something, too ashamed to correct the villagers."

"I wouldn't have stood the inaccuracy for a moment," El Capitán said.

"Go on, please, I'm getting hungry."

"Yes, we were bound for Cuba. A disastrous mission, the last attempt to maintain our stronghold there. The Americans were waiting, and they trapped us in the harbor at Santiago. I was the youngest captain in the fleet, but I'd seen battle before, and I knew this one was hopeless. I told my superior officers that if we stayed to fight, we would be slaughtered down to the last man. We needed to fire up the coal furnaces and make a run for it. As they say, discretion is the better part of valor. And I'm not ashamed to say I believe that dictum, unlike the officers who died that day. They said the bottom was too foul, we would run aground, and certainly many ships did as they foolishly fought. After most of the fleet had been lost, I decided that the admiral was out of his mind, and I took control of our vessel. The men respected me, and they followed me without hesitation.

"We turned and pushed for the open sea. I myself supervised the work in the coal room, pushing the men to stoke the furnace. The coal the government gave us was of poor quality. I'd personally requisitioned better, but it was delayed and never made it before our departure. Who knows how many of the other ships might have made it if they'd had decent coal. As it turned out, none of the ships in the Spanish Armada returned except mine. And I paid the price.

"Two American ships were in pursuit. They would overtake us. I sent the men from the furnace room and shoveled every last brick of coal into that furnace myself, pushing it far past the point of safety. I knew it could blow, but there was no other way. The fire raged. We pulled away from the American vessels, and the furnace exploded. *Gracías a Dios,* the Americans had turned around and didn't realize we'd stopped dead in the water. The explosion maimed me, in a particularly humiliating fashion, as you no doubt are aware.

"But that humiliation was not enough. When we made it back to Barcelona, I was court-martialed. They would have hung me if I hadn't already been wounded, and if it hadn't been so clear that the mission had been suicide from the start. Instead, I was forced to resign, but everyone knew what that meant, including my father. I think he died from the shame of it.

"I worked a frigate for many years after that, trying to forget about the dishonor I'd caused my family, about my own humiliation. But then I came to understand that I'd saved those men. They were alive because I had the sense to know when we were licked. There is no glory in death. Not even a military one. I knew that, and now those men are married with children, children who run laughing through the plazas of so many Spanish villages. Children I knew I could never have. It was then I decided to settle and take a wife of my own. I wanted at least to have the trappings of family life. Why I chose this godforsaken village is beyond me, but I did try to live a respectable life. I did try. I suppose my father's ghost was still haunting me. Well, no more."

The ghost of El Capitán faded. Though Juan Rodrigo was hungry, he knew he must return to the village and tell El Capitán's story to any villagers who would listen. He went to the bar first. But the moment he arrived, a frantic Tesifón met him. "Where have you been, Juan Rodrigo?" he said between breaths. "Carlota is in labor, and I fear it's not going well."

They ran together to Tesifón's house. Father Joaquín was already there along with Dr. Gonzalez. As he entered the bedroom where Carlota lay, Consuela turned to him, her face taut, not able to disguise the fact that she blamed him for the way things had gone.

"Will she live?" Juan Rodrigo hesitated upon entering, not out of fear of Consuela's wrath, but because of the feeling of imminent death hanging in the air.

"Your daughter will be fine," Consuela said, signaling with her head to the cook to bring the infant she held in her arms to Juan Rodrigo. "The mother has very little time left." And with that, Consuela's face changed, becoming the color of ashes.

Juan Rodrigo took the infant from the cook and gazed at the tiny face. The eyes stared into him, and he had the sense that they already saw him as all there was in the world. How happy he was to finally have a child, no matter that it was not a boy. Someone who relied on him and loved him. Someone he would give his life for. The feeling overwhelmed him.

He went to Carlota's side. "I can't take the burden by myself, *mi paloma*. I need you. I need you now, not only for the beauty you bring to my life, but for your common sense." He knelt next to her, running his fingers through her hair as he had done only the previous night. It seemed impossible that his life was changing so fast.

Carlota's eyes were closed, and she never reopened them. She died as Juan Rodrigo knelt beside her, his head upon her lap, the baby in the crook of his arm. As Carlota left her body, she kissed her newborn baby and ran her fingers across her husband's head and the hair that was already beginning to grow gray. Juan Rodrigo felt the touch as one might feel the wing of a butterfly that brushes against the back of your neck, and he knew she was gone.

He lay with her body through much of the night, Consuela taking care of the baby. But then he thought of El Capitán's words: *You are the gravedigger.* And he thought of the fact that in the morning he would be digging Carlota's grave, and his spirit raged. He cursed his own father and his grandfather before him for becoming gravediggers. Suddenly he didn't want to see Carlota; he didn't want to know her. Better to be a stranger to those you bury. He ran from the room.

A nightingale sat, singing, in an olive tree outside Consuela's house. Juan Rodrigo cursed the bird. "To hell with you and your kind!" he yelled. "You swarm like a cloud upon Fulgencio, but you do nothing to save *mi paloma!*" And with that he picked up a rock and threw it, hitting the nightingale in the head and knocking it from the tree. The wounded bird fluttered about the ground, and Juan Rodrigo walked up to it, staring into its eyes. "To hell with you!" he said again. "I never want to see another bird in this godforsaken town again!" He crushed the bird's head with his boot and walked away into the night, unaware of the chorus of cooing, trilling, and chirping that rose from the trees around him.

Never had the birds felt such rage in another being. The power of that rage acted like a gale-force wind, pushing the birds from their roosts, from their nests and homes, knocking them about in the air, until all the birds in the village swirled about in one great mass. The great Red Kite said to the black-spotted dove, the one who everyone said was headstrong, that they must fly away quickly or be carried who knows where by Juan Rodrigo's anger, and so the birds, including the doves that sat in the orange trees, all followed the Red Kite out of the village, over the cliffs, and across the sea.

Juan Rodrigo wandered throughout the night, too caught up in his own despair to notice the flight of the birds. In the morning he went to his house to check on his burro. Then he grabbed his pick and shovel and climbed the hill to dig Carlota's grave. This time he didn't fight the warm shock of air that breathed into him as he hollowed out the hole in the ground. But he didn't welcome it, either. Instead, he sat down in the grave, almost like a ghost himself, and watched as Carlota walked toward him. She sat beside him, taking him in her arms and caressing his head while she told him her story.

With each word, with each stroke of her hand on his head, she let him know that she forgave him for missing the birth. She told him how pleased she was that he'd heard Manolo's, El Capitán's, story. That she'd been plagued with guilt over her actions, and that now she understood. And she made him promise to tell Manolo's story to the villagers, and to tell her story to her sister and brother-in-law, and in time to their daughter. At the mention of their daughter, Juan Rodrigo finally looked at her. "What am I to do with her? I can't raise her by myself."

"You will," she said. And though she knew it was true, that he would be a fine father, she worried for Juan Rodrigo as one worries for a child once it leaves home to find its place in the world. I am a mother after all, she thought. But the child is not who I thought it would be. "You will raise her, and you'll do it better than most mothers," she repeated, almost as much for herself as for him. "But you must control your temper, Juan Rodrigo. The birds may not forgive you as easily as I have."

"I do not want to see them ever again," he said, though his eyes held a sadness that begged to be forgiven. "You were my only *paloma*. They do nothing but remind me of you."

"The birds speak truth, my love," Carlota said. "Don't be so quick to dismiss them."

"Truth!" Juan Rodrigo replied. "This cemetery has always been called *la tierra de la verdad*, but I've failed to see whatever truth can be found here. The only truth I know is that I will miss you."

Carlota held him in her arms for a moment before she left, singing to him, a song that reminded him of doves.

That afternoon, Consuela and Tesifón led the procession from the church to the cemetery and found Juan Rodrigo still sitting in the grave when they arrived. They buried Carlota, and after spending the next few months with Consuela and Tesifón, Juan Rodrigo took his daughter, Esperanza, back to his own house, where the burro was quite happy to see them. Consuela made sure the baby was supplied with milk, relying on goat's milk when the wet nurse went dry. Consuela visited Juan Rodrigo and the baby often, though there was still a trace of blame for Juan Rodrigo hidden beneath her joy at seeing the baby. She felt, somehow, that Juan Rodrigo's presence at the birth, his love, might have pulled Carlota through, and she refused to let go of that feeling.

When Esperanza was two and appeared as healthy and strong as any child, Consuela and Tesifón invited Juan Rodrigo for dinner and there told him that they were moving to the city. Tesifón had another idea, one that would make the new horseless carriages more efficient, but it would take both the financial capital and the intellectual resources of the city to make it happen. Besides, Consuela said, the village contained only sad memories for her. The epidemics had taken their toll on her friends, and with Carlota's death, she saw no reason to stay. She'd remained two years, as it was, to make sure Esperanza was healthy, but now it was time to go. Of course, they wanted Esperanza to visit them for long periods during the summer. They would sell the bar to Pedro, who'd wanted to purchase it for a long time; Tesífon apologized to Juan Rodrigo, saying they felt that he would have enough responsibility with the child.

"WHY IS IT THE DEAD can only speak to me once to tell me their story? Well, all except for the girl in white," Juan Rodrigo said, gazing at the single olive he held in his hand. "What I wouldn't give to be able to talk to you again, Carlota." And with that, he heard the sound of a bird singing along the cliffs; this time he was sure it was a nightingale. The bird landed in the branches above him. He couldn't help but smile upon seeing it. *Imagine, after twelve years. I didn't know if I'd ever see another.* "Thank you," he said. "Does this mean I'm forgiven?" he asked the nightingale. But the bird didn't answer.

He placed the olive in his pocket and walked home, aware that as he passed under the olive and almond groves, there were birds rustling within the leaves, preparing their homes. And so that is how Juan Rodrigo was left alone to care for his daughter, a difficult job for any man, much less a poor one. But she was the hope that kept him going, the simple joy on her face balancing the memories weighing down the faces on those of the dead.

The Story of Dorotea

THE NEXT DAY, when Juan Rodrigo went outside to relieve himself, he noticed his daughter's stockings and dress had already been scrubbed clean and hung out to dry along with the rest of the wash. Esperanza sat on the stable fence, petting El Viejo.

"A beautiful morning, eh, *bonita?*" Juan Rodrigo said, searching his daughter's reaction for any sign of forgiveness for his stupidity the night before.

Esperanza stepped down from the fence, not looking at her father. "Can I go to the village?"

"Of course," Juan Rodrigo said, wanting to say more but taken aback by the fact that she still seemed upset. This is not going to be easy, he said to himself. How can an old man raise a young woman, especially one so strong-willed? As he watched Esperanza climb up the path to the village, he felt alone for the first time in years, not since the time, so many years ago, before Carlota, before the ghosts began speaking to him. It had been that same feeling that drove him to find consolation from Pepita's house of ill repute: the feeling that, unlike his father and grandfather before him, he was nothing but a man who dug holes in the ground, then covered them up again. He wasn't a storyteller, reworking truth, shaping memory to ease a family's pain or give meaning to a friend's death. He buried bodies, nothing more.

Later in the week, when he was called to attend another family in mourning, Esperanza said she had schoolwork to do and couldn't go. She'd always gone with him before, even when Doña Villada had a test planned for her the next day. She'd study in a quiet room while the family mourned, or occasionally out in the barn. But this time Juan Rodrigo went alone. He was gloomy as he walked, knowing that he'd been falling into these moods more and more lately; it seemed that as Esperanza grew, needing him less, he doubted his own ability, not just as a father, but as a member of the village. The fear and hatred of so many of the villagers that had never bothered him before now seemed to rankle, though he would never admit it. He did not want to see the ghost of Dorotea Oliveira; he wanted nothing more to do with stories. After all, what story could be told of him? That he was two times a widower, that he couldn't handle his own daughter anymore, that she needed a mother yet he'd failed to provide her even that. There was no essence to pass on in death, no legacy, no story to be told. If there were, would Esperanza want his? he wondered. No. Do not marry, *mi corazón*, for nothing lasts. Prepare to live alone.

Dorotea's daughter, Rosalia, answered the door, dressed in black, with a red poppy in her hair. It was this oddity in the normal raiment of grief that first caught his attention, that and the smell of her skin as she kissed his cheek in greeting, like an olive grove in autumn rain. Hers was different from the spring smell of Carlota, yet he found himself pondering the scent and the flower as he attempted to pay his respects to those who mourned inside. Juan Rodrigo had never paid particular attention to Rosalia, beyond the fact that she was one of the few widows in the village who hadn't attempted to trap him with her good cooking. Rosalia's husband had died the year before, leaving her alone with her mother. But on this day, Juan Rodrigo not only noticed her but found himself hesitating to leave her side as he greeted the only other mourners in the room, Dorotea's closest friends and shopping partners, Matilde and María.

Contrary to his previous reluctance to hear the ghost of Dorotea, Juan Rodrigo found himself shoveling the earth quickly, anticipating the encounter, formulating questions about the character of Rosalia. Why didn't she have children? Who'd worn the pants in the family—she or her husband, Ricardo? Is she happy here, or does she long for the city? But it turned out that Dorotea was quite a talker, and she'd appeared with her own agenda regarding the story she wanted to tell. Dressed all in black, her hair pulled into a tight bun, her hands tucked into the shawl she had wrapped about her waist, the way she'd worn it so often in life, she approached Juan Rodrigo. Her mouth opened wide, and she took a deep breath, as if she would need all that air to tell her story. The shadows over her sunken eyes were dark, but Juan Rodrigo knew they were no more haunting than they'd been in life.

"I always had men around me," she said finally. "They liked my smell!" And she laughed, a laugh that was more like a cackle, dry and harsh.

Juan Rodrigo inhaled the air about him. It was hard to distinguish anything from the smell of the olive trees and the dusty earth, which he associated so much with the cemetery. But as he allowed the smell to linger in his nose, he detected also a faint odor, not unlike the one his burro gave off when he hadn't been scrubbed for a month. If that was her smell, Juan Rodrigo thought, she would do better not to brag about it!

"Couldn't keep them off me," Dorotea went on. "My sister, Alita, was so jealous, why, I remember the time when Jesús came all the way from . . ."

In death, as in her old age, Dorotea returned in memory to those moments that were happiest for her, one of them being the time as a young woman when she'd fought with her sister over her first boyfriend and won. She'd been the type of woman raised on romance books, and she and her sister had fought over many men, though few of them turned out to be real prizes. Dorotea's first two husbands represented two of those victories, and they drank heavily and beat her often before they left the village.

"They were good men, though," she continued. "Hard as stone. I liked that. A man's got to be a man. Few women understand that. I never minded knowing my place. Not like today's women. They think they run the marriage. You take my Rosalia. . . ."

Juan Rodrigo perked up, hoping to hear something, but just as quickly Dorotea changed subjects, moving on to her third husband, Rosalia's father.

She'd adored him, and he was a good man, at least until he grew old. He'd always been a hard worker; if there was no work to do around the house, he'd ask neighbors what he could help with. Confined to his chair in his old age, he grew bitter and made Dorotea wait on him, pushing her past the point of exhaustion, insulting her all the while. Yet Dorotea not only endured, it was what she lived for.

"Dorotea," Juan Rodrigo interrupted, growing impatient. "You skipped a part in your story. You'd mentioned your daughter. . . ."

"If he was happy, I was happy," Dorotea continued on, talking right over Juan Rodrigo, as she'd done so often with her husband and daughter when she was alive. Once Dorotea began talking, she didn't need an audience. Before he was confined to his wheelchair, her third husband would get up and leave the room, sure that his wife hadn't even noticed.

"One thing a man needs is a woman to care for him," she said. "That's my little secret." And in that moment she looked like a girl in her twenties, talking about the plot of her favorite romance. "Just because a man is strong doesn't mean he can get by without the attentions of a woman, especially as the man gets older. Why, I remember my Salvador. . . ."

In her last years with her third husband, Salvador, she'd had no further thought than to make sure he was happy, no matter how often he berated her. And once he'd died, she revisited the time with Salvador in her mind, that and her youth, turning all the men into charming gentlemen and considerate lovers. Juan Rodrigo couldn't help but feel sorry for her as she recounted her story. It seemed to him that though so many failed to draw lessons from their own lives while living, they should at least have learned something in death. But then, remembering his recent moods, he reminded himself that he should know better. Who is to say when it is time for another to learn a lesson, if we rarely learn them ourselves? He wondered what he would tell Rosalia; then again, he expected she already knew her mother's ways. Strange, he thought, but of all the women in the village, Rosalia seemed the least concerned with flattering the men. Perhaps she'd learned the lessons for her mother.

Indeed, Rosalia had a keen eye as a child, and she'd understood much of her mother's life. Still, she was grateful as Juan Rodrigo sat beside her on the sofa, telling her all he knew. She questioned him about her mother's early life, unconcerned by the fact that old Matilde and María raised their eyebrows whenever she delved into a particularly unflattering point. The two older women were the only others in the living room, as Rosalia wanted no one but her mother's closest friends in attendance. The women hovered before the door to the kitchen, as if guarding the food they'd brought to help Rosalia through her difficult time. They dressed in black, appearing in life very much as Dorotea did in death: deep-set frown lines about their mouths from all the times they shook their heads in disdain at hearing the latest gossip about one villager or another. In their hands they each held a rosary, which they fingered nervously as they watched the couple on the couch.

Rosalia had suspected that her mother's fond memories of her first husbands were false, having heard the gossip in the village. But whenever she'd questioned her mother on it, Dorotea would look about her, like a cat taking in its surroundings before a nap, then smile and tell her the most fabulous stories of how she and her former husbands would picnic in the hills, or camp on the beach. It had all sounded so lovely that Rosalia began to doubt the gossipmongers.

For Juan Rodrigo's part, he found he had trouble concentrating. The incongruity of the flower made him smile, and the intoxication of the scent stayed with him, but it was more than that. Here was a woman who'd lost her husband the previous year, and now her mother, a woman who'd never cultivated friendships in the village and so now found herself alone in the world, and yet she sat and listened to him with a strength and dignity he'd not seen before, as if it was simply another day in the long sentry of existence. Desperation clung to other women in her situation, but not Rosalia. She was interested in her mother's life, grateful for the story, but beyond that Juan Rodrigo couldn't discern anything. She was a mystery; and Juan Rodrigo needed a mystery, perhaps more than anything else at that moment. For his life had become too focused on his daughter. He realized that, in his own way, he was also becoming bitter—not where it was noticeable yet, he told himself. But he could tell. He didn't like the feeling of competition he'd had with El Romancero, and he didn't like the way he sometimes wished to teach people lessons through the stories—too much like Doña Villada, he thought. Yes, he could see himself like Dorotea's poor third husband if he didn't watch out, and so he needed a mystery, though he didn't know he needed a mystery.

She offered him coffee. Matilde let out a gasp; María dropped her rosary. But Juan Rodrigo said he must get back to his daughter, who'd suddenly decided it was so important to finish her homework. Still, he lingered, wanting to speak with her alone, needing to tell her about Esperanza's becoming a woman; he felt so unsure in that regard. But the living room suddenly seemed very small, and the eyes of Matilde and María began to feel like those of vultures circling about, watching the final death throes of their prey. He found that he couldn't bring himself to speak, nor could he muster the courage and charm to corner her privately, not with those eyes always upon him. And not, he thought, after so many years without practice.

Sensing Juan Rodrigo's hesitancy but thinking it was due to the fact that he was a poor man and hesitant to ask for payment, Rosalia reached for her purse.

"No. No," Juan Rodrigo said. "It's part of my duty, my obligation to the village."

"No one owes this village any obligations," Rosalia replied. "Least of all you." She gazed at him curiously.

Feeling as if he'd misspoken, Juan Rodrigo explained, "I may be poor, but my needs are few. Just enough to keep myself and my daughter out of trouble." He glanced around the living room, taking in the oak dining table, the buffet, and the china cabinet, with at least a few fine pieces in it. Rosalia was not rich, but neither was she poor. A nervous laugh escaped his mouth, surprising him, and he cut it short. Rosalia continued to stare at him. Matilde and María whispered to each other. But Juan Rodrigo paid no attention to them, for he found Rosalia's stare more uncomfortable than those of the vultures, if one can imagine that as possible.

"You do a fine job of raising your daughter," Rosalia said, breaking the spell. "She is not of an easy disposition, but you are fair with her."

"I take that as a compliment," Juan Rodrigo said, regaining his composure. He was proud of how he'd raised his daughter, despite his current worries. Carlota had been right. He'd done well.

"Still, I feel I should pay you something, if only so that your daughter may have a nice dress to wear to school. She will be a woman soon."

Juan Rodrigo felt himself flush at this remark. Why had he not foreseen the changes in his daughter, if this woman could tell so easily? "People often give milk, eggs, bread," he said, sticking his hands in his pockets and feeling like a schoolboy.

"Nonsense!" Rosalia exclaimed. Matilde and María shut their mouths and crept closer, their fingers now tightly clasping the rosary beads. Juan Rodrigo looked at the floor, growing frustrated with himself. He was the man; he should be handling the business dealings. Yet he'd given in to this woman. The strange thing was that he felt as if it was for his own good. Rosalia would not take advantage. "I would like to do something for that daughter of yours, Juan Rodrigo," she continued. "She comes by here every so often just to view my mare. She hides behind the scrub oak, thinking I don't see her."

"I'm sorry, Señora Oliveira, you should tell her that you don't want—"

"I let her think she is going unnoticed, because secrecy is half the fun of youth, Juan Rodrigo! The mare is going to foal any time now. I'd like your daughter to have the foal."

"Señora Oliveira, I couldn't accept," Juan Rodrigo replied. "It's too gracious a gift."

"You underestimate the value of your services," Rosalia said, her gaze lingering on Juan Rodrigo. Matilde and María renewed their whispers.

"At least let me pay you something for it." It had already occurred to Juan Rodrigo that Esperanza would love the horse, and that perhaps it was a good thing to give her the responsibility of caring for it.

"Nonsense!" Rosalia exclaimed again with a ferocity that settled everything. Juan Rodrigo simply said thank you. The hint of a smile played on both of their lips. Matilde and María scuttled back to the kitchen to resume their vigil; they would have much to talk about in the village.

"Esperanza leaves soon to visit her aunt in the city," Juan Rodrigo said as he was leaving. "I would rather not have her go, but that is a different story."

"Consuela is a strong-willed woman."

"Yes," Juan Rodrigo replied, thinking to himself, She is not the only one—this village seems to breed them like rabbits! "Let me know when the foal is born, and I will send Esperanza to care for it. Then when she returns from the city, she will continue to care for it until the foal is ready to leave its mother."

"Very good," Rosalia replied, giving her cheek to Juan Rodrigo. As he kissed it, he allowed himself just the slightest intake of breath. Yes, he thought to himself, an olive grove in autumn rain, when the loam is dark and the pungent scent of the earth clears the nostrils! After, he gazed across the room, briefly catching the eyes of the two old women, daring them to look back.

THAT EVENING OVER DINNER, Juan Rodrigo broke the silence by telling his daughter about the foal she would soon have. She shrieked and jumped with joy, almost knocking the dinner plates off the table.

"But you must understand that the responsibility for the foal is yours," Juan Rodrigo said. "You will watch over it until you go to the city, then when you come back—"

"Oh, Papá!" Esperanza interrupted. "I don't want to go to the city now. How can I?"

"You must go," Juan Rodrigo replied. "You promised, and Aunt Consuela is expecting you. Besides, you were so excited to go before."

"But, Papá, I have the horse now."

"The horse will be here when you get back."

"Papá!"

"You gave your word, Esperanza. In my house that means something. And Rosalia has agreed to watch over the horse when you are gone. It's only for a month."

"A month!" Esperanza exclaimed. "That's forever!" And she stormed out onto the porch once again.

Juan Rodrigo smiled to himself, as things did not seem to have changed as much as he'd thought. She was still his daughter.

The following Sunday morning, the foal was born. With school out for the year, Esperanza wished to spend all day with the foal, but she was now required to spend mornings working with the other women of the village. They gathered early in the northern fields to plant potatoes, beans, tomatoes, and melons. Early summer, along with olive-picking season in the first part of the year, were the times when gossip, which was always the village pastime but was normally confined to whispers behind closed doors or in the congregations of women who loitered about after church, transformed itself into a cacophonous festival of sound and gesture, a din so deafening that even the crickets stayed away from the fields when the women gathered there. And this particular time, the talk focused on Rosalia and Juan Rodrigo. Matilde and María had planted the seed, and that seed, as well as the fact that Rosalia did not take part in these seasonal gatherings, was all the women needed. *She is a strange one, that Rosalia. Well, that's why she's a perfect match for the gravedigger—who else could put up with his ghosts? I would put up with his ghosts, if only to feel the strength of those arms about me. Oh, Leti, you know you want to feel the strength of something else!* But other words, in other parts of the field, were not so kind. *Rosalia is just another whore if she goes with that man. You know he still visits Pepita? Yes, I have it on good authority. He's been the ruin of many women. Just look at his past. Well, you know Rosalia is not much better. They say she knew about her husband's shenanigans. She knew and she did nothing. If my husband so much as thought of another woman, he would get no more from me. What are you saying, Susana, no more sex?* Por Dios, *I could never do that. No, melon-head, no more cooking!*

Unlike most of the girls her age, who liked to work side by side with the older women so that they, too, could partake in the gossip and feel more like the adults, Esperanza, not wanting to hear the talk, confined herself to working with the younger girls, for which she also became the object of gossip. But only the mornings were spent in the orchards and fields. Immediately after lunch, Esperanza ran to visit the foal, spending the rest of the day at the Oliveira house. Rosalia looked on with pleasure, teaching Esperanza how to care for the foal. They decided together on the name of Bella. The two women talked much during this time. At first their talks were confined to the horse and its care, but soon Esperanza found herself confiding in Rosalia and thinking once again of the mother she'd never known. Rosalia lacked the golden eyes of Sofia, but there was something about her: a way she had of looking at Esperanza that made her feel more like a grown woman, a way her father could never understand, no matter how hard he tried. And, for her part, Rosalia saw a bit of herself in Esperanza: not simply a headstrong girl, but a girl different from the rest, one whose differences would bring her much loneliness.

Esperanza had never been away from the village. This fact, along with her attachment to her horse and the newfound relationship with Rosalia, made her loath to leave for the city. Her father, for reasons of his own, spent most of the morning on the day she was to catch the coach repairing and cleaning the henhouse, cursing all the while. "Why did I agree to such a stupid idea?" Then throwing the shovel aside, which he'd been using to scoop up the hen droppings: "'It will give her culture, Juan Rodrigo,' Consuela said. Typical! She has all the culture she needs right here!"

"I will miss you, *mi corazón*," Juan Rodrigo said as they stood at the edge of town, waiting for the coach. It was late as usual. "You are all I have, all I've had for many years. It will be strange without you here. I don't know why I agreed to let you go."

"Because at the time I wished it, Papá," Esperanza replied. "And because Aunt Consuela said that if you didn't agree, she'd come and get me herself."

"Yes, she did threaten to do that, didn't she. And I'm always a sucker for your wishes. It is my weakness."

"Don't worry. I won't take advantage."

"You already do!"

"Papá! It's not true. And I'm excited about seeing the city. Excited and scared." She went to her father and hugged him.

"The world is open to you, *mi corazón*. There's no need to be scared."

"I love you, Papá."

"I love you, too." And smiling, though tears were beginning to form in his eyes, Juan Rodrigo mistakenly thought that his daughter was once again his child, forgetting that most changes in life are irreversible, not least of all the metamorphosis from a girl to a woman.

PART

8

The Story of Paola and Ricardo

THREE WEEKS AFTER Esperanza left for the city, Juan Rodrigo once again found himself in the cemetery, digging yet another grave: this time for old Julio, a fine man who'd said little but raised ten wonderful children and countless grandchildren, spending most of his final years in his shed carving beautiful pieces from ash trees for them all. Though he'd spoken little in life, he had plenty to say in death, and Juan Rodrigo spent the entire day listening to the old man. Juan Rodrigo was tired and hungry. He hadn't been himself lately. At first he'd attributed it to Esperanza's absence, but when his coughing grew worse, he knew he was growing ill. On this day, he was not looking forward to traveling to the village to repeat Julio's long tale. So, as he packed up his shovel, Juan Rodrigo was pleased to see Rosalia climbing the hill to the cemetery, thus giving him an excuse to remain.

He looked about him and spotted the grand tomb of Don Bernardo. A miniature Parthenon, it was the perfect place to hide. At least all of Bernardo's money had gone for something useful, Juan Rodrigo thought. Then he laughed at himself as he crept along the side, trying to get a good view of Rosalia as she walked through the graveyard. *Secrecy is half the fun of youth,* she'd said. Well, in that case, I'm reliving my youth! he thought. The area around the tomb was overgrown with weeds and the all-too-common scrub oak. The cracks that ran through the stone were filled with dirt. Juan Rodrigo dug his finger into one of the cracks, scraping away the dirt, thinking that, in the end, even the rich do not escape.

Rosalia's walk through the cemetery was more of a march; she didn't sing to herself or cry, as Juan Rodrigo had seen so many others do when they came to pay their respects. Instead, she seemed very matter-of-fact, almost in a hurry. But instead of going to her husband's grave, she first went to the grave of Señorita Pacheco. Paola Pacheco died young of consumption. She'd never been healthy, and her frailty lent her a particular beauty. Many men in the village had tried to court her, despite knowing that she would not be long for this world. But, as far as anyone in the village could tell, she never gave herself to any of them.

Paola's family kept the grave covered with fresh flowers, but they often complained to Juan Rodrigo that the flowers were missing when they'd visit the next time. One by one, Rosalia picked the flowers off of Paola's grave, then marched over to her husband's grave and placed them there. Juan Rodrigo thought it all very strange, but the strangest was still to come, for Rosalia then lifted her skirt and squatted over her husband's grave, peeing on the flowers and the tombstone. Juan Rodrigo was shocked, yet he found himself leaning forward, peering around the corner of the tomb, trying to get a better look as she squatted there.

Then Rosalia stood, arranged her skirt, kicked a little dirt over her husband's grave, and, without saying a word, walked out of the cemetery and down the hill.

Juan Rodrigo gathered his pick and shovel, smiling now, for he understood one more mystery in the village. He walked back to the village ready to tell Julio's tale, forgetting about his hunger and fatigue. And he found himself thinking of the curious character of Rosalia. She was a strong woman to be sure, Juan Rodrigo thought. But things got to her; yes, Paola and Ricardo at least had gotten to her.

Carlota would never have done such a thing. Like her sister, she would've been appalled by the sight of Rosalia squatting over the grave. No, Juan Rodrigo felt the stirrings of attraction, not because Rosalia reminded him of his love, but because she was so different, and that difference eased the pain in his heart at Carlota's passing, reminding him that there are many strange wonders to be savored in this life.

"I'd never heard that one," Esperanza said, "though I wish I had. I would have teased Rosalia about it."

They both sat atop the boulder that Esperanza had been hiding behind earlier. The surrounding pines and poplars watched them, occasionally commenting on this or that part of Juan Rodrigo's tale, though Juan Rodrigo only heard their whispers as leaves rustling in the wind.

"She would not have appreciated that coming from you," Juan Rodrigo said to his daughter. "I don't know what got into me. I must have become carried away."

"Yes, you seem to be inserting parts that have little to do with me," Esperanza replied. "What about my story?"

"It is all your story." Juan Rodrigo wrapped his arm around his daughter. "We cannot say how the lives of others intersect with our own, how the course of their lives influences the choices we make. So I tell the story as it comes, taking the side roads, the twists and turns, as they present themselves."

"I understand," Esperanza replied. "But I want to hear how you tell the part about Antonio and I."

"I'm getting there." Juan Rodrigo stood to stretch. It had been a difficult day, and he didn't know if he had the energy to finish the story.

"And about Bella." Esperanza stood as well, tugging now on his arm. "Tell me more about Bella."

The pines and poplars whispered to one another once again. *She is a willful girl,* an old pine said. *She would not have survived long, anyway. Life would have had many lessons for her.* But a young poplar, with scarcely any branches, became irritated at these words. *You cannot predict how a life will turn out,* the young poplar said. *There are so many possibilities, so many influences, any of which can change a life forever. Didn't you hear what the old man said?*

The argument was followed by a great shaking of branches and bending of boughs, which caused Juan Rodrigo to pause and turn toward the sky before continuing with his story.

9

The Story of Esperanza

Soon Esperanza returned home, and in the weeks that followed, she visited the foal every day after her chores were done, spending the afternoon brushing her and making sure she had enough food, but mainly just talking to her. She told Bella things she would never dare tell her father: the change she'd noticed in her father's health since she'd been away—she woke often to his coughing fits in the middle of the night—and how, since returning from the city, the men seemed to look at her differently, particularly Don Alfonso, the pharmacist, and Señor Miguel, Doña Villada's son, who was grown and this year was going to help his mother at the school. But always her conversations would come back to her great love for her classmate Eugenio. She'd found herself thinking of him often when she was away.

She could spend entire afternoons espousing his magnificence to her horse. In her innocence, Esperanza didn't realize that Eugenio was not completely right in the head. His parents, as punishment, often lowered him down their dry well, making him sit there overnight, and those long nights in the cold, dank well, searching for a glimpse of the moon to light away the horrors he'd imagined, had their effect on him. Esperanza couldn't have known this, as only Father Joaquín was privy to the knowledge: a knowledge only hinted at in Eugenio's confessions. And, to his credit, Eugenio was a kind boy, never disobeying the teacher, and generally considerate of the feelings of his classmates. It was one such incident that first attracted Esperanza to Eugenio. One of the younger boys had wet his pants, and the other kids were making fun of him during recess. Eugenio threatened to beat up the next boy who said a word. That would have been enough to impress Esperanza, but then he walked the young pant-wetter home, making sure everyone understood that the boy was now under permanent protection. Eugenio would not show the cruelty inherited from his parents until many years later, when he had his own family. Then he would have many children, and none would escape his wrath.

Rosalia Oliveira often stood on her porch, listening to the soft murmurs of Esperanza's voice as she cared for the foal. She couldn't pick out the words and had too much respect for another's privacy to eavesdrop, but as she stood on the porch listening, feeling the intensity with which the young girl talked to her horse, she couldn't help but feel the girl's loneliness. Esperanza had never had many friends. Rosalia wondered if it was because her father was the gravedigger, or was it part of Esperanza's nature? Rosalia's character was one that eschewed the company of others, and she saw some of those same traits in Esperanza—and she couldn't help but feel the girl would have a difficult road.

Sometimes, when Esperanza became carried away with her daydreams, it would be nightfall when Rosalia would have to pry her away from the barn. On those nights, she made a special dinner for Esperanza, knowing that Juan Rodrigo's idea of a good meal was blood sausage and bread.

Each time, Juan Rodrigo arrived shortly after dark and waited, fuming, in the parlor until Esperanza had finished eating. Rosalia escorted Esperanza to her father, knowing her own presence would help calm Juan Rodrigo's temper. She'd noticed the way he shyly averted his eyes when she approached. And how those same eyes would gaze at her when he thought she wasn't looking.

"How many times have I told you, Esperanza? You must be home before nightfall." Juan Rodrigo stuffed his hands in his pockets, telling himself that his daughter was too old for a spanking.

"I'm sorry, Papá." Esperanza lowered her head, making her large eyes appear even bigger. "I love Bella so much that I lose track of time."

"You say you're sorry, but then you do it again the next time." Juan Rodrigo yanked his hands from his pockets and shook them in exasperation. "I've a good mind to give that horse back."

"Papá! No!" Esperanza looked at Rosalia, her eyes imploring. "I'll be good, and soon she'll be old enough for us to keep at our house, and you won't have to worry."

"She's right, Juan Rodrigo," Rosalia said, placing a hand on his shoulder. "Let the girl be a child a little longer. The time for responsibility is coming soon enough."

And her words had their effect on Juan Rodrigo, for he wondered why he wanted his daughter to become responsible when all he saw each time he looked at her was the four-year-old he'd carried on his shoulders. "The world is a hard place, Rosalia," Juan Rodrigo replied, knowing his speech ran counter to his own thought. "You know that better than most. And she was not born into privilege."

"Perhaps not," Rosalia replied, "but one never knows what the future holds."

"Even a gravedigger can see the future when it's this clear. She'll have to work hard, Rosalia. You know it as well as I."

"Not if her aunt takes her to live in the city." It was not quite what Rosalia wanted to say, and, knowing that, she paused, her hand leaving Juan Rodrigo's shoulder and clutching her apron. Then, as if her hand knew it needed something else to do to distract the mind, it began smoothing out the apron, even though one could plainly see there were no wrinkles. "Or maybe the child will have a mother once again to guide her," Rosalia said at last.

The words were not lost on Juan Rodrigo. He rubbed his crooked nose, then, feeling suddenly exposed, he scratched his head purposefully. "The city is worse," Juan Rodrigo replied, quickly turning for the door.

"You didn't always speak that way of the city," Rosalia said, following him.

"I was foolish then. I don't want my daughter to make the same mistakes." Juan Rodrigo took his daughter's hand. "The foal will be old enough to leave her mother in another month. If you are late again, we will not be taking her home with us. Do you understand?" And though Juan Rodrigo's words were harsh, he was thankful for the presence of his daughter's hand in his, the security and purpose bestowed by the warmth that radiated there.

"Yes, Papá, I understand."

Rosalia looked on with hopeful eyes as Juan Rodrigo and Esperanza walked down the path from her house. She wondered why he had never remarried. The child needs a mother, she thought. And Juan Rodrigo needs someone to soften his bitterness.

THE NEXT DAY, before Esperanza could ask permission to visit her horse, Juan Rodrigo told her they were going to the village.

"But why, Papá?" Esperanza sat on the steel milk bottle that propped open the front door. "School begins next week, and then I won't have any time to see Bella."

"That's exactly why I want to take you into town," Juan Rodrigo replied. "And I'm not worried about you having time to visit that horse of yours. I'm sure you'll be able to see her once the school year is over."

"Papá!" Esperanza screamed.

Juan Rodrigo could not contain his smile.

"Doña Villada won't make me stand in the corner with Bibles in my hands!" Esperanza said, laughing. "I'll do my homework fast and well, and I'll still see Bella every day. They'll say I'm the smartest girl in the village!"

"Of that I have no doubt," Juan Rodrigo said. "And the most mule-headed!"

They stopped at the shop of Mercedes Manrubia, the seamstress. She'd worked out of her house at the far end of the village until her parents had come to live with her. Since then she'd found the walk to the shop she'd opened in the center of the village, and the work she did there, a refreshing change from the loud voice of her mother, and the complaints of her father, aimed at provoking pity.

"Mercedes was a good friend of your mother's," Juan Rodrigo told Esperanza each September when they made a visit to her shop.

"My daughter is a woman this year, Mercedes," Juan Rodrigo said, hugging his daughter close to him. Mercedes smiled at the way Esperanza hugged her father back, and how she gently broke away to look at the secondhand dresses Mercedes sold. "She needs something special for school," Juan Rodrigo continued. "Something that says, 'I am a beautiful woman and not to be trifled with!'" Laughing at his own wit, he looked at Esperanza, gauging her reaction. Then, with his arm around Mercedes, he whispered, "But not too beautiful a dress, you understand. I don't want the boys getting ideas."

"I've just the thing for her," Mercedes replied. Then, pulling out a bolt of cloth from the back room: "Have you ever seen such beautiful material?"

Acting like the ladies she'd seen in the shops for so many years, Esperanza walked slowly to Mercedes, her lips pursed together, as if appraising the quality of the cloth. But Mercedes noted the girl's wide eyes, and the way she left her hand on the green cloth, rubbing it over and over.

"It's beautiful, Papá, don't you think?" Esperanza asked, clearly worried that the cloth was too expensive.

"Fitting for a Persian princess," Juan Rodrigo replied, "but not for the daughter of a gravedigger."

Esperanza dropped her hand and stomped her foot, then catching herself, and wanting to appear the lady, walked to the window to examine a simple red dress on display there. Mercedes smiled. The girl was headstrong, but Juan Rodrigo had raised her well, she thought. Now it was Mercedes' turn to take Juan Rodrigo by the arm and whisper.

"You will have your Persian princess, old friend," she said. "I wouldn't dream of charging you, not even for a hundred such dresses! You healed many wounds the night after Florentino died. Your story may not have resolved everything, but it went a long way toward what he and I should have done years before."

Juan Rodrigo started to protest, but Mercedes turned immediately to Esperanza, raising her hand to silence him and saying, "Your father loves you very much. You'll look like a goddess born from the green sea."

Esperanza turned, joy upon her face as she realized what Mercedes was saying.

They stopped in La Plaza de Los Naranjos for chocolate and *churros* before returning home. With the exception of Juan Rodrigo's work in the bar and Esperanza's school, they came to the center of the village just once a week, on Wednesdays, for groceries and basic supplies. So this trip was a treat, and Juan Rodrigo wanted his daughter to feel that way. They lingered at their table outside the café until the morning sun hovered directly above them.

"I'm glad the birds forgave you, Papá," Esperanza said, listening to the chorus coming from the trees around them.

"I never said they forgave me," Juan Rodrigo replied. "They just realized I was an old fool and not capable of bothering them anymore!"

"I never dreamed they would be so beautiful and that there would be so many different kinds," Esperanza said. "When people spoke of the birds, I pictured them to be like the bats, since they were the only thing I'd seen that could fly."

"Yes," Juan Rodrigo replied a bit absentmindedly, as this particular trip to the plaza had made him wonder what it would be like if Carlota were with them now.

"My favorite are *las palomas*," Esperanza said. "They've made this plaza their own."

"The doves lived here before I drove them away," Juan Rodrigo said. "It's good that they've returned, but I still can't say I'm happy when I see them."

"Why?"

"They remind me of *mi paloma*," he said. "That's what I called her, my dove."

"I know," Esperanza said, taking his hand in her own.

The clang of bells came to them from down the main street. As the noise grew, they heard a fiddle dancing above the clamor, and above it all the rise and fall of one voice, like the mournful cadence of a river when spring's water has nearly run dry.

"The gypsies," Juan Rodrigo said.

"Really?" Esperanza turned in her chair, peering to the corner from which the sound emanated. "They've never been here before."

"Yes, they come but rarely. To trade what they have for what they need."

"Their music is beautiful." Esperanza rose, wanting to run to them as they emerged, but Juan Rodrigo held her back.

"What kind of people have no home?" he said. "They're always speaking of devils and demons, things that can't be seen or proven. I don't like them."

"But, Papá, you talk with ghosts."

"That's different. I'm the gravedigger, and the ghosts need me," he said. "The gypsies celebrate the other world."

The man with the fiddle was the first to enter the plaza. He wore a mismatched suit. Two men with guitars, similarly dressed, followed him. A group of women in red and black entered behind them, clapping rhythmically and stomping their feet. Then came the decrepit wagons, the squeaking of their wheels drowned out by the music. Children and animals ran in between the wagons: goats, chickens, cows, even a goose. A man dressed in a blue shirt with green-striped pants, and wearing a hat with a single long feather, danced among the children, slapping his legs and feet and clapping his hands. To Juan Rodrigo it was as though chaos had been unleashed upon his beloved plaza, but to Esperanza there was magic in the movement and the music and the ululation of the singer.

A boy of about fifteen with dark hair and eyes, and a loop ring through one ear, sat atop one of the wagons. Clearly proud of his role as driver of the only cart with a horse, he sat erect, tapping a branch against the horse's flank, talking to it as the procession made its way around the plaza. Esperanza saw him before he spotted her, intrigued by his calm assurance with the horse. She studied the way in which he used his stick, as a reminder, not as punishment.

The music stopped, and along with it the procession. The boy, whose name was Antonio, raised his gaze to take in the plaza and immediately zeroed in on a slender girl with dark brown hair sitting next to an older man with a crooked nose and a grimace on his face. Antonio immediately noticed the girl's eyes, even from across the plaza, for there was gold laced within the brown. The way they shimmered in the light beckoned to him like a dream, like the times when he awoke in the middle of the night in the cave that served as his home only to see the rock of the cave entrance gleam under the moonlight.

When Esperanza noticed the boy staring at her, she turned away, pointing another bird out to her father, who simply huffed and signaled the waiter for the bill. The plaza was still then; even the birds waited for what might happen next. The gypsy women pulled peppers and garlic and cloths from their wagons. Not a word was said as they prepared their goods, as if they were a well-rehearsed dance troupe preparing for a show.

An older woman with a cracked and worn face, and most of her teeth missing, walked to the center of the plaza and let out a sound not unlike a rooster: "Aiieeeee...ki...ki...ri...ki...ki..."

The other women joined her, holding up their wares and calling in a variety of trills and warbling. The birds, fluttering in the trees, seemed disturbed by this competition, and rose from the trees, flying about the plaza before settling down again. Juan Rodrigo laughed at that. "You think you're the only ones that can sing!" he yelled to them.

Many of the villagers seemed more disturbed than the birds by the shrieking song of the gypsies; they covered their ears, some even their eyes, and left the plaza. Juan Rodrigo was not so easily offended, but he was also not a friend of the gypsies. He rose, signaling Esperanza to follow him. She remained, enraptured by the sound.

"Esperanza, don't make me tell you twice," he said. "Remember my words about your horse." That was all Esperanza needed to hear to pull her from the spectacle, though she threw a last glance over her shoulder, noticing the holes in the boy's red sweater and the fact that his pants were too short for him.

A WEEK LATER, on the first day of school, Esperanza wore her green dress. Doña Villada scowled when she entered the classroom, commenting that ostentation is a sin.

"When did Jesus refer to green dresses?" Esperanza asked. "Or was it one of the Commandments?"

For that she did not have to stand in the corner of the classroom, but she did have to spend an hour after school cleaning her mouth out with Doña Villada's own special soap: She called it "Brine of the Sea," and Esperanza thought it very fitting since it tasted like salt water and almost made her sick.

As she made her way along the path that led through the cliffs from the school to her home, Esperanza stopped many times, turning to look. She was sure someone was following her. At one point, she climbed into a small alcove that sat at about eye level in the rock face, and waited. That way she would be able to catch whomever it was, but no one appeared. Not appreciating the fact that it was she who had been outsmarted, she grew angry and called out, "You don't fool me. I'm too smart for you. Now, show yourself, or I'll tell my father, and he'll sic the ghosts on you!" In reply, she heard a voice, not unlike that of the gypsy singer she'd seen in the plaza, a wail that did not frighten but rather filled the listener with both wonder and sadness. "If you are a gypsy," she yelled, "stay away. My father has no use for gypsies! And I'm nearly home. He has probably heard me already and comes with his ghosts!" But Esperanza heard nothing more. She climbed down from her hiding place and ran the rest of the way home.

Her father was in bed taking a *siesta* when she arrived. "Papá!" she called, shaking him awake. "There's someone in the cliffs."

"What do you mean someone, a man or a woman?" he asked, coughing and wiping the sleep from his eyes.

"Yes, a man. Singing," she said.

"Too bad it wasn't a woman!" Juan Rodrigo replied. "Well, let him sing." He rolled back over on the bed.

"Papá!" She sat on the bed, exasperated. "It scared me."

"I guess you won't be visiting your horse, then," he said with a wry smile, but then coughed again.

Instead of answering, Esperanza chewed her fingernails, staring out the window, as if deciding what to do. "Nothing will stop me from seeing Bella."

"That's my girl," Juan Rodrigo said. "No Rodrigo is afraid of singing. The wind sings through the cliffs and sometimes the ghosts grant us a verse, but we are not afraid of them." He sat up in bed and Esperanza could see he looked clammy and pale.

"Papá, are you sick?"

"Yes, I've got a bit of something. All I need is rest." Seeing the concern in his daughter's face, he beckoned her with his hands, hugged her to him for a long time, and said, "Don't worry about me. Go to your horse. She needs you right now. I need to sleep. And if you hear any singing, tell him to come here and sing to me!"

Esperanza eventually left, not because she wanted to see her horse, though she desperately did, but because she thought she might persuade Señora Oliveira to make a special soup for her father. Rosalia agreed to make the soup, a rich broth of vegetables. The smell alone would raise the dead. And Esperanza went to care for her horse.

When she approached Bella, the horse made a soft whinnying sound.

"I'm happy to see you, too," she told her horse. Then she gently brushed her down, whispering in her ear the stories she'd thought up in the time since her previous visit. Bella stomped one foot excitedly when she liked a certain part of the story and flicked her tail nervously when Esperanza reached what she called a "bad part." Being young, Bella had trouble distinguishing between story and reality, and she didn't understand that these "bad parts" were mere fiction. So, when Esperanza, becoming carried away with the telling of her tale, and hoping to get a reaction out of Bella, described in detail how a fierce fire, whipped up by the winds, encircled the village, and how she and Bella had to face it, calling on the rain to extinguish the blaze, Bella didn't like it at all. She flicked her tail and wildly threw her head about, knocking Esperanza to the ground. Esperanza understood that she'd gone too far and immediately calmed Bella with the touch of her hand on the young horse's neck and her soft voice in her ear. "I'm sorry, *bonita,* I should have known better."

Bella nuzzled against Esperanza and made a face that, if one thought a horse was capable of smiling, one would have surely seen as reflecting the most contented of smiles.

That evening, Rosalia waited on the porch with her shawl wrapped about her and the soup in a kettle beside her. "I'll walk you home," she said. "It's getting dark and your father would be upset if I let you go alone, especially with this singing man roaming about." She gave no hint of the joke, except in the warmth of her eyes, but Esperanza only frowned. She didn't like being made fun of, and she'd told Rosalia about the singing as one woman to another.

Juan Rodrigo was awake when they arrived, having cursed himself for allowing Esperanza to go so late. He'd hoped she would be back before nightfall, and when she was, his relief overcame whatever embarrassment he felt over having a woman in his house again, and he invited Rosalia inside.

She did not comment on the state of the house, nor did she let the slightest hint of her shock betray itself in her face. Rather, she moved to the side of the main room that Juan Rodrigo called simultaneously a living room, bedroom, and kitchen, and placed her soup kettle upon the stove. She did not touch a thing in the house until after Juan Rodrigo had his soup before him, then she casually moved about, picking up a shirt here and a sock there. Whether it was because of her natural manner or his own hunger, Juan Rodrigo didn't even notice. But though Esperanza also enjoyed the soup, she made sure to watch how Rosalia handled herself in the house, curious to know how mothers behaved.

"You're looking better already, Juan Rodrigo," Rosalia said as he sipped the last of the soup from the bowl. Somehow she'd managed not only to pick up all the clothes but arrange them neatly in the drawers of Juan Rodrigo's only dresser.

"And I'm feeling better, too!" he said. "I've lived too many years to let a little chill get me down."

"Is that what it was?" Rosalia asked. "I hope it isn't the flu. It's been so bad these last few years."

"It can't get me, or who would the ghosts talk to?" he said. "They wouldn't allow that." He winked at Rosalia and then immediately cursed himself for doing so. What was he thinking?

Rosalia didn't turn away.

Esperanza noticed the wink and also the awkward manner in which her father said good-bye. Rosalia lingered in the main room, as if with a word from Juan Rodrigo she would abandon everything and stay with them. Esperanza knew her father sensed this, and she wondered at the prospect of having a mother. As Juan Rodrigo showed Rosalia to the door, he spoke her name twice, hesitating each time, "Rosalia . . . Rosalia . . ." Both women waited, simultaneously afraid and excited by what he might say. Esperanza liked Señora Oliveira. She wouldn't mind at all if she lived with them, especially if it meant she could eat such soup every day.

Rosalia closed her eyes for the briefest of seconds, hoping to see her dead husband's face, praying that he might guide her, that he might give her his blessing. But her husband said nothing, and all Juan Rodrigo could bring himself to say was, "Thank you. You've made me feel much better."

THE NEXT DAY, on the way home from school, Esperanza noticed a flicker of light coming from the alcove where she'd hid the previous day. She climbed inside and found a candle burning beside a flower. She'd never seen a green flower before. Then, once again, the mournful voice rose from the mountains around her, but this time she understood the words: "O my nights, my days are filled with a burning hunger. But I am sustained by the petals of the green flower!"

She jumped out of the alcove, hoping to surprise the singer. When she landed, she heard footsteps in the trees. She was proud of all the time she'd spent climbing rocks; surefooted, she knew she'd catch the singer. But the chase along the cliffs went on and she didn't seem any closer, until at last she caught sight of a red sweater as the boy darted down another slope and then beyond a grove of pines. She knew immediately who it was and spent the rest of the day thinking about the boy who was so proud as he drove his cart.

She arrived home dreaming of the boy only to find her father again in bed.

"Papá, you need medicine stronger than Rosalia's soup," she said, sitting beside him.

"I'm fine." Juan Rodrigo sat up in the bed. "It's just a mild case of that flu," he said, though he feared the sickness went deeper than that. "Run along to your horse. I'm going to rest. I'll be better in a couple of days, you'll see."

"Enough of this nonsense," she said. "I'm going to the pharmacy."

"You sound like your aunt Consuela," he replied, taking her hand. "I should have never let you spend that month with her."

"To the pharmacy," she repeated, giving him a stern look, a look that, in the end, did not remind him of Consuela but of his wife. "Don Alfonso will know what to do." Speaking that name out loud made her afraid, though she wasn't completely sure why. It had to do with the way he looked at her. "Don't worry about a thing," she said, not wanting her father to read her thoughts. "I'll be back before nightfall, and you'll be better by tomorrow. Then

I'll take you to see Bella. She's getting bigger every day. Soon she'll be able to carry you!"

DON ALFONSO PRIDED HIMSELF on keeping his pharmacy modern and fully stocked. In the absence of a real doctor, Don Alfonso diagnosed those who came to him, and even made house calls when patients were too sick. In this event, he left the pharmacy to his son, Emilio, who was in his early twenties, and a bit odd, though no one could put their finger on exactly what it was. Don Alfonso was excessively proud of his son, and though normally it would not have been strange for a father to be proud, Don Alfonso's pride smacked of ostentation and made poor Emilio that much more timid. Esperanza saw nothing wrong with the boy. She liked the way he sometimes confused words or mispronounced them; for example, he couldn't say the word *science,* which caused his father no end of embarrassment, as Don Alfonso worshiped all that was remotely scientific. Esperanza hoped that Don Alfonso would be making a house call so that she wouldn't have to feel his eyes upon her, but when she walked into the dark store, that is exactly what she felt.

Though Don Alfonso's pharmacy had all the modern conveniences, he was obsessed with the idea that the new electric lights were bad for the eyes, and he kept his lights low, forcing customers to stand a moment in the doorway while their eyes adjusted. Esperanza didn't wait in the doorway, though, for Don Alfonso to approach her and take her by the hand. Instead, she marched to the black marble counter before he could step out.

"My father is sick," she said. "He thinks it's the flu, but I fear it may be something worse."

Don Alfonso, nevertheless, did step out from behind the counter, reaching for her hands. "My dear," he said. The sweet smell of his cologne nauseated her. "My dear," he said again. And she looked up at his towering frame. He was a big man, both in height and in girth. And he was nearly bald, though he combed the few remaining gray hairs across his head. No matter what the time of year, he wore a white shirt with a bow tie and a black suit coat, though in the fall and winter he also wore a gray wool sweater under his coat. He bent his head to kiss Esperanza's hand. As his thick lips pressed against her flesh, Esperanza cringed at their wetness. "Tell me his symptoms," Don Alfonso said, putting his arm around her now and leading her to one of two wood chairs that stood against the side wall.

"He sleeps all the time, and he feels clammy," she said, pulling away just enough to maintain a distance from Don Alfonso, to let him know that she was no child. "And I think sometimes when I look into his eyes that he does not see me, as if he is suffering under a spell." Esperanza sat in the chair furthest from the pharmacist.

"You talk like the gypsies," Don Alfonso said, sitting beside her. "I am a man of science, and science is the one true light, the light that will take man out of the darkness of superstition." He patted her knee. "Science will cure your father."

"I would be very grateful if you could do something." Immediately upon saying it, Esperanza felt that somehow it was wrong, that she'd made a mistake.

"I'm sure you would," Don Alfonso said. "I'm sure you would." And he patted her knee again before rising and crossing behind his counter. "Your father is a poor man, Esperanza. But I respect him. He works hard, and I pity him now that he suffers." He pulled down a large bottle of white powder and mixed it with another bottle of pink. "Dissolve this in water and give it to your father twice a day. He'll be better soon."

Grateful, Esperanza rushed forward. As she reached for the bottle, Don Alfonso grabbed her hand. "Remember, my dear," he said, his eyes devouring her, "the miracles of science are not cheap."

THAT NIGHT, Esperanza gave her father the medicine and the remainder of Rosalia's soup, then said she was going to bathe him, but he wouldn't hear of it. Still, she heated the water for the bath before sitting on the porch while her father soaked. She decided to write a note to the gypsy boy and leave it in the alcove on her way to school the next morning. She was proud of her ability to write. Once, when the teacher had them write a story, she'd written about a girl who waited by the sea for her father to return on a ship. He was a great sea captain and had been absent for many years. The girl took responsibility for raising herself, but she was tired of it; she wanted to play, to dance with the spirits in the mountains. When she finally saw her father's ship returning, a great storm rose from beyond the mountains and pushed the ship back out to sea. Doña Villada had given her an F for that story, saying it was obviously one of her father's creations. Though many people in the town didn't appreciate Juan Rodrigo's stories, there were few who mistrusted him altogether. Doña Villada was one of them.

Esperanza wrote throughout the night, telling the gypsy boy her fears for her father's health. How she thought he was dying of loneliness, that he was the type of man who needed a woman, though he was too proud to admit it. How she tried to help him but how sometimes she felt his loneliness was beyond her. How she knew her father loved her dearly, more than anything in the world, but that he needed something more, something she couldn't give him. She wrote about the time she spent in the city with her aunt and uncle, and how she missed her father terribly, but how she also had guilt over the relief she felt: the freedom from the responsibility of pleasing him, of keeping him happy. And then she remembered the moving picture to which they took her. Consuela and Tesifón had been quite shocked. They'd taken her because the new moving pictures were the thing to see and the place to be seen. But Esperanza would never forget the image of the devil rising from the smoke about him as he tormented that man Faust. And the death of Gretchen. She'd never seen anything like it. Her aunt took her from the cinema before it was over, but it was too late, the images had their effect on her mind. She fell ill for a week after that, and her aunt swore she'd never forgive herself. Yet there were also parts that were magical. She wanted to describe the moving picture in detail to the boy, yet found that the face of Mephistopheles still haunted her.

Her aunt didn't understand, and Esperanza was too ashamed to tell her. It was not the movie that had affected her so much, but rather the fact that the movie had brought out her fears of the ghosts she'd lived with: the spirits that needed her father. They took him from her; that was part of it, but not all. She realized then that she was truly her father's daughter. She shared his discomfort with the unseen world, and while he'd gotten used to the ghosts by necessity, she had not. There were some she didn't mind, those that brought joy even in death, but others—she remembered the fear that came over her the night Father Ramon's spirit entered the house. It was then she acknowledged the heart of her fear; her father's sickness was rooted in his dealings with the ghosts. The look in his eyes told her everything. The weight of the ghosts, their lives, their hopes and regrets, was overpowering him; he was not meant to be a gravedigger.

She tried to tell all this in the letter to Antonio, though she did not yet know his name, nor how he would respond. But she felt sure that he would understand. She'd recognized a part of herself in him when she saw him driving the cart that day, and then again when he sang to her. A pride, but a pride born of responsibility.

The next day, she left the letter, along with a lock of her hair. When she returned after school and checked the alcove, the items were gone. Dancing and singing to herself on the way home, Esperanza felt that maybe now she would have someone who would understand.

Eugenio was waiting for her where the path forked to her house. When she first saw him, she felt the urge to run but didn't. Instead, she smiled and danced before him. Eugenio revealed the flowers he'd been hiding behind his back. His smile was a warm one, and Esperanza wondered why she'd felt a tinge of fear that first moment upon seeing him.

"How's your father?" he asked, walking beside her.

"How'd you know he was sick?"

"I saw you come out of the pharmacy yesterday, and you wouldn't be getting medicine for your burro!"

"El Viejo could certainly use some medicine!" She laughed, and realized she was happy for the company.

But then there was silence, and Esperanza could tell Eugenio was preparing to say something. He stopped, stuffing his hands in his pockets. When he spoke, he stammered, then stopped again, taking a deep breath before saying, "Would you go to the All Souls Dance with me?"

Esperanza hadn't expected the question and wasn't sure what to say. "But it's not for another six weeks."

"I know," he said, still looking nervous. "But you're so pretty. I thought I better ask before anyone else does. Of course, your father would accompany us."

Esperanza blushed. No boy had ever called her pretty before. Her father called her *bonita* all the time, but that was different. "I hadn't thought about the dance. It seems so far away, and with my father being sick . . ."

"You don't have to answer right now," Eugenio said, seeming relieved. "Just remember that I asked you first." With that he turned and ran down the path that led to the village where most of the children lived.

Juan Rodrigo was out in the yard, working on the burro's long-neglected pen. He watched his daughter twirling and dancing her way up the path to the house and said to the sky above, "Carlota, what have you done to me? She's going to be one like you who talks to the birds!"

"So you are feeling better, Papá," she said, dancing in circles around him. "I'm glad!"

"I can see," he said. "And I can see that something else is making you happy. I'm growing dizzy from watching you!"

"Let's go together to see Bella today, Papá. I so want you to love her the way I do."

"I don't know if that's possible," he said. "But, yes, we must go see her today. It's time to take her home. That's why I'm working on making this stable stronger. El Viejo here may get ideas and follow your horse right out!"

"Oh, Papá! I'll be able to ride her soon." She stopped twirling now and ran around Juan Rodrigo, imitating a cantering horse.

"Not until we can afford a saddle," he said. "But we can work on breaking her in until then.

"But, Papá, it's not fair. I don't need a saddle."

"There will be no discussion about it," he said, suddenly getting serious. "I will pay for half of the saddle. You must work to pay for the other half."

"Then I'll carry groceries for Señora Faura, and help Señora Ortega with her garden. Oh, and Señora Mercedes, she's always wanted me to help her in her dress shop. Maybe she'll agree to pay me a little bit."

"Maybe," Juan Rodrigo said. "But now let's go see your horse."

THE NEXT DAY, on her way home from school, she skipped along the path, barely able to contain her excitement. Surely there would be a note from the boy. They could write their deepest feelings to each other; maybe he would even write her poems. She would read them in her bed at night, then write answers conjured from her own fancies: How he would meet her on his white horse. How they would sail across the sea to start a life together. Of course, her father would come with them.

But there was nothing in the alcove. Climbing down, dispirited, she began to walk the path back to her house, when she heard the song, accompanied by the wind whistling through the pines: "I am sustained by the petals of the green flower . . ."

She turned in the direction of the voice, catching a glimpse of the red sweater disappearing down into a ravine that cut through the mountain. She had him this time, as there was only one way out of the ravine, and she took off down the mountain. Cutting through thick brambles, she tore her green dress but didn't stop to examine it. She saw him now strolling through the ravine, walking proudly, sure in his feeling that he'd escaped. Stepping down through the boulders that led to the only other opening in the ravine, she dropped the last few feet, landing directly in front of the boy, startling him.

He didn't try to run but simply smiled. *"Me llamo Antonio,"* he said, extending his hand and bowing slightly.

"Why do you sing to me?" Esperanza asked.

"Because your eyes dance with the same fire that is in my heart," he said, smiling again.

He spoke exceptionally well, Esperanza thought, not at all like Eugenio. But the intensity of his gaze frightened her, and she bent down to examine the tear in her dress.

"I caught it in the brambles," she said.

"You shouldn't have been running, you could have fallen."

"You sound like my father."

The boy recoiled. "I am my own man," he said.

"I didn't mean anything by it," she said. "I can tell that you are." She sat down on a rock, and he sat beside her, taking the torn hem in his hand.

"The women in my village could fix this for you."

"Señora Mercedes can do it better than any gypsy woman," she said. The boy dropped the hem and stood. He tossed a small rock across the ravine, and Esperanza wondered why she'd said such a thing. Her father didn't like the gypsies, but what did she know of them?

"I'm sorry," she said, then paused, not knowing what else to say. "I'm going to work for Señora Mercedes. I'm saving to buy a saddle for my horse."

"I have a horse, too." The boy sat beside her once again. "But we use him to plow the fields, and I'm not allowed to ride him. Not yet. Does your horse listen to you, or do you have to bribe him with sweets?"

"Mine is too young for work yet. But I talk with her. And she's brown, with a white spot down her nose and white around her feet. She's beautiful."

"Your dress is beautiful," the boy said. He looked as if he wanted to say more, though he had little need for words, as Esperanza knew what he was thinking. His openness revealed his awkwardness, and, realizing it, the boy feigned interest in cleaning the dirt from his hands.

The combination of his sincerity and her own rush of feeling threatened to overwhelm Esperanza. "I didn't know that green flowers existed," she said.

"Neither did I."

The moment became too much for them, and Antonio jumped up to show her how he could have climbed out of the ravine at any point if he'd wanted to, that he really wanted her to catch him and knew she would come down through the chute between the rocks. Esperanza didn't believe him, especially when he almost fell halfway up the steep side of the ravine.

They ran through the ravine then, and as they played, he told her of the caves beyond the Rio Yátor where his family lived, of the music they woke to every day and the stillness within the caves at night. Esperanza thought it sounded magical, but then he explained how he felt trapped there, as if the caves could only hold small lives, and he knew his would be big. He talked of leaving for the city, as her own father had once talked to her mother, though Esperanza never knew this. "Soon. Very soon I will go, and I'll take my horse with me."

"My uncle could help you get a job there," she said. "He's very influential."

"You have an uncle in the city?"

"Yes, of course. Didn't you read my letter?"

He paused before answering. "It was beautiful," he said finally. And as he spoke, his face flushed.

"I'm glad you liked it. I'll write you another. I'm very good at writing letters."

She and her father brought Bella home from Rosalia's house that afternoon. Esperanza stayed outside talking to the horse until bedtime. Juan Rodrigo smiled to see it and said to his wife, "Maybe she is different from you, after all. She does not have the spirit of the birds in her, but of the horse!"

Esperanza told her father that she was helping in the village and so would be late coming home from school. But in actuality, she and Antonio began meeting every day in the ravine. They could not meet closer to the boy's encampment because Esperanza would never make it back before dark, not unless she rode her horse. They would talk to each other until they were sure there was no more to say, then they would begin again, finding a secret area of their hearts yet to be expressed. It was at these times that the intensity in Antonio's eyes sometimes frightened Esperanza, and she would break away, showing him the tracks of a beetle in the dirt, or the rocks that sparkled in the side of the ravine, the rocks her father used to bring to her when she was little.

When she returned from her afternoons with Antonio, she cared for her horse, and then in the evenings, just before supper, her father showed her how she must work to tame Bella if she was ever going to ride her. She learned quickly, though, truth be told, she didn't apply much of Juan Rodrigo's knowledge. Bella listened to her without the use of the switch. Esperanza could indeed speak to the horses!

ONE AFTERNOON two weeks later, when Esperanza and Antonio sat on their favorite rock, leaning against the side of the ravine, holding hands, they heard a noise—the crack of a branch, or the crunching of gravel—from somewhere in the rocks above. A few pebbles fell, hitting them in the head. Antonio grabbed Esperanza and yanked her away from the ravine wall. Many rocks, the size of melons, broke free from the ledge, crashing down on the boulder where they'd been sitting. Eugenio stuck his head over the ledge; tears were in his eyes.

"Why are you spying on us?" Esperanza stepped forward, embarrassed, yet at the same time angry with him for uncovering her secret.

"Why do you sit here with this gypsy?" he asked.

"It's no business of yours who I sit with," she said, realizing that she was really angry with herself for keeping the secret in the first place. Her father had taught her to be honest. She wanted to say she was sorry—to Eugenio, to Antonio, and to her father—but somehow the tears on Eugenio's face irritated her. What right had he to think she had wronged him so?

"You were going to go to the dance with me," he said, standing now, looking down upon them. And then he was gone.

When she arrived home later that afternoon, her father was waiting for her, belt in hand.

"You told me you were working," he said. "You lied to your own father to be with—"

"With whom, Papá?" Esperanza yelled back, defiant.

"With Antonio. I see Eugenio has been to see you."

"At least he knows how to tell the truth!" Juan Rodrigo replied. "But you! You sneak about with a gypsy!"

"That's why I couldn't tell you, Papá," she said, coming toward him now, sadness on her face, not for the fact that she was in trouble, nor because she'd lied, but for the situation that had forced the lying upon her. She remembered the look on Antonio's face when she'd said that Señora Mercedes could fix the dress better than any gypsy. She didn't want her father to be that way; she knew he didn't mean it. "How could I explain that I was friends with a gypsy boy, when I knew that you would react like this?"

"So it's better to lie to your father, is that right?" With that, Juan Rodrigo slapped his belt against the side of the doorway where he stood. He inhaled deeply, readying himself for another tirade, when he started coughing uncontrollably, spewing up phlegm.

"Papá," Esperanza said, rushing to him. "You mustn't get upset. You're not well." She fit herself under his arm, helping him inside. Sitting him on the bed, she fetched a glass of water.

Juan Rodrigo studied his daughter. He knew that physically she was becoming a woman, but he hadn't realized that the changes involved more than that. He wondered if her talking to horses was the childish fancy he'd thought it was, or if she indeed believed in invisible worlds like her mother. "What do you see when you look at me, Esperanza?"

She brought him the water and sat beside him, moving the belt from the bed and taking his hand. "I see a father who loves his daughter very much," she said.

"Is it so bad for a father to love his daughter, to want her to be safe? To be happy?"

"Of course not," she said. "But what about your own happiness?"

"My happiness is your happiness," Juan Rodrigo said. "You're all I live for."

"But don't you see, Papá?" she said. "That is what's suffocating me. That's why I must lie. I know it's not right, and I'm sorry, but I feel the weight of your life every day."

"No, *mi corazón*, that's the last thing I want," Juan Rodrigo said. "Maybe I try too hard to make things right for you. Maybe I demand you spend too much time with me. I don't know."

"I only know what I feel, Papá," she said. "And lately I've felt almost as if you were the ghost, and it was my responsibility to set your life straight."

"What should I do?" Her father looked at her as if he no longer knew what to do.

Esperanza studied her father's eyes, amazed. It was the first time that he appeared the child to her. The feeling frightened her. "I don't know," she said.

Then, regaining himself, Juan Rodrigo puffed his chest and reached for the belt once again. "But this gypsy boy," he said. "He is not good for you."

"We're just friends, Papá," she said, though she knew it wasn't true. But she hadn't yet fully admitted that even to herself.

"Gypsies have no homes," he said, and Esperanza got ready to hear her father's complaints about the gypsies once again. "What kind of people have no homes? And I don't like their magic. It's the work of the devil!"

"Antonio doesn't believe in magic," she said, but again she questioned whether she was telling the truth. Content to gaze in each other's eyes, to feel the touch of each other's hands, they'd never talked about the unseen.

"You don't know the stories I've heard about the gypsies," Juan Rodrigo continued. "They lie. They steal, even from their own kind. And worst of all, they say they take children in the night and drink their blood."

"Papá," Esperanza exclaimed. "You can't possibly believe such lies."

"It's true," Juan Rodrigo said. "Why, the ghost of Florentino himself told me that once. On his way back from Almeria, he stumbled upon a gypsy camp in the night and saw the bodies of children scattered about."

"You told me yourself, Papá, that Florentino drank too much, especially on his trips. That's why he and Mercedes argued so," Esperanza replied, folding her arms before her, deciding she was not about to give in, nor would she run to the porch, frustrated, as she usually did. No. She did not believe her father's stories this time.

"You doubt me?" Juan Rodrigo said, but instead of his temper rising, as it used to do, his anger seemed to seep from him.

"Yes."

They stared, one at the other, each determined not to give in. Then Juan Rodrigo put down his belt. "You are a wise woman," he said to Esperanza. "Not about the gypsies—there you are mistaken—but about me. I will be a better father. I won't suffocate you."

Esperanza smiled but did not lower her arms.

"Still, a daughter must not lie to her father," Juan Rodrigo went on. "And lies, while harmless in a child, never befit a grown man or woman."

"I understand, Papá. I will not lie again."

"I have learned something today, but you must show you have learned something, too," he said.

"Yes, Papá."

"Promise me you will not see the gypsy boy again."

"Papá!"

"He is bad luck. Nothing good can come of your time with him."

"Didn't you hear what I said, Papá?" she cried out. "You're wrong about the gypsies. The ghosts don't always tell the truth!"

"Promise me," he said.

Her father looked so earnest, she found herself unsure what to do. If she could only explain the way she felt when she and Antonio were together, the way he made her feel older, for the first time like a woman to be desired, to be loved. But if she told her father that, he would never understand. And he seemed to need her so. His eyes begged her to be true to him, saying, *I've had all the sadness I can handle in my life. I've lost my wife, and I can't bear to lose my daughter. You must help me through.* And she realized then that he'd learned nothing during their talk, but she accepted it and loved him anyway, and when she opened her mouth she said, "Yes, Papá, I promise. I will not see the gypsy boy again," though it hurt her to do so.

She wrote a letter to Antonio explaining everything and placed it in the alcove on her way to school the next day. Then, in the afternoon, she went to work for Señora Mercedes and was pleased with herself as she sat learning the trade of dressmaker. But that evening as she cared for her horse, she heard Antonio's mournful voice rising from the ravine, drifting from tree to tree: "O my nights, my days . . . what wind has carried away my green flower? And what hunger must I endure now that she is gone?"

Bella turned to her, cocking her head as if asking, *Why do you not answer?* Esperanza's only reply was to hug her horse to her. "I can't, Bella," she whispered, and her horse responded with a soft whinny to show she understood.

The voice haunted her so much throughout the night that she wondered if what her father said was true about the magic of the gypsies. And in the morning when she woke, she heard it again, breaking through her window with the first light of the sun. If her father heard it, he said nothing, and they sat through breakfast together speaking of the people in the village: *Señor Azevedo had a horrible toothache—did you hear that? And the little Bermeja girl seemed so sad. It's not natural for a six-year-old to wander the streets with such a look. Do you suppose there is something not right at home?* But Esperanza heard very little of this, until her father said, "You never want to hear my stories anymore, Esperanza. Why is that?"

She almost told him how when she was young the lives seemed so wondrous, that she had loved hearing of the strange things people said and did. It hadn't mattered to her that they were being told to her father by the ghosts of the recently departed. But lately the stories made her sad, partly for the effect they seemed to have on her father, but also because so many people seemed trapped in the village, their lives unfulfilled. She believed Antonio when he said their lives were bigger than that. At a time in her life when she was so hopeful, she couldn't bear to believe that so many had died having lost hope. Again she thought it had all started that night with the visit from the spirit of Father Ramon, but, shuddering, she stopped herself from thinking about it, and answered her father. "I don't know," she said. "I'm so busy living now that I'm older, that I have no time to hear the stories of the dead."

Day after day, the voice of Antonio haunted her until soon a month had passed. Señora Mercedes now gave her more responsibilities in the dress shop, and Esperanza had learned to do the measurements properly. But her mind was not at peace. It wasn't just the voice; she missed her time with Antonio and felt as if a part of her had been taken away.

Finally, one afternoon she told Señora Mercedes that she would not be able to make it the following day, as her father needed her help. She figured that lying to Señora Mercedes was not the same as lying to her father, and if she was gone just this one afternoon, her father would never know, and it wouldn't really be like lying to him. The next afternoon, while her father worked in Pedro's bar, Esperanza quickly returned home and went directly to her horse.

"Bella, I need your help, for the voice no longer comes from the ravine, but down in the valley near the river. It's a long way, and I can't make it there on foot and be back before nightfall. Will you help me, Bella? Will you carry me to the river?"

Bella's great, wet eyes looked at Esperanza, telling her that she would do whatever Esperanza wished, for never had someone taken such good care of a horse. And Esperanza jumped astride Bella and galloped after the voice that beckoned to her.

Juan Rodrigo was enjoying a short break, sipping his wine outside the bar with his friend Pedro Martinez, when a large black crow landed upon the back fence post and stared at the gravedigger, not saying a word. Pedro tried to shoo it off, but it wouldn't fly, so the two men sat drinking their wine and joking with the bird. Yet the jokes were more to put the men at ease, for Juan Rodrigo didn't like the bird's look, not at all.

Riding down the mountainside, coursing through the maples and elms, edging along the Rio Yátor, Esperanza felt free as she never had before, as if by simply breaking the boundaries of her village, she had become another person. It was different from her trip to the city the previous summer when she had stayed with her aunt and uncle. There, she was still expected to be the daughter of Carlota and Juan Rodrigo. Racing through the valley now, she had no fear and felt sure she could face the devil from the movie *Faust* that had scared her so. The singing grew louder as she traveled along the river, until she felt as if she were riding upon the voice, letting it carry her to her new home.

Antonio stood before a grove of elms where the oxbow in the river calmed the water. It looked like one of the few places to cross the great river, and Esperanza wondered if the caves where Antonio's family lived were near. He smiled when she approached.

"Your horse trusts you," he said. "That is a good sign. You must be a kindred spirit of the gypsies, but then again you are the green flower."

Esperanza fought the sound of her father's voice rising in her head. "Thank you," she said. "Bella really is a fine horse." They gazed at each other, until Esperanza once again spoke, more to break the power of the silence than anything else. "But why do you call me that, really?"

Antonio smiled and, moving to help her down from her horse, answered with a question of his own. "Why did you stop coming to the ravine?"

"Didn't you get my note?" she asked, feeling the earth beneath her feet and wondering at the difference from the freedom she felt on the horse.

"Yes," he said, but he turned away.

Esperanza approached him, resting her hand on his shoulder, aware that the gesture felt quite different than the childish hand-holding they'd done in the past. "I'm sorry, I should have known."

"Don't give me your pity," he said. "We gypsies don't need to read. We rely on the ability to see where others can't." And with that he turned to Esperanza, and she saw the purple and red bruises along his cheek.

"Who has hit you?"

"No one!" Again he turned away, this time walking toward the river, where he sat upon a rock overlooking a small, sandy inlet. Esperanza followed him, sitting beside him on the rock. Her hand caressed his cheek, feeling the wetness of tears there. They sat together, saying nothing, yet satisfied in the glimmering moment where they were free to exist for each other and no one else, free of the responsibility of family and village. The sun descended behind them, the warmth of its rays fighting to the last against the onslaught of the early October chill. But Esperanza and Antonio knew nothing of the sun's struggle as they sat, the cold not bothering them.

Eventually, Esperanza told him she must return home; he kissed her, lightly and briefly. They both smiled afterward, and again she caressed his face, then mounted her horse and set off through the field along the river.

In autumn, as dusk settles upon the valley, the snakes leave the woods, searching for warm rocks near the river on which to bask under the last rays of the sun. It was one such snake, a mud snake—though why they are called mud snakes is anyone's guess, since they are shiny black in color, while mud is brown— who being young and not having seen a horse, raised its head before Bella, hissing and generally trying to defend itself. Of course, Bella was terrified, as she was also young and had not seen a snake before. She didn't want to jump, but she panicked and Esperanza tumbled to the ground, hitting her head on the same rock the snake had occupied.

Fortunately, Antonio had seen the accident and was at her side moments after she landed. She was unconscious. The snake had fled, being more frightened of the horse than the horse was of it, if that can be believed. So Bella stood calmly as Antonio carried Esperanza and set her upon the horse. She let the boy mount and listened to his whispered words to run home as fast as she could.

STILL UNNERVED by the presence earlier of the crow, Juan Rodrigo paced before the stable in front of his house, cursing at his poor burro, when he really meant to curse at himself, and coughing in between expletives. His condition was returning.

When Antonio arrived, Juan Rodrigo took his daughter from the gypsy without looking at him, then carried her inside. Antonio waited outside the house with Bella and the burro. Fortunately, it had not been a serious injury, and Esperanza was already coming to when her father laid her on the bed.

"Where am I, Papá?"

"In your house where you belong," he answered.

"Were you telling me one of your stories just now?"

"Yes," he said, wanting to humor her until he was sure she was all right.

"It was so beautiful," she said. "I'd forgotten how beautiful they could be!"

"I'm glad you liked it," Juan Rodrigo said, already wishing he hadn't deceived her.

"Who was it?" she asked. "There was a girl riding a horse, and she seemed so happy."

"Forget about the story," Juan Rodrigo said, bringing her a glass of water. "Drink and rest, *mi corazón*."

"I thought for a moment that I was the girl, and that I had been dreaming, but then it didn't feel like me, and I knew it was one of your stories." Esperanza then caught sight of both Antonio and the burro peering in through the doorway; the horse was still thinking about the snake and stayed in the stable, where Antonio had left her. "I'm confused," she said. "What's going on, Papá?"

"Nothing. They are concerned about you as I am," he said. "They want to be sure you are all right."

"It wasn't one of your stories at all, was it, Papá?" she asked.

Juan Rodrigo wiped the small trace of dried blood from her forehead. He had no answer for her, and was now angry with himself for lying. "No," he said. "I thought it would help you, that's all."

"I understand, Papá," she said, and with that she smiled and reached for her father's hand, knowing he needed her touch.

Once she was asleep, Juan Rodrigo went outside and sat against the fence post beside the gypsy boy. "Thank you," he said, then nothing more for a long time. The sun having set hours before, the chill of night settled within their bones.

"I want to marry her," Antonio declared.

"What!" Juan Rodrigo rose and stood before him. "She is thirteen. Not even of age. And you . . . you are a gypsy!" In the stable, both the burro and Bella heard Juan Rodrigo's rising anger and kept their distance.

"I will wait," Antonio said. "I wanted you to know, and to ask your permission."

"There will be no permission!" Juan Rodrigo kicked the fence post to emphasize his point, and Antonio stood. It was then that Juan Rodrigo noticed the bruises on Antonio's face, but he saw them solely as a reminder of the life of the gypsies, and he grew more determined to keep his daughter from them. "She is my daughter, and she'll do as I say!" he yelled. "And you! You'll stay away from her. You are bad luck. The crow tried to warn me, but I didn't listen. Leave here, and do not come back!"

The boy stood where he was. "I love her," he said, "and I wish to be near her."

"You are a boy!" Juan Rodrigo yelled. "What do you know of love?"

Though Antonio was a boy, he knew enough to keep his gaze on Juan Rodrigo and wait until the old man stopped pacing about. Then he spoke: "I know that love, if it comes into our lives at all, flies in on the wings of a bird, and that the bird cannot be contained, no matter how we try to hold it in our hands. And though we cannot hold it, I know that we are fools if we ignore it."

Juan Rodrigo studied the boy. He saw himself in his youth, and he wondered what had happened to that boy from so long ago. Where was the child who sat beneath the great olive tree in the cemetery making up his own stories as he watched his father talking with the ghosts? And where was the young man who'd brought crystals to Carlota in the plaza? He stepped forward, wanting to put his arm around this boy, to tell him that he was right, that sometimes the young were wiser than the old.

But he didn't. "Go, please," he said, dropping his gaze to the dirt, somehow not able to embrace that passage of time that changes a boy into a man, to accept the way in which it breaks and embitters us so that we no longer treasure the ardor of the young, but rather see them only as a reminder of our own failings. "Go," he said again. "She is my daughter." And when he raised his head a moment later, the boy was gone.

The next day, when Esperanza woke, the horse was nowhere to be seen. She ran down the pathway to the village, only to find her father returning along the same path.

"You shouldn't be running so soon after your injury," he said to her, trying to smile, but knowing that she was angry with him, and that he now had to face that anger.

"Where is Bella?" Esperanza stood before him. He gestured for her to come closer so that he could hold her and explain, but she wouldn't move. "Where is Bella?" she asked again.

"I returned her to Rosalia," he said. "She could use the money the horse will bring. It is difficult—"

"No, Papá! She was my horse. How could you?" Esperanza broke into tears, and Juan Rodrigo wondered if he'd been too rash.

"I understand, *mi corazón* . . . ."

"No, you don't understand," she said from behind the tears. "How could you understand and still do something like that?"

"The horse is dangerous," he said. "I was worried about you. . . ."

"You weren't worried about me." She turned on him. "You want to keep me with you, always. You don't want me to grow up!"

"Esperanza . . ."

"You're so alone, Papá," she said, "even with the company of ghosts. And I can't be there for you, not forever. I love you, Papá, but I can't." And with that she broke down completely, running from him in the direction of Rosalia's house.

Rosalia Oliveira, as always, proved to be a good listener. She'd foreseen what would happen when Juan Rodrigo stubbornly demanded she take back the horse, and she knew it would only be a matter of time before he relented. The only thing to do now, she told Esperanza, was to wait. Her father had acted out of love, and that same love would eventually bring her back her horse. In the meantime, Esperanza visited Rosalia every day. Each day her father came to pick her up, much as he had before, only this time more grudgingly. At home in the evenings, she waited on the porch for the voice of Antonio, but there was not even a whisper from the valley below.

After a week passed, Rosalia decided that Juan Rodrigo was nearly as stubborn as his burro. She invited Esperanza and her father for dinner, knowing that Juan Rodrigo rarely passed up the opportunity for a good meal, and when he sat patting his belly, and commenting on how much he enjoyed the food, she glanced at Esperanza; they knew they had him.

"Juan Rodrigo, never in my life have I seen a man like you," Rosalia said. "You promised your daughter a horse and then at the first sign of trouble you give it back!"

"She lied to me!" Juan Rodrigo said, sitting up in his chair, his sated stomach making it difficult for his eyes to focus in on the attack.

"I lied because you forbade me to see him, Papá," Esperanza joined in. "I am a woman now. You can't treat me like a girl."

"Esperanza," Juan Rodrigo began, "don't start. . . ."

"She's right," Rosalia said. "The problem is you don't know how to treat her!"

Juan Rodrigo flung his hands in the air. "What are you talking about? I don't know how to raise my own daughter? She's my daughter, and I'll raise her as I see fit!"

But Rosalia met his gaze and matched his temper with a fire all her own. "You have raised her well, Juan Rodrigo, but you raise her like a man. You need a woman," she said. "And she needs a mother." She paused as if sounding her own heart, then threw down her dish towel, saying, "Now, when are you going to stop beating around the bush and ask me to marry you?"

They were all silent. Juan Rodrigo stared at his plate and then began eating his beans. Esperanza smiled as she looked back and forth between Rosalia and her father. Surprised at her own comment, Rosalia shakily cleared the empty plates from the table. While she was in the kitchen, Esperanza whispered to her father, "Do you love her, Papá?"

"How do I know if I love her?" he snapped, and jumped up so brusquely, he spilled his wine on the table and onto his clothes. *"Por la Virgen!"* he exclaimed, then stepped into the kitchen. Esperanza waited, hopeful, but alone in the dining room. After a few minutes, she heard laughter from the kitchen, and she smiled. She would have a mother after all.

When they left Rosalia's house, they stopped by the barn to pick up Bella, Juan Rodrigo feigning indignation the entire time. Rosalia asked them to wait, then stepped into one of the stalls and pulled out an old saddle. "It was my late husband's. May he rest in peace," she said, handing the saddle to Juan Rodrigo. "Perhaps she will be safer with this."

As they walked home, Esperanza was dying to ask her father what had happened in the kitchen, but she was afraid of saying the wrong thing. If she fired her father's temper, he wouldn't say a word the entire night, and she couldn't stand the idea of not knowing. As they reached their own home, she could bear it no longer. "What were you two laughing about in the kitchen?" she asked.

Juan Rodrigo smiled at the memory of it. "I told her she was too forward," he said. "These things take time."

"But why were you laughing?"

"I said that she nearly gave me a heart attack with her proposal, and being dead, what kind of husband would I make!"

As Esperanza slept, Juan Rodrigo sat on the porch, staring at the moon. "Forgive me, Carlota," he said. "The girl needs a mother, and, yes, I need a wife."

Days rolled into weeks and autumn brought rain with its passing. Esperanza and Juan Rodrigo had many pleasant meals at Rosalia's, and though a wedding date had not been set, it was clear their courtship was a happy one. Juan Rodrigo did not relent in his wishes that Esperanza stop seeing the gypsy boy, and Esperanza played the dutiful daughter, but in the afternoons, she met Antonio in the ravine, where they talked about their future lives together. Like Juan Rodrigo had in his youth, Antonio dreamed of moving to the city, where he would be an important businessman, perhaps dealing in leather goods—his gypsy connections would help him there. Esperanza, for her part, was agreeable as long as she could bring along Bella and El Viejo. Since the burro had been around her entire life, she saw no reason why he wouldn't live with them still, giving rides to their children. Her father's remaining with them was something she didn't question.

But the rain that came with winter did not have a salutary affect on Juan Rodrigo. He coughed all night and once, in the morning, there was blood on the collar of his nightshirt. Esperanza had noticed it when she did the wash, though she didn't say a word to either her father or Rosalia. Pushing aside her fear, she went directly to Don Alfonso.

His full lips pressed against her hand, then, arm around her waist, he took her into the back room.

"The blood is not a good sign," he said. "You were right to come to me. I have just the thing for him, but it will necessitate that I make a house call and administer the medicine myself, once a day for a week." His hand inched toward her. "My services are not cheap," he said, his hand resting now upon her, his fingers tracing the outline of her budding breast.

Confused, Esperanza stood a moment, fear coursing through her, along with a strange heated rush not unlike when Antonio touched her cheek. She backed away.

"Don Alfonso, my father spoke to me of men like you. I'm not a silly child," she said, trying to make herself sound assured. "My father needs the medicine, and you will give it to me."

"Why should I give it to you?" Don Alfonso said, adjusting his bow tie and stepping closer. "You can't pay for it. The medicine of science is expensive."

"We will pay," she said, but her voice was barely a whisper.

"Oh yes," he said. "Your father the gravedigger. And does he support you well, talking to ghosts?"

"I'm working now . . . I'll pay."

"Yes, I know you will," he said, and he pressed himself against her.

Esperanza stood, as if she were already dead, and Don Alfonso was a coffin, enclosing her. His hand was not sliding down *her* stomach, but that of a corpse, of the woman who would be her when she was lying in her grave. Yet from within that cold stillness, Esperanza kicked back. She didn't know where it came from. Her foot seemed to have reacted of its own volition when it kicked Don Alfonso in the shin. He weakened his grasp, and Esperanza bit him on the arm. He screamed, releasing her, and she ran from the store.

She ran all the way home, but because it was early on a Saturday, Juan Rodrigo was still working the bar. She thought for a moment of going to Rosalia, telling her everything, but then thought better of it. Rosalia would tell her father, and who knew what he might do with his temper. It would only make his sickness worse. She had to find Antonio. She had to get away from the village, if only for a little while.

With the rains of winter, the Rio Yátor flowed strong, and Esperanza sat in despair on the rock overlooking the river, where she and Antonio had sat that afternoon weeks before. The gray sky did nothing to lighten her mood. She tried to talk with Bella, but her horse was skittish, perhaps remembering the snake from the previous visit. So Esperanza sat, alone, worrying about her father, and wondering if she would ever leave the village or if she would become trapped there. Always before she had been sure of herself, sure of the fact that she and Antonio would live life as they chose, but now she felt for the first time the forces that worked in a village to break a person. Funny, she thought. When she was young she'd been afraid of the outside world; now she was afraid of her own home. She wondered what her father would have done if her mother had lived.

From somewhere within the trees on the opposite bank of the river, she heard a fiddle, then the strumming of guitars and the rhythmic clap of hands. Antonio emerged from the woods followed by his people: the men in their mismatched suits, playing a variety of instruments, the women, braceleted and dark, hands clapping, hips jangling, following behind the men. The music lifted her spirits immediately, but she didn't smile until Antonio danced for her, slapping his legs and stomping about. They played song after song, until she rose from the rock and began to dance as well. The crowd of gypsies on the other side cheered as she danced, and Antonio twirled about, signaling for her to cross the river and join him.

"How?" she yelled over the music.

But he simply gestured to the river, and where before she had seen nothing, now there were rocks scattered across, big enough to step on and close enough that she could move from one to the other with little fear of falling.

The gypsy caves were not at all what she expected. Though the entrances were small, the insides expanded outward. The walls were painted white, with pictures hanging from them. There was an abundance of furniture, and lace curtains decorated a side opening in the cave wall. Though light shone through the window, it was not enough, and the caves were lit by torchlight.

Wood shelves adorned with glasses and plates lined the kitchen area. They cooked their meals over a fire pit, which sat beneath the only other opening in the cave, a chimney hole. The caves were big enough to hold several families, and it seemed that's exactly what they did. Esperanza tried to pick Antonio's parents from the tableau before her, but they all looked like good possibilities.

Everyone moved with a purpose, and all the time music filled the air. An old man continued to play the fiddle while sitting in the corner of the cave. Women carried water, herbs, and chickens ready to be plucked. A group of men sat smoking in the central area of the cave. Esperanza supposed that was their living room. It was clear they were preparing for a feast.

Antonio grabbed her shoulders from behind, attempting to frighten her. "What do you think?"

"How many live here with you?" Esperanza asked.

"Four families in this cave, because it's one of the biggest," he said. "In most caves, just two families."

"Are there any girls who live here with the other families?" Esperanza lowered her gaze.

"There are two, but they are very young, and certainly can't compare to a green flower." He grabbed her hand and led her to the kitchen. The women talked and laughed as they prepared the meal. Antonio sat with Esperanza for a few minutes and then left to finish some chores. Esperanza was not used to the company of so many women and found herself moving toward the back corner of the kitchen area. One of the women, an old, dark one dressed in a blue skirt and dirty white blouse, grabbed her and led her to the washbasin. There, the women handed her various vegetables to be scrubbed. They laughed at the slow manner in which she worked, for although she was a hard worker, and had cooked many meals for her father, those meals usually consisted of reheating blood sausage or salt cod.

As if simply another step in a dance, the women moved from preparing the meal and setting the table to gathering the men. Soon wine was poured, and music and talk rang through the cave. Esperanza sat next to Antonio and, not sure why she was nervous amidst such cheer, held his hand. Antonio stared at her, smiling while he ate, and soon she forgot about her worries at home.

"Always before we ate dove," one of the men yelled out over the table. "Now it's chicken."

"How can you be so barbarous, Fernando?" another man said. "The birds and the gypsies are one and the same."

"Yes," another said. "We feel their anguish, because we know what it means to see the end of the world. The weight of visions is heavy—it's a wonder they can fly at all!"

"Tonight we drink to those birds that have not yet flown," an old woman with legs nearly as thick as an elephant's said, standing, raising her glass. "We drink to the birds and to ourselves, the only ones who see into the invisible world and feel sorrow at its loss."

Then the old man began to play again, and guitars, accordions, jugs all appeared so fast that Esperanza wasn't sure where they'd come from. The old woman who made the toast finished her drink in one gulp and began to dance. Everyone at the table, children and old alike, rose, clapping their hands and stomping their feet to the rhythm resounding through the cave. They made a circle around the old woman as she danced, her hands twirling snakelike in the air. She called to the children to dance with her, and one by one they entered the center of the circle, mimicking her movements as if learning the rituals of an ancient rite. Esperanza studied the women's feet. When the woman first rose to dance, Esperanza thought it impossible; her legs were too thick. And now, watching her dance, she still didn't know how she did it. Her legs barely moved, yet somehow the writhing of her hands and the slow undulation of her hips created the illusion of movement in her legs.

The dancing went on for hours. Entranced, Esperanza didn't notice the cave getting darker about her. Without shifting tempo or cadence, the women gathered up the dishes, dancing with them to the kitchen. A man with a mustache that only partly hid a cleft lip called to Antonio, and Esperanza was once again left alone.

"Are you of this world, or the other?" a voice whispered in her ear.

She turned to see an old man with yellowing eyes and scarcely any teeth smiling at her. Esperanza returned his smile, though the question had disturbed her. In his bent shape, he was no taller than she.

"You can see me, can't you?" Esperanza replied. "Here," she said, grabbing his hand. "You can feel me."

The old man moved his hand slowly up her arm, like a blind man searching the wall in front of him for an opening.

"You see, I'm no ghost," Esperanza continued. "I should know, my father talks with enough of them."

"Maybe he has gypsy blood in his veins," the old man said, raising a cigarette to his lips. He kept his other hand on Esperanza's shoulder.

"He wouldn't like to think that," Esperanza answered, shrugging her shoulder so that the old man's hand fell to his side. The old man laughed, a harsh laugh that unsettled Esperanza not a little.

"Very few would acknowledge their gypsy blood, yet many have it! I see by your eyes that it is true. You have it, so you must have gotten it from someone."

The mention of her mother gave Esperanza pause. She remembered the gold-flecked eyes of the old woman Sofia. It was her only way of imagining her own mother.

"And what do you know of the green flower?" Esperanza asked, wanting to change the subject.

The old man raised one eyebrow, studying the girl. "The green flower," he said, then puffed at his cigarette. "I thought from your eyes the gypsy blood was in you, but now I know."

"What is it?" she asked. But she really wanted to tell him that when Antonio sang of the green flower, she felt something stir inside her, something strange and deep. It was like the feeling she had when she was little and she'd spin around and around until she fell down. The feeling she had when she tried to get up and walk. A feeling that she didn't belong in this world at all.

"The green flower exists in both worlds," the old man said, continuing to observe her. "Not like the gypsies or the birds. We are able to see the unseen, perhaps even touch it on rare occasions. The ghosts are the same. Only the green flower lives in both places."

"What do you mean?" Esperanza asked.

"It's like the ghost that bit that poor boy."

"Can you see ghosts, too?" Esperanza's old jealousies resurfaced as she recalled the times she listened to her father talking to the four-year-old girl, Ursula.

The old man waved his hand at her. "For us it's easy. Yet they usually can't take on real, physical form."

"What do you mean, 'real'?"

"There was one the other day that bit a boy right in the face, drawing blood," he said. "Many, after that, saw the disembodied head of the spirit moving along the dark edges of the river."

"My father's ghosts aren't mean," she said, but then she thought of Father Ramon.

"Not all of ours are, either," the old man said. "Some are bad and some are good, just like the gypsies. Yours are but thin whispers of shadow. Ours live among us. They do not hide behind rasping curtains. We know of what stuff they're made."

"Maybe the green flower is like one of your ghosts," Esperanza said, almost asking. "Something that exists in this world and the other, a magical bridge connecting the two."

The old man laughed. "Magic. I don't know what that is," he said. "What your people call magic for us is the way the world works. But yes. The green flower is something rare and precious." He gazed at her now, puffing on his cigarette. "Something rare and precious, indeed," he said.

Esperanza wished he would stop staring at her. The intensity of his gaze made her feel as if she were truly invisible.

Shouting broke out, and Esperanza turned to see Antonio arguing with the man with the cleft lip. She didn't understand the words, for they were speaking Calé, but she understood that the argument was about her. The man kept pointing in her direction.

Antonio stood, unflinching, until the man's tirade was done, then he turned to go to Esperanza, but the man grabbed him by the shoulder, raising his fist as if to strike. Esperanza screamed, and the man looked up, his eyes emanating disgust. He checked his hand, clearly debating what to do. Esperanza's presence seemed to have some effect on him, for he dropped his hand and let Antonio go, then turned back to the other men, lighting a cigarette and laughing.

"He says you must go," Antonio said. "But I told him that you could stay, that you are one of us, and that I would take you back in the morning."

Esperanza looked about her, seeing the shadows that lingered in the corners, realizing that time had passed rapidly while she'd been in the caves and that darkness had now fallen. "But I can't stay," she said. "My father will be worried, and he's sick." The thought of what her absence would do to her father upset her, and Antonio saw it.

"I'll take you back tonight, then," he said. "I'll ride with you to your house and then return to my home. I'm used to the darkness."

And so they went, Esperanza watching closely as they approached the river, fearful of the disembodied head the old man had talked about. Seeing Bella, still in the moonlight, she felt much better.

A short distance from her home, Esperanza reined her horse in and Antonio dismounted.

"Meet me where you crossed today, at the river's edge," Antonio said in rushed breath. "In two weeks, when the moon is waning."

Esperanza sat atop her horse, stunned. She'd dreamed of leaving with Antonio, but always it involved her father and El Viejo. "I can't," she said, barely able to get the words out.

Antonio stilled her trembling hand with his own. "I'll marry you in the city," he said. "We can begin our lives there. You will love it. I hear it's alive with sound."

"But if it's so alive, how will we hear the voices of our past?" Esperanza said.

"Come with me," Antonio said, too much heated by the moment to listen to the past.

Esperanza tried to give weight to the thoughts and images in her mind, but they were jumbled. Afraid to show herself unsure, she said, "I will." And with that, Antonio smiled and was gone.

Her father and Rosalia were waiting for her when she arrived. Juan Rodrigo, perhaps calmed by Rosalia's presence, or perhaps feeling too deeply the sickness, did not fly into a rage as he'd so often done. Instead, he listened to his daughter as she told her story. She told nearly everything, deciding to leave out only the conversation with Antonio. She told about the gypsy caves and finally about her reason for venturing there, about what had happened at Don Alfonso's pharmacy. And while Juan Rodrigo did rise and pace the room, swearing at the chairs, the table, and kicking the bed several times, he did not run immediately to Don Alfonso's door, as Esperanza had feared.

Rosalia said softly, "I know how to deal with him."

"Yes, string him up by his *cojones!*" Juan Rodrigo yelled, but Rosalia laid her hand on his, saying, "Leave Don Alfonso to me." And he looked at her with such pain, a look that said, *She is* mi corazón. *I would die for her, but sometimes it seems even our own deaths cannot guarantee the protection of our daughters. How can you, a woman, protect her?*

But Rosalia only repeated, "Leave Don Alfonso to me." And Juan Rodrigo relented, though he kept up his cursing throughout the night.

Rosalia took Esperanza with her the next morning because she wanted her to see the nature of Don Alfonso's cowardice. It was Sunday, and Rosalia knew Don Alfonso would be sitting in the front of the church. All the better to suit her purpose.

The church was large, much too big for the needs of the village, and separated into three sections by great stone pillars that reached up to a vaulted ceiling painted blue to look like the sky. Father Joaquín, high in his gold pulpit, almost choked in the middle of his sermon when Rosalia walked in, as she was not one to attend church—not since her husband had died, at any rate. Rosalia and Esperanza nodded to the villagers as they passed down the aisle: a warm smile to Isabel in her blue chiffon, a nod to Enrique wearing his only tie—too short—and a cold but polite glance reserved for Matilde and María, who sat scowling in the center section. Matilde's husband, Jorge, didn't see the need for church and would find almost any reason to get out of going: On this day he had to attend to his onions. Don Alfonso sat with his son, Emilio, just two rows in front of Matilde and María.

Rosalia and Esperanza scooted in beside Don Alfonso and his son, Rosalia asking Emilio if he wouldn't mind moving so she could sit next to his father. Being a polite boy, Emilio obliged her. Don Alfonso took one look at her and stood to leave, but Rosalia's firm hand on his knee made him think twice. Father

Joaquín continued, though his sermon didn't have the usual eloquence, as he kept stopping himself to glance down at the front row.

"I have always known you were a beast, Don Alfonso, but this time you've gone too far!" Rosalia said none too softly.

"I don't understand to what you are referring," Don Alfonso replied, keeping his voice a whisper, and signaling with his hand to Rosalia that she should do the same.

"Then let me refresh your memory," Rosalia said, her voice louder than before. "Keep your hands off Esperanza or any other girls, for that matter."

Father Joaquín raised his voice to be heard above her.

"I've done nothing to be ashamed of," Don Alfonso whispered back, shaken, and glancing at Father Joaquín, as if looking for help.

"At least you'd never get very far," Rosalia said, looking him directly in the eye, her hand tightening on his knee, "since you can't get it up!"

Don Alfonso attempted to rise again, and this time Rosalia slapped him down in his seat. Father Joaquín appeared to have lost his place on the page and was searching through his notes. "If you do not stop this at once," Don Alfonso said, "I'll have to talk to the authorities."

"To whom?" Rosalia said. "No one will help you." Then, leaning in to him, she whispered, "You recall your late wife and I were very close."

Don Alfonso's eyes widened.

"She confided many secrets to me over the years, not the least of which was your impotence." She made her voice so soft that she had to press her lips against Don Alfonso's ear to make sure he heard. "And the fact that Emilio is not your son."

"That is a lie!" Don Alfonso yelled. Father Joaquín stopped his sermon, gazing directly at them. Don Alfonso rose. This time, Rosalia didn't stop him, and he walked rapidly down the aisle.

Rosalia and Esperanza followed, leaving the perplexed Emilio looking after them.

"You see my point," Rosalia said once they were outside the church. "I believe Esperanza asked for some medicine for her father, and I believe you still owe her that medicine."

Don Alfonso stood there a moment; his son emerged from the church. "Is there something the matter, Father?" he asked.

"No, my son," Don Alfonso said, raising his hand. "Nothing wrong. These kind people are simply in desperate need of my help."

"The miracles of silence, right, Father?" Emilio said.

"Of science, dear boy. Science will save the world from the accursed darkness." And with that, Don Alfonso instructed Emilio to remain at the church while he took the poor people in need of his help to his pharmacy.

NOT WANTING TO WAIT ANY LONGER, Rosalia moved in with Esperanza and Juan Rodrigo the next day. Of course, it could not have been the other way around, as the gravedigger must always live outside of town. If Rosalia wanted to be with Juan Rodrigo, she would have to adopt his way of life. And that is what she did. "Let people talk," she said. "I know what's real, and what is manufactured by the gossip of a village!" And Juan Rodrigo laughed, as he had long since ceased to care about what people said of him. Being a gravedigger, living on the outskirts of town, one learned quickly that you couldn't live by the rules of a village.

But what they didn't count on was the sheer volume of noise that a village can produce when it feels its unwritten rules are being thwarted. It started with the muffled sound of a few cow horns on the first day Rosalia moved in. By the next day, it seemed as if practically every man in the village was blowing a horn or conch, creating such a racket that Doña Villada had to shut down school because the students could no longer hear her. On the third day, a few drunken men even kept up the horn blowing at night, so that no one could get any sleep. And one such drunken old man, named Belasko *de la botella,* for he always had a bottle in his hand, even went so far as to recite amorous verses, with an admittedly vulgar slant, beneath Juan Rodrigo's bedroom window. Because he'd always felt sorry for Belasko, Juan Rodrigo escorted him home, not even attempting to explain the complicated reasons why he and Rosalia no longer worried about marriage.

"What do they think they are doing, Rosalia?" Juan Rodrigo asked when he returned home. "None of them even has the courage to come to my house and blow the horn in my face, except for poor Belasko."

"That's because they are afraid of you," Rosalia replied.

"Me? No, they are afraid of you! But do they honestly think that by depriving the entire village of sleep they are accomplishing anything?"

It was not until the fifth day that Rosalia decided she'd had enough. She forced Juan Rodrigo to accompany her to the village. They walked arm in arm through the main plaza, daring anyone to make a sound. Being a generally harmless lot, the villagers stood silently on the sidewalk, or sat motionless in their chairs outside the café, watching them as they passed. No one dared to lift their horn until Matilde and Jorge entered the plaza. Upon seeing the couple daring to walk about in full daylight, Matilde yanked the conch out of her husband's pocket and brought it to her lips, but Jorge knocked it to the ground.

"Not out in the open, Matilde!" he said.

Rosalia took it as an invitation. "We are decent people," she exclaimed. "Is it that you have nothing better to do than to close the village down with your racket, to make it so not even the children can sleep at night?"

The villagers watched. Matilde tried to pick up the conch, but her husband placed his foot on it.

"If anyone objects to our living together, let them say it now, to my face," Rosalia continued. No one said a word, not even Matilde, who was looking angrily at her husband. Later, when enough time had passed that the villagers talked about that day, it was generally agreed that, at that moment, the village had never been quieter.

In the week that followed, Esperanza watched as Rosalia nursed her father back to health, forcing him to take the medicine Don Alfonso had given them, and making him eat her curative soups. He didn't mind the latter, though he made a fuss because Rosalia seemed to like it when he complained, as then she could take pride in the fact that he needed her to care for him in spite of himself.

Esperanza didn't see Antonio, but she knew the day was fast approaching when she'd promised to meet him, and her thoughts were continually on that subject. How could she leave her father? And if she did leave, how could she tell him? She spent the days sitting on the stable fence talking with Bella, but she never seemed to arrive at a decision.

On the morning of the day she was to leave, Esperanza rose early, before breakfast, and walked to the wood's edge where she and Antonio had discussed their plans.

"I can't go with you," she said, as if she were speaking with Antonio. "Though my heart is with you, I'm tied to this place. I don't understand it, but I feel it when the sun goes down at night and the world is silent, except for the calling of the nightingale. Then I think of my father's stories, and I know they connect me to this place. That I belong."

"I used to think that you could talk to the birds like your mother, then to horses, but now I know it was all foolishness," Juan Rodrigo said, approaching behind her. "You were talking to yourself the whole time."

"Papá!" Esperanza screamed. "You scared me. And I was not talking to myself."

"I see," her father said. "Did the trees prove good conversationalists, then?"

"You can't treat me like a child, Papá."

"I know. I know," Juan Rodrigo replied. "You keep saying that."

"Because you never learn."

"Let's spend the day outside," Juan Rodrigo said. "Spring is in the air, though winter is only half over. I can feel it! Why don't we take a picnic down by the pond where poor old Sofia used to live?"

Esperanza hugged her father, for it sounded like a wonderful idea, and they walked back to the house together. At the breakfast table, as they planned their picnic, Esperanza studied her new mother, the sureness of her movements in the kitchen and the joy she seemed to radiate as she attended to Juan Rodrigo, and the way her father sat there, contentedly, letting Rosalia care for him. And she knew that in some way, her father's need for attention brought happiness just as Rosalia's need to care did. She thought about the horns that blew in protest of their way of life, then she thought that maybe they were like the gypsies after all, existing to help one another out of common need; and, imagining the expression on her father's face if he knew what she'd been thinking, she broke into a fit of laughter.

But throughout the picnic and into the afternoon, Esperanza's conscience plagued her. She didn't want Antonio to think that she'd lied to him. She needed to see him, to explain. And so she decided to approach both her father and her new mother that evening and ask them for permission to take the horse that night.

"What do you mean, you want to ride Bella tonight?" Juan Rodrigo replied. "That's impossible. It's far too dangerous."

But Rosalia, sensing that Esperanza had a motive other than a moonlight ride, placed her hand gently on Juan Rodrigo's shoulder and simply asked, "Why?"

Esperanza opened her mouth, thinking she was going to explain about her promise to Antonio and her realization that she couldn't keep it, but when she spoke, she found it difficult to tell her father that she'd made a promise, however fleeting, to leave him. In the end, all she said was "I cannot tell you my reasons. I ask you to trust that they are true ones."

Juan Rodrigo rose from the table. "Trust!" he exclaimed. "You're going to see that gypsy again, aren't you?"

Esperanza lowered her gaze by way of acknowledgment.

"She's asked us to trust her, Juan Rodrigo," Rosalia said. "Maybe we should. She is old enough."

Normally, Esperanza would have joined in the argument, but this time the guilt at her own betrayal held her in check. She hoped Rosalia's words would be enough.

"She's obviously not old enough, if she wants to go on midnight rides through the mountains." Juan Rodrigo walked to the door. "No!" he shouted. "We've had enough disobedience in this house. From now on we listen."

Both Esperanza and Rosalia wanted to point out that it was he who was not listening at the moment, but neither did, for his stance showed a determination he'd not had since becoming ill, and neither of them wanted to do anything to turn the course of his recovery.

"Yes, Papá," was all Esperanza said. Rosalia rose to clear the table.

That night, Esperanza played the dutiful daughter as Juan Rodrigo told her a story and tucked her into bed. But after he left her, Esperanza lay awake, listening to their conversation, waiting for the moment when her parents went to bed.

Juan Rodrigo went first to the shed where he kept his pick and shovel, and there he pulled out an old, rusty lock, which he placed on the stable gate. Then he went to the porch, where Rosalia sat waiting for him.

"There must be many stories that could be told about that grouping that looks like crows sitting atop a great olive tree," he said, pointing to the sky.

Rosalia laughed. "You are a crazy old man, Juan Rodrigo."

"Me, crazy?" he exclaimed, grabbing her hand and kissing it, then holding it as he turned to her. "I've seen you in the cemetery, Rosalia. No wonder nothing grows on your husband's grave!" And he burst out laughing.

At first Rosalia's face froze. Fearing he'd misstepped, Juan Rodrigo tried to stifle his laughter. Rosalia blushed. She pulled her hand away and hit Juan Rodrigo hard on the shoulder. Still unsure of her reaction, Juan Rodrigo rubbed his shoulder, looking questioningly at Rosalia. Now it was her turn to laugh.

"It's a strange life, Juan Rodrigo," Rosalia finally said.

"Strange indeed!" He slapped her leg softly. "And what are we to make of it? How are we supposed to understand it if life won't hold still long enough to let us get our arms around it?" he asked, now trying to wrap his arms around her.

Rosalia pushed his arms away, playfully. And gazing up at him, expecting to find the face of an amorous old man, she instead found the face of a little boy. How odd it is that one who faces so much sadness and death still retains so much of the innocence of youth, she thought. Perhaps that's what keeps us going. Then thinking more on it, she shook her head. No. Better yet, it is childlike stubbornness!

"Rosalia, *mi cielo*, you still haven't answered me."

"I was thinking, Juan Rodrigo."

"Thinking what?"

"That we weather the changes because we must. What else is there to do?"

"It isn't very encouraging." Juan Rodrigo chuckled. "I had no idea you were such a cynic."

"I'm not." She held his hand, squeezed it. "The funny thing is that I'm very happy."

"Me, too," he said, squeezing her hand in return.

"And I was thinking that though we have no choice about what befalls us, we do choose the friends we share this life with." Then she gazed into Juan Rodrigo's eyes. "And the lovers," she said.

Juan Rodrigo smiled. "Yes, Pedro Martinez is a good friend. I believe I chose him well!"

Rosalia hit him again, if anything, harder than before, and they resumed their laughter.

As was their custom, Rosalia went to bed first, leaving Juan Rodrigo a few moments of reflection before he joined her. But this night it was not to be. Soon after Rosalia left, a familiar chill passed through him, traveling up his neck and settling near the top of his head. A feeling he knew too well. He dropped his gaze to meet that of Ursula's. The four-year-old girl stood at the edge of the porch, wearing the same white cotton dress she always wore. It was a very pretty dress, Juan Rodrigo thought. Her parents must have loved her very much. But this time she wore a wreath of flowers in her hair, and in her hands she held a nosegay.

"You're dressed for a special occasion," Juan Rodrigo said.

Her large, round eyes strained, as if she were struggling to see in the darkness.

She opened her mouth to speak. *"Viejo . . ."*

Wearily, Juan Rodrigo closed his eyes and waited. He'd never liked this moment. "Who has died?" he asked finally.

"It's who will die."

Opening his eyes, he said, "Go away, then!" and shooed her away with his hand. "I don't want to know who is going to die. Your job is to tell me when they've died, so I can do my job."

"This is different."

Juan Rodrigo stood. "I will not listen to you tonight, Ursula. Why do you come? Tonight was such a joyful night. Did you not hear our laughter?"

"*Viejo*, we don't always want to hear what the wind whispers when it talks with the cliffs, but we must listen." Her voice was soft; the expression in her eyes remained the same. "You are the gravedigger."

"I know who I am!" Juan Rodrigo yelled. "Why must everyone continually remind me of this?" He raised his hands to the sky, clenching his fists as if he would bring down the stars. "Now leave me alone!"

"But you don't have to dig this grave, not if you listen."

"No!" Juan Rodrigo stepped off the porch, walked toward her. "I'm tired of listening! You bring me nothing but grief, and you bear sadness for others. I want no more of it in my life. Leave me!" He swatted at the air where she stood. Her body shimmered, then dissolved into moonlight.

Juan Rodrigo woke to Rosalia's kiss. Smiling, he wiped the sleep from his eyes. Perhaps the ghost of Ursula had only been a bad dream, he thought.

"What, my love?" Rosalia gazed into his troubled face.

"The girl, Ursula, visited me last night. I keep telling myself it was a dream, but it was not. I fear for Pedro. I'd like to go see him."

"Yes, of course." Rosalia took his hand, caressing it.

"Perhaps Esperanza will want to come."

"Yes," Rosalia replied. "She and Mercedes made a shirt for his birthday."

Juan Rodrigo smiled. "I'd forgotten. It's this Thursday. How do you and Esperanza have such keen memories?"

"All women have keen memories."

"Well, I dare not forget either of your birthdays, or else I'll never hear the end of it!"

Juan Rodrigo peeked through the doorway that led to Esperanza's room. The blankets were rumpled; it was hard to tell if she lay beneath them. "Esperanza," he called. But there was no answer. He stepped into the room, trepidation falling over him. "Esperanza," he said again. He ran through the house and out the front door.

"What is it?" Rosalia asked, but she also received no answer.

Juan Rodrigo saw immediately that Bella was eating peacefully in the stable, and for the moment, his heart felt at ease. "Esperanza, you gave me quite a fright," he said to the air about him. Bella and El Viejo raised their heads, wondering at their master.

"What is it?" Rosalia said again as she approached Juan Rodrigo. And it was this second time of the question being asked that put doubt in Juan Rodrigo's mind. *The girl tried to warn you last night, you old fool!*

"She's just left for school early," he said. "That's all, or maybe she wanted to work on that shirt at Mercedes' shop." But his hands trembled even as he said the words.

"It's not like her to leave without saying anything."

"I'll check in town," Juan Rodrigo said, already moving. "You go to the school, we have to be sure."

"*Válgame Dios!* When I find you, Esperanza, you better not even think of leaving the house for a month!" The anger kept his fear at bay, but one presentiment gnawed at him as if he'd had something rotten in his belly, and try as he might, the image of the four-year-old-girl remained in his mind. *But you don't have to dig this grave, not if you listen.* She had been warning him. He walked, and as he walked, the cracks in the dry earth seemed to him great chasms.

"Juan Rodrigo," he said to himself as he approached Mercedes' dress shop. "If anything happens to her, you will never forgive yourself."

Mercedes answered the door able to see immediately that something was wrong. "What is it, old friend?" she asked.

"Has Esperanza been here?" It felt to Juan Rodrigo as if he could no longer speak. His rigid jaw cracked in its attempt to form the words.

"No," Mercedes replied. "Should she have been?"

Juan Rodrigo shook his head, then turned back, gazing at Mercedes as from an immense distance, as if he were already falling and needed to hear a voice, to feel a hand, anything human that might save him. Sensing this, Mercedes reached out to him, but Juan Rodrigo turned away, already setting the judgment upon himself, not allowing himself to feel a comforting touch. *What an insect you are that you think of your own misery. She may still live.*

He dug deep for the words, pushing them up from inside the well of guilt and despair that rose within him. "Mercedes," he said. "Get Pedro and his boys. Find anyone that can walk and search the cliffs. My Esperanza is gone!" And then, though he was already breathing heavily, he ran down the path to his house. *You boneheaded fool! Why didn't you listen? Esperanza was right. It is you who needs to learn!*

A large black crow sat atop one of the fence posts of Juan Rodrigo's stable. Bella and El Viejo stayed clear of it. As Juan Rodrigo approached, the bird called out, "Cawww . . . Cawww!" It was as if the bird's cry signified everything Juan Rodrigo had feared. He rushed the bird, but the crow did not move.

"Fly, you son of a bitch!" Juan Rodrigo cried. He picked up a rock and was about to fling it, when the bird's eye caught his own. No words passed between them, nothing conscious, but Juan Rodrigo felt the presence of another living creature, one that had done nothing to harm him. And that presence, at least for the moment, halted his anger. The killing of the bird all those years ago had not relieved his pain. He knew that much. He dropped the rock. "I have no time for you now, bird," he said, walking past the crow.

"Venga, Viejo," Juan Rodrigo yelled to his burro as he opened the stable gate. "You still have strength to carry me, you stubborn burro. You must have the strength." He placed the old saddle upon its back.

"She was not at school," Rosalia said, coming down the porch steps. "What has happened, Juan Rodrigo?" she asked, her voice trembling. "I fear the worst."

Juan Rodrigo turned for a moment, reaching out for Rosalia. He wanted to hold her to tell her what a fool he'd been. But then he felt the presence of the four-year-old girl behind him. He turned as Rosalia ran to him. "I don't have time to talk," he said as he prepared the saddle. "*Por la Virgen, Viejo,* hold still, or I'll tighten it so hard, it'll break your back!"

The hairs on the back of his hand stood on end, and he knew by the touch that it was Ursula's icy hand that held his and not Rosalia's. The burro backed away from the presence of the girl. "Hold still, goddamn you! Let me climb on!"

"*Viejo,*" the ghost said.

"My love," Rosalia called, grabbing his other hand.

"No!" he screamed, flinging both hands away. "You cannot do this to me!"

"I'm sorry, *Viejo,*" the ghost went on.

"Juan Rodrigo, what has happened?" Rosalia cried again, falling to her knees.

"No!" Juan Rodrigo attempted to mount his burro, but skittish of the ghost and the temper of his master, it once again backed away. Juan Rodrigo fell to the ground but didn't get up, his back arching with the sobs that racked him. The ghost, Rosalia, and the burro waited.

Juan Rodrigo watched his own hand push the dirt, first one way and then the other. His hand no longer belonged to him as it clawed now at the dirt, tearing into it. He wanted so badly to hurt the earth. His fingernails snapped as he dug into the parched earth again and again. It's digging my own grave, he thought. Good.

Rosalia bent over him, whispering, as if beseeching, in his ear. "My love, my love . . ." She would not yet allow herself to imagine the full possibility of her fear.

The white dress dipped in front of Juan Rodrigo as the little girl bent to place her hand once again in his. *"Venga, Viejo,"* she said. He hoped his hand would hit her, swat her down. "Come, *Viejo,*" she repeated. "They will not find her, but you can. The black bird is waiting."

Juan Rodrigo watched the sun burning its way through the morning sky. He watched, waiting for it to set so that this cursed day would be over. Again he thought, Maybe it was all a dream. But the sun did not move; its heat continued to press down upon him. He stood, though he didn't remember getting up. The great black bird took flight.

Juan Rodrigo turned to Rosalia. "Stay here," he said. "In case Esperanza returns." Just words, he thought. Words to comfort the mind until it adjusts to what the body already knows.

Rosalia nodded her head, pressing her hands together as if in prayer. She had been through so much, she thought. But she could not weather this loss. Not the loss of one so young.

The flight of the crow led him through the cliffs below the village, the cliffs that led north to the valley and beyond to the Río Yátor. Juan Rodrigo had known where they were headed all along. And so, as he made his way around the balancing boulder that marked the difficult route down through the sandstone cliffs to the narrow rock bridge that crossed the gorge, he found himself talking to his Esperanza as if he were following her and not the black bird.

"So you chose the shortcut to the river, since I locked up the horse," he said. Esperanza ran before him in his mind.

"This way will be faster," she said. "I won't make it back by morning if I take the easy path. And I must tell Antonio. It wouldn't be right, Papá, if I didn't."

He descended through the crevice that led to the spires like the fingers of an immense hand guarding the narrow bridge, knowing that he should never have been able to climb these rocks, but that somehow he was, his focus intent on finding his daughter.

"You could have been late, *mi corazón*," he said. "I wouldn't have been upset if you would've come home after breakfast. Just this once."

"You're lying, Papá," Esperanza replied, peeking out from behind one of the spires. "You would have forbidden me to ride Bella for at least a month, or worse." Then she disappeared again.

Worse, Juan Rodrigo thought to himself. What could be worse than that which has come to pass?

"And besides," she said, "I'm good in the rocks."

"Yes," he said, "you have always been an excellent climber."

The crow sat atop the tallest spire, overlooking the stone bridge. The drop on each side of the bridge was nearly one hundred feet. The black bird called to Juan Rodrigo, and he followed. When he reached the tall spire, the crow flew away. Juan Rodrigo searched far below the bridge. At first he couldn't see anything. His eyes were tired. He tried once more to conjure the vision of Esperanza running through the red rocks, but he could not do it. Then he spotted her, lying one hundred feet below, like a broken stick. His first impulse was to jump and be with her.

Papá, don't do it! the voice of Esperanza screamed, though she had not yet learned how to speak so as to be heard from the other world. *Do not waver like a poplar in the wind atop the cliff! Please, Papá, be strong. Do not jump! I slipped on the bridge. On a little pebble. It was so stupid, and it hurt at first, but I'm fine now.*

Juan Rodrigo stood a moment more, as if willing the breeze to push him from the narrow stone bridge. Then he climbed down the cliff face, scarcely aware of who he was or what he was doing, only knowing that he must reach the bottom.

Papá, don't cry! Por favor, *be strong! I can't watch you cry, Papá. Not when I know it's for me, not when your body shakes like Miguel's poor dog, Hannibal, after those boys beat it and dragged it through the streets. Don't cry when I can't comfort you, and when I don't even know if I'll see you again.*

He knelt beside her, took her limp body in his arms, and at last his mind knew as well as his heart that she was dead. He didn't cry, nor moan in anguish. Instead, it was as if the wail sounded inside his body, low and deep, a dirge that started in the bone, shattering it, ripping muscles, rending sinew until the body no longer functioned. He collapsed on the ground, his child still in his arms.

I'm sorry, Papá. I'm sorry. It was my fault, and now I've hurt you. Please, forgive me for disobeying you!

And though Juan Rodrigo did not hear the words of his daughter, he must have felt some part of her sadness, her feelings of guilt, for he bent his head, kissing his daughter on her forehead stained with blood and dirt. "I love you, *mi corazón*," he said. "I will always love you."

Unable to carry the body all the way through the cliffs and back to his house, he made for the village, breaking out of the rocks just below the church. Will alone pushed him, the desire to see his daughter back at home, in her own bed. Otherwise, he could not have made it.

He carried his daughter through the village and, though tears fell from his eyes, still no sound crossed his lips. He passed through La Plaza de Los Naranjos. Villager after villager came out from their houses, from the café and the bar, each one asking, "What has happened, Juan Rodrigo?" and "Where are you going with your child in your arms?"

He walked on, not hearing them, untouched by their calls, until Mercedes ran out of her dress shop. She repeated the questions the villagers had already been asking, as if there would ever be answers: "What has happened, Juan Rodrigo? Where are you going with your child in your arms?"

Juan Rodrigo stopped at the edge of the plaza, turning to his friend Mercedes, but was unable to speak. She ran to him, attempting to help him with his burden. He pulled Esperanza violently to him, and that action, the taking possession of his daughter, released the anger and grief welling within. At last, the keen escaped from his body, filling the air with a cry so horrible that all in the village felt the weight of his guilt and grief. Mercedes backed away, fearful of the sound, but more fearful of the man, for his face was so contorted at that moment that she scarcely believed it was the face of her friend.

"I am the gravedigger," he said. "And I'm going to the cemetery to bury my heart." He left Mercedes wailing in the street.

As he climbed the path to his house, Rosalia ran to him. But he did not stop or change his step, and Rosalia was left clinging to him until she, too, fell, moaning in the dirt.

He placed Esperanza carefully in her bed, tucking the covers in around her. "There will be no wake, *mi corazón*, no stories," he whispered to his daughter. "I'm sorry, but I'm through with it all." Then he turned from his daughter and left the house.

He grabbed his pick and shovel and slung them over his shoulder, and with a gesture of his hand, he signaled for his burro to follow. They climbed slowly up the pathway to the cemetery, silently. Rosalia remained in the house, weeping over the body.

The four-year-old girl sat in the dirt, waiting for them. Once again, she took his hand, and all three continued on. At the spot beneath the olive tree, they stopped. Juan Rodrigo gazed out over the sea.

The burro watched as his master reeled before him. Afraid that his master might fall down, the burro stepped closer. But his master didn't fall. Instead, he looked out to the sea in the distance on one side, then to the valley below on the other. "It's a good spot," his master told him. "Good as any." The burro watched the flies gather around his master's face and the fact that his master did nothing to stop them. At last, his master placed his foot upon the shovel and pressed it to the ground, then paused. The burro had never seen his master like this. He looked as if he'd carried a heavy burden up a mountain—yes, that was the only way he could explain it—and that he was going to stop and not move again as he, himself, had so often done when asked to carry too much for too long.

"*Tengo que decirle algo. Un cuento muy triste,* I have to tell you something. A sad story," Juan Rodrigo told his burro, then pushed the shovel into the earth.

On the night she was born, the gypsies came out of their caves, smelling jasmine in the air . . .

"THAT WAS A BEAUTIFUL STORY, PAPÁ," Esperanza said, still sitting next to him under the shade of the olive tree. "It made me very proud to have you as my father."

"Nonsense! I cried like a baby in the telling of it," he said, the tears still flowing down his face.

"It's because you cry that I'm proud."

"It is I who am proud," Juan Rodrigo replied. "Your willfulness stems from my blood. You are a Rodrigo, though your mother rolls her eyes at the thought." He smiled at his daughter, then squeezed her hand in his, expecting to feel the wintry cold. But though he did not feel warmth, he did not feel the cold. There was simply an absence. It was then that the ghost of the four-year-old girl rose, handing her nosegay to Esperanza, and walked through the cemetery and down the hill. Juan Rodrigo watched her go and found that he was unsure whether she was fading in the light as she walked or whether her image was growing more defined.

"Why do you look so surprised, Papá?" Esperanza asked, rising before him.

"Your hand," he said, and for a moment it seemed that was all he would say. Then he continued, "Your hand, it did not hold the icy coldness of death."

"Yes," she said. "I don't understand it. You always told me the ghosts had difficulty perceiving things clearly in this world, but it appears the same to me as when I lived. Except there is much more here now. And it is all clear. I could see Ursula, Papá!"

"Yes, I noticed. Now you don't have to be so jealous." He winced at the reminder of the past.

"It is very beautiful here, Papá."

"Like a rainbow," he said jokingly.

"No," Esperanza said. "Rather, like the feeling one has standing in the mist after the rainbow fades."

Juan Rodrigo smiled.

"What will you do now?" Esperanza asked.

Juan Rodrigo shook his head and heaved a great sigh. "Maybe it's time that there was another gravedigger in this village. I certainly wouldn't mind the competition!"

Esperanza laughed, though she saw that her father was at least partly serious. They stood together silently, gazing at each other.

"Will you come and see me?" Juan Rodrigo asked at last.

"Yes."

"Are you able?"

"I don't think that I'm like other ghosts," she replied.

Now Juan Rodrigo laughed. "Well, you certainly weren't like other children!"

"Go now, Papá," Esperanza said. "They need you. I will come back from time to time. Though you must learn to get on without me."

"I've been trying to learn that my entire life," he said. "I knew the day would come when you would leave me, but I did not imagine it would happen like this." And with that, he opened his arms. Esperanza stepped into his embrace, and he hugged her to him. Then, as the tears once more began to flow from his eyes, he realized she was gone.

Rosalia, Mercedes, and Pedro waited for him at the bottom of the hill. Somehow the encounter with the ghost of Esperanza had eased his pain, and he, in turn, tried to relieve that of his friends. They were sure they would have to hold him up, but it was he who placed his arms around them. Pedro and Mercedes looked as if they took on the full blame themselves for not finding Esperanza in time. And Rosalia. When Juan Rodrigo looked at the vacant expression on her face, the way the eyes occasionally rolled back in her head, he worried that she would not survive this loss.

When they returned to the house, it seemed the entire village was there: Enrique, Isabel, Ana, Martina, María and Matilde, poor Jorge, Father Joaquín, Doña Villada and her son, Miguel, Pilar and her children, Elena and Iago, even old Fulgencio showed up in black with only the slightest hint of color in his tie. A few of the younger children were there as well: Pedro's boys, Eugenio, little Anna, the Bermeja girl. Somehow it pained Juan Rodrigo to see her. But it was to Rosalia in particular that he addressed Esperanza's story once everyone had gathered together on the front porch. For, yes, he wanted to tell her story; he needed to. One could not shirk off being a gravedigger so easily. The presence of Esperanza on the hill had given him strength and now it was time to pass that strength on. He put everything he had into the story, every last bit of his art, hoping that he would reach Rosalia, praying to bring her back at least a step or two from the abyss.

At first she didn't even seem to hear. She sat in the dirt beside the porch, drool dripping from her mouth. Juan Rodrigo was sure he would lose her. It was only when he reached the part with Esperanza on the horse, riding through the valley to meet Antonio and feeling more free than she'd ever felt, that Rosalia's gaze shifted, and where before she looked into darkness, she now seemed to be searching for something to latch on to, something to bring her back. Her gaze fixed itself on the stable. Juan Rodrigo turned to see Antonio standing beside El Viejo. He gestured with his hand for the boy to join them, but he would not.

The villagers stayed most of the day, the women cooking a supply of food that would last Juan Rodrigo and Rosalia a month, the men chopping wood and fixing things around the house. In the evening they buried the body of Esperanza.

The Story of Juan Rodrigo

IT WAS NOT UNTIL the next morning when Juan Rodrigo woke up that he truly felt the weight of his grief. The presence of Esperanza and the story had helped him the day before, but now he faced her empty room. He sat beside her bed and didn't know if he would ever get up. He sat there for three days, Rosalia now the one supporting her love, feeding him, caressing his head, and telling him stories of her own—things only she'd learned about Esperanza during their brief time together.

On the morning of the fourth day, Juan Rodrigo rose from the floor beside Esperanza's bed and walked to the cemetery. He had not seen her, as she'd promised, and he thought that perhaps she could only appear atop the hill where her grave lay.

She was waiting for him with a perplexed and somewhat irritated look on her face. Juan Rodrigo was not expecting it, and instead of rushing to her, as was his first instinct, he paused, unsure what to do.

"You didn't exactly tell the truth about you and Mamá."

Juan Rodrigo stood, hoping to see the expression on her face change, but, if anything, it only became more disapproving. "If you recall," he said, gathering himself, "I never got around to telling you the whole story. Only bits and pieces."

"You told me it was everything." Esperanza stormed over to him. "Once the birds returned, you told me the story, and you said that was everything."

"It *was* everything, *mi corazón*," Juan Rodrigo replied.

"Hardly!"

"Esperanza!" Juan Rodrigo stomped his foot now, hands gesturing in the air. "Are you calling me a liar?"

"Yes," she said.

With horror, Juan Rodrigo realized that his daughter may have found out his secret from the gossip told beyond the grave. He decided he'd better tell her the truth, or at least as much truth as he had to. "If you're referring to my time with Pepita," Juan Rodrigo went on, blustering about, "well, I didn't feel it was fit for your ears."

"I thought the storyteller's job was to tell the truth," Esperanza said, sitting atop her own gravestone.

"It is," Juan Rodrigo replied. "Sort of." He turned to his daughter, his face pleading. "The storyteller's job is to get at the truth, and I did when I told you of my love for your mother."

"But was there not truth in your love for Pepita?"

Juan Rodrigo stared at his daughter, uncomprehending. Why did she always seem to know more about the goings-on in the village than he did? She looked even more grown up, if that were possible, as if she'd become the woman she'd always wanted to be. "It was a . . ."

"It was what?"

"Well, yes, we had a kind of love." Juan Rodrigo turned away, looking for a place to rest. He suddenly felt very tired.

"Go on."

"That's it? 'Go on'? Is that all you have to say?" Juan Rodrigo leaned heavily against the olive tree. "Aren't you happy to see me?"

"First I want the truth."

"They gossip too much in the other world," Juan Rodrigo said.

"Then by all means clear it up for me." Esperanza rested her head on her hand, appearing as if she could wait a very long time.

"You have to understand, *mi corazón*, that I had been a widower for seven years before marrying your mother," Juan Rodrigo said. "That's a long time for a man to be alone."

"I understand that part," Esperanza said. "But why Pepita? She's so fat. She spends half her day sitting on the porch inviting the kids to pull bugs out of her hair, and Papá, she's a whore."

"Don't use words like that," Juan Rodrigo said, his strength returning with his role as father. "Not in my presence. Besides, she wasn't always like that," Juan Rodrigo continued. "At one time she was almost beautiful."

"Tell me about her, Papá." Esperanza slid down from her gravestone and sat on the dirt.

"Well, she had broad hips and . . ." Juan Rodrigo found he couldn't go on. The words just wouldn't come out. "I can't look at you when I speak of her," he said finally, turning to gaze out over the sea. "Let me see now. How do I begin?" he said, as if talking to himself. "She had a round face that glowed, no matter what her mood. She could be sad, but somehow her face turned that sadness into something joyous. I loved her sense of humor. My God, could she tell a joke, and one after another—vulgar, too. That's what got me through the hard times, the years right after Josefina's death, and then the years your mother was married to El Capitán. And her house, it was not dingy or dreary, as are so many of those places."

"Papá," Esperanza interrupted. "How many of those places have you been to?"

Juan Rodrigo turned to her and gave her a stern look. "None of your business, child," he said, then gazed back over the sea. "I remember sitting there, sometimes all night, just drinking and talking with Pepita, while her girls went about their work. It's funny, you know, she collected art. Who would have thought it? But there were paintings decorating the walls. And in each room, above the bed, Pepita insisted that there hang a crucifix. That's how she was, very proper about certain things."

Esperanza rose and went to stand near her father, taking his hand. "And did you make love with her, Papá?"

Juan Rodrigo looked again at his daughter, taking his time, considering her as he, perhaps, had never done before. Yes, she was a woman now, though it saddened him to think that she would never know what it felt like to embrace another body that way. "At first we made love, whenever I could afford it," he said. "But as time went on, Pepita overlooked my lack of funds. We each brought something to the other. Her humor eased my pain, as I've said, but it was the softness of her touch, the way she took me into her arms without question, without demand for anything in return, that kept me a part of the living during those times. And I think I brought her a few laughs, too. I know she always appreciated the joke about my nose! It was not a relationship of passion, but one of humanity."

"Do you see her still?"

"No," Juan Rodrigo replied, no longer surprised by his daughter's frankness. "We lost contact a long time ago."

"Though there was a time when she went crazy over you, wasn't there?"

"Esperanza!" Juan Rodrigo exclaimed. "Who have you been talking with in the other world?"

"You say the relationship was not passionate, but when you left her for Mamá, she threw her girls into the street, causing quite a scene in the village. She must have loved you more passionately than you know or admit?" Esperanza let go of her father's hand and twirled in circles before him. She knew she had him and enjoyed watching him attempt to talk his way out of it.

"You never let me off easy, did you, Esperanza?" Juan Rodrigo shook his head. "Yes, there was a difficult time," he went on. "She knew of my love for Carlota. We'd told each other everything during our nights at the bar or in bed, but I suppose she thought that love was as hopeless as I did. I remember her half-clad girls walking the streets during the light of day. For a week, the men stopped their work and gathered in the plaza just to watch. The women, of course, were in an outrage. Never had there been whores walking the streets of a decent Spanish village—they kept them locked in houses, and the women were determined to get them back into Pepita's house. They banded together, Consuela taking charge as usual, and marched to Pepita's door, demanding she take them back. But Pepita wouldn't listen. She sat brooding in her porch chair, and when the women of the village approached, she let loose a string of vulgarities that would have frozen Cordoba in August! Most of the women returned home, shaken, but not Consuela. Very few things got to her, and though she liked to appear the lady, she knew how to let a curse fly when she needed to.

"Everyone thought she was going to give Pepita an earful, as she did with anyone who crossed her, but not this time. Instead, Consuela sat with Pepita throughout the afternoon, waiting for her to talk. No one would have believed it. She sat down next to Pepita, saying, 'I'm not leaving until you tell me what has happened. We can't have your girls wandering the streets. So do not think you will get rid of me.'

"Sometime after nightfall, when the gawkers gave up who'd been waiting around to see when Consuela would hit Pepita, or at the very least give her one of the verbal tirades she was so famous for, Pepita slowly turned to Consuela, saying, 'My heart is broken.'

"I had no idea that I'd broken her heart," Juan Rodrigo said. "But she told Consuela everything about us. Consuela was, of course, horrified, as her sister was about to marry not only the gravedigger, but a good-for-nothing whore chaser! Still, she kept her head and promised Pepita that she would talk with me.

"And talk with me she did! The very next day, she found me in the bar and threatened to cut my *pistola* off, the same as El Capitán's. I must admit she had my attention. She told me I had to go and straighten things out with Pepita immediately or she would tell Carlota of my indiscretions."

"And did you?"

"Yes, yes, I was not about to lose Carlota again. I'll never forget the way Pepita's house looked. It was a mess. She'd always kept things so neat. There wasn't a cleaner whorehouse in Andalucia! But now, in just a few days, there were clothes and bedsheets strewn about the place, and food everywhere, for Pepita had taken to eating. And that wasn't all. Pepita had not kept herself. Her hair was a mess, her dress rumpled and torn, and worst of all was the vacant look in her eyes. I recognized that look. I knew it well: the look of one who cares no longer for life. I took her in my arms, as she had done with me so many times. How could I not? That's what our relationship had meant to me: a place where we traded despair for the comfort of another's touch. And she was good. Very good. I must admit, I abandoned myself to her passion, and it shook me. She'd made her point. What was I to do?"

"You mean that you realized you loved her?"

"I mean that I realized I had love for her, and that it would not be an easy thing to break away. Maybe that's what Consuela expected. Maybe that's why she sent me there. I knew I was in love with Carlota, but it's difficult to throw away a relationship of seven years. Strangely, it seemed to have the reverse effect on Pepita. Maybe it was the fact that I'd finally given her a gift to ease her pain, instead of the other way around. I don't know. All I know is that she called her girls back from the street and cleaned up her house again. I was relieved that it seemed to all be over. Though Consuela told Carlota of my long-standing affair with Pepita anyway, as I had a feeling she'd do."

"What did Mamá do?" Esperanza asked, sitting under the olive tree, obviously interested, as she had learned even more from her father than she'd expected, more than she'd heard from the ghosts.

"She was upset at first," Juan Rodrigo said, joining his daughter under the olive tree. "But in the end she forgave me. After all, it had happened before she and I were engaged. We were eventually married and Consuela could say nothing more."

"Most of it happened before you were engaged," Esperanza reminded him, "but that last visit was while you *were* engaged."

"Well, yes, but I didn't mention that," Juan Rodrigo replied. "No sense in hurting her."

Esperanza leaned close to her father, smiling. "Just that one time?"

Juan Rodrigo shifted his weight about, as if trying to get comfortable. "Of course, just that one time. What do you take me for?" he demanded.

"You're overreacting, Papá," Esperanza replied. "Now I know you're lying."

Juan Rodrigo stood. "*Eso no puede ser!* No one could know about that. How could you find anything out, even on the other side?"

Esperanza simply stared up at him.

"José Pérez," Juan Rodrigo exclaimed, recalling his dear friend who'd had his own secret affairs. "Now I know what you felt like. *Un bicho malo, eh?* Well, it seems that I'm something worse!"

"Well, Papá?"

Juan Rodrigo turned to his daughter, defeated. "I suppose it's time the truth came out," he said. "Though it pains me to say it, and truth be told, I think I'd forced it from my memory. I could not forget about that last time with Pepita. And Carlota, well, at first your mother was a bit inexperienced in bed." Juan Rodrigo turned to the grave of his wife: "Forgive me, Carlota. I know we both learned how to appreciate each other, and in time there was no better lover than you, but you must admit that at first our adventures in bed were lacking." He returned his attention to Esperanza, who sat in the dirt, smiling. She seemed to find it all quite amusing. "I found Pepita's sudden change of mind distressing and found that for the first few months of my marriage I couldn't get her out of my head. Finally I went to see her. Not to indulge myself, mind you, but just to talk."

"Papá, I'm not a child. It's time you talked straight with me."

Juan Rodrigo again glared at his daughter, attempting to summon his fatherly rage, but he had no stomach for it, and his face instead took on the look of a man who has been beaten. He continued. "At first we did talk. We talked into the night as she poured glass after glass of cognac. I've always been a sucker for cognac. And then, I don't know what happened. It just seemed as if everything was so natural, like we were living five years before and I was on my weekly visit. After we made love, Pepita pulled me to her on the bed, taking my face in her hands. 'That was for us,' she said. 'That was the real thing. It was not a gift from one to the other, but a blessing for all that we've given. Now go to your wife and do not come back here again.' I grabbed my shirt and pants, and with a last look at Pepita lying on her bed, the crucifix above her, I ran out and never returned."

"I think I believe you, Papá," Esperanza said, standing now, moving to her mother's grave. She stood over it, head lowered, staring intently at the earth, as if still trying to discern how her mother looked in life.

"You better believe me," Juan Rodrigo said. "It's the truth!"

"You've finally admitted it," Esperanza said, her gaze remaining on the earth.

"Yes," Juan Rodrigo bellowed. "I suppose I have. And it feels good. But what I don't understand is how did you know. Who told you?"

Esperanza said nothing but kneeled down before the grave. She took a handful of dirt and sifted it through her fingers.

"Carlota!" Juan Rodrigo exclaimed. "Impossible! How could she have known? If she did, she would have never forgiven me."

"She did know, and she did forgive you," Esperanza replied. "And there's one thing more."

Juan Rodrigo sank against the olive tree as if pushed by an unseen force. Rolling his eyes, he said, "What more could there be?"

Esperanza finally turned her attention from the grave. She approached her father, but without the clever smile of hidden knowledge this time. What she had to say would shock her father, and she knew it. "You have a son," she said.

"A what?" Juan Rodrigo's head fell back against the trunk of the tree.

"A son," she repeated. "From Pepita. A boy, named Santi."

"And did Carlota know about this, too? Something that even I didn't know." Juan Rodrigo fought to stand up again. "If it's true at all. I don't believe it!" Now that he'd regained himself, he paced back and forth before the olive tree.

"It's true. But Mamá didn't know. It is something that I know. He is your son, from your last encounter with Pepita." And with that Esperanza smiled. "I always wanted a brother," she said.

"I don't—" Juan Rodrigo tried to speak but couldn't. His pacing no longer easing his agitated nerves; he wandered now about the gravestones, trying to find his way. "What do I do? I know him. I've seen him in the village. He is seventeen now, a grown man."

"I must go now, Papá," Esperanza said, running to her father, hugging him. "But I look forward to more conversations."

"I must admit that I'm not sure I do, not if they're all like this," Juan Rodrigo replied, holding his daughter close. And then she was gone. "Though it was good to see you," he said to the empty air. "It was good to see you."

Juan Rodrigo told Rosalia nothing of Esperanza's visit. Instead, he sat quietly through a lunch of *habichuelas*, thinking. After lunch, Rosalia suggested that they take a walk through the ravine that Esperanza loved to play in so much, but Juan Rodrigo absently waved her suggestion away, saying, "I think I'm going to work outside a bit. The henhouse needs cleaning."

He worked throughout the afternoon but found that he could not concentrate. "I'm sorry, Leti," he said to one of the hens after checking under her for eggs for the third time. "It's that I've come to realize that the truth of my own life is not what I believed." Leti didn't appear to hear him, or if she did, she didn't understand, as she pecked at his hand when he tried to move her back into her nest. If she'd understood, she would have had more sympathy. Juan Rodrigo picked up the shovel, preparing to scoop up the shit that covered the floor of the henhouse. It was only when he found himself sitting on the bench, surrounded by the hens and holding the shovel, the shit still covering the floor, that he decided he would go and see Pepita.

Strangely, her house was not far from the bar where Juan Rodrigo had spent so much time. *Why did I never drop in to see her before? Surely, an old friend deserves that much.* And she was more than that, he thought. As he approached, he found that he was sweating, though it was not hot. What if she refused to see him? What if she didn't acknowledge him as the father? Thoughts and worries swirled inside his head so much that by the time he reached Pepita's door, there were great patches of sweat under each arm, and he wasn't at all sure he would be able to face her.

The girl who answered was scarcely eighteen, though she already had the appearance of a woman in her late twenties. She will not last long, Juan Rodrigo thought. Pepita should send her back where she came from. The girl showed him in, and Juan Rodrigo saw that at least the physical aspect of the place had not changed that much in seventeen years, although there was more artwork lining the walls; the whorehouse had a better collection than any museum in Andalucia! And through the open doors, Juan Rodrigo could see the beds all meticulously made, a crucifix hanging over each one. Pepita sat in a wooden rocker in the corner beside the bar.

"Like a ghost from the past, you return, Juan Rodrigo," Pepita said, her heavy, wrinkled hands shifting the woolen blanket about her legs, her blue polka-dot dress not quite reaching her swollen and blotched ankles.

"You are looking well," Juan Rodrigo said, nodding his head to her and looking about for a chair, as if seeking permission to sit.

"I'm sorry about your daughter," Pepita said, drawing her gray hair into a bun. "She was a fine girl, and beautiful."

"She was the best thing God gave me," Juan Rodrigo replied.

"I thought gravediggers didn't believe in God." She signaled to the girl who'd answered the door, asking her to bring them each a cognac.

Juan Rodrigo smiled. "Oh, we do," he said. "But because we are familiar with his tricks, we are more wary."

With that, Pepita smiled as well. The girl brought the drinks and the two toasted each other silently.

"You are right about children being the greatest gift," Pepita said finally. "They teach us many things. Without them we would be lost."

"And less tired," Juan Rodrigo said, and now they both laughed, and for a moment it seemed as if time had not just stopped but reversed itself, and they were sitting as they used to so long ago. "I joke," Juan Rodrigo continued. "But my Esperanza taught me many things. She is still teaching me."

Pepita raised her eyebrow and took a sip of cognac. "Oh," she said. "And what does your daughter teach you?"

"That I have a son," Juan Rodrigo said, letting his gaze fall on Pepita.

Pepita shifted her blanket about her once more, those great, prunish hands smoothing it over her knees. Silence settled between them as each took another sip. "He is a good man," Pepita said quietly. "He knows how to work hard, but more than that, he treats me well. He treats his own mother well, even when others don't."

"Yes," Juan Rodrigo replied. "I have seen him many times going out of his way for others, but why didn't you tell me?"

"That is not an easy thing to answer."

"I would have cared for him. At least I could have given you money to help out."

"What money?" Pepita's voice rose. "You have always been poor, Juan Rodrigo. It is my fate that I pick the poor ones. You could not have provided anything. You had all you could do to care for your daughter. No. Santi's welfare was my responsibility. I knew that from the moment I felt him growing inside me. Your life and mine ran along separate paths."

Juan Rodrigo gazed at Pepita with renewed respect, though his anger at her for not telling him had not subsided. "There are few women as tough as you," he said. "And few men, for that matter! I simply wish I would have known."

"Well, you do now," Pepita said, and it was her turn to take in the man who sat in front of her and measure if there had been a change in his character. His hair was grayer, his face more lined than the last time she'd seen him, but the nose was just as crooked. "What are you going to do?"

Juan Rodrigo sat back in his chair, looking as if he was just now considering the thought, when in reality he'd been thinking of nothing else since that morning. "I would like to see him," he said at last.

"Yes," Pepita replied. "But what then?"

"I will tell him that I am his father, and I will care for him," Juan Rodrigo said. "I will get him a job at the bar, maybe teach him the trade of digging graves." He stopped, catching himself. Would he teach him that trade, when he, himself, had sworn to quit so many times? "I don't know what I'll do, but I am the boy's father. He should know that."

"Should he?" Pepita replied.

"What do you mean?"

"I mean that Santi is young, and that he is tempestuous like all men his age. If you tell him now," she went on, "at a time when he is trying to establish himself as his own man, he will only hate you."

"That's when a boy needs a father," Juan Rodrigo replied. "To model himself after."

"Santi has grown up without that model. He is used to it."

"Are you saying I'm a bad model, Pepita?"

"No," she replied. "Only that having a father now would confuse him. He is doing well. If you come into his life now, he'll resent the fact that you weren't there for him. But if he becomes his own man, then he will have something to be proud of, not something to be ashamed of, when he meets his father. And that pride will help him to accept you, in time."

"At least let me get him a job at the bar," Juan Rodrigo said.

"He has a good job at the mill," Pepita replied. "He is a strong boy, Juan Rodrigo. Trust in him."

Juan Rodrigo took a last sip of cognac, feeling as if he'd lost yet another child in the space of one short week. "How will I know when it's time?" he asked at last.

"You will know."

"You are a strange woman, Pepita," Juan Rodrigo said, smiling.

"And you are a strange man—at least that's what people say!"

They sat together sipping their cognac. Finally, Juan Rodrigo rose from his chair and bent to kiss Pepita on the forehead, but at the last second she turned her face to him and kissed him on the lips. "Careful," she said. "I'm still the best there is."

"Of that I have no doubt." Juan Rodrigo smiled. But before leaving, he turned to Pepita once again. "It was good to see you," he said. "Let us not be strangers again."

"I'm too old to take you in my bed," Pepita replied. "And besides, you have another woman now."

"I'm not talking about *that*, woman!" Juan Rodrigo exclaimed.

"I know," she said, her face betraying nothing.

Yes, it had been good to see Pepita again, he thought. It's a mistake to let so many years pass without seeing a friend. But his heart was still sore at the loss of a son he'd never known. And on the way home that evening, he spent much time imagining what his life would have been like with Esperanza and Santi. They would have got on well, he thought. And then the thought that nearly stopped his heart: Maybe if Santi had been there, none of this with Esperanza would have happened.

THAT NIGHT, while sitting on the porch, he told Rosalia about the missing pieces of his life. She listened quietly, not saying a word, until he told her about his visit to Pepita that day. Then she nestled her head on Juan Rodrigo's shoulder, taking his hand in hers, and said, "Pepita is a wise woman. But though you may not be able to be his father, I don't see why you can't be his friend." Juan Rodrigo squeezed her hand in his, for she had found a way to ease his heart.

"But I am an old man," he said. "What would he see in me?"

"Just that, an old man," Rosalia replied. "But at least you are a funny one, and a dirty one at that. You could teach him to swear."

"Rosalia, *me cago en la* . . ."

"Any young man could benefit from your tutelage in the art of the curse!"

11

La vida es un soplo

THE NEXT DAY, Juan Rodrigo went to the cemetery to tell Esperanza of his visit to Pepita, but instead of his daughter waiting there for him under the shade of the olive tree, he found Antonio. The gypsy boy had visited her every day, watering and caring for the green flower that now grew from atop her grave. It was a single flower with many blooms, like an azalea, but green all over, with only the slightest hint of yellow coming from the stamens inside. Juan Rodrigo stood in wonder at how the flower could have grown so fast.

"I could have sworn it was not there yesterday," he said.

"Oh, but it was. It just took a trained eye to see it," Antonio answered.

"Is this some sort of gypsy magic?" Juan Rodrigo asked as he sat down beside the boy.

"It is a type of magic, perhaps, but it is not gypsy, though the gypsies have long known about the beauty of the green flower."

To Juan Rodrigo, Antonio seemed much older than he had before, no longer a boy. "What will you do now?" he asked, echoing the question his daughter had asked him five days before.

"I'm leaving this place," Antonio replied, his voice firm. And Juan Rodrigo understood that he meant it. "I'm going to the city to make my fortune. I do not want to be in the country anymore."

"Do you think you'll make it amongst the *payos?*"

"I can work as hard as any other," he said. "I'm just as good."

"I believe that," Juan Rodrigo said, holding the gaze of the boy in his own.

"And you?" the boy asked.

Juan Rodrigo thought for a moment, then smiled, because he had an answer where before he had none, and that is something, he thought. That is something. "I'll remain here where I belong."

"Nothing holds you here," the boy said. "Why do you stay when all that you have here is pain?"

Juan Rodrigo winced a bit at the remark. There was truth in it. Yet he would stay, he felt sure of it. "Like you, I always thought I would leave this place," he said. "Only I never did. It used to eat at me, make me bitter. But today I think I am part of this place. I no longer want to leave."

"That is good," said the boy.

"Tell me," Juan Rodrigo said. "Do you think that a boy your age can be friends with an old man?"

"I don't see why not," Antonio responded. "We are, and you're not even a lover of gypsies."

Juan Rodrigo laughed at that, slapping the boy on the back. "I must admit, you are changing my mind in that regard!"

The two of them sat together on the hilltop the remainder of the day, Antonio talking more of his plans, and Juan Rodrigo giving advice when he could. When they parted, they knew it was for the last time.

Juan Rodrigo continued to visit the cemetery each evening, caring for the green flower, telling it stories just as he'd done with Esperanza each night at her bedside. Esperanza kept her promise and did visit her father from time to time, and the tales she told him of life in the other world pleased him. They spent many nights together on the hilltop under the stars trying to top each other in their storytelling art. Juan Rodrigo often complained, as he'd done with El Romancero, that her stories were too fanciful, that they didn't get at the truth. But, as always, she was ready for his arguments, pointing out the fabrications in his own life story and reminding him that truth was different in her world, that magic and fancies existed there side by side with reality. And how could he argue with her?

Occasionally, Rosalia joined them on the hilltop. In many ways, they existed much as they had before: Esperanza coming and going at will; Juan Rodrigo complaining about his work, his health, and eventually about his age; and Rosalia warming his heart with her humor and his stomach with her cooking. Esperanza smiled as she watched them together. If her father had known a year ago what would befall them, he would never have believed it, calling it gypsy magic and the work of *el diablo*. But here they were, a small band of gypsies existing upon the bridge between both worlds. Yes, the way she saw it, there was little difference between her family and the gypsies; they both understood the marriage between the living and the dead, the bond between the invisible and the known, and the affinity the light has for the dark.

Juan Rodrigo made it a habit of stopping by the mill each day, at first pretending that he had business there, negotiating the price of flour for Pedro at the bar. He asked for Santi personally, saying that he was known as an honest man. And Santi came out of the mill, confident, and pleased with himself, as he'd been told of Juan Rodrigo's comment. He was a tall boy and skinny for his age, yet he worked harder than anyone at the mill. Juan Rodrigo could see that. Pepita was right. The boy worked as though he had something to prove, and he would not rest until he proved it all by himself. Juan Rodrigo went to the mill day after day, and soon he found that Santi approached him to talk. And Juan Rodrigo listened. He listened as he'd not done with his daughter, for he had at least learned that lesson. He listened to Santi talk of his hopes to run the mill himself someday, and he offered advice when he could, though he was careful not to say too much.

Over the years, they met at Pedro's bar, where Santi would buy Juan Rodrigo a drink and tell him of his progress at the mill, or of his hopes to win the heart of one woman or another. Then, one night, Santi arrived with one of those women on his arm and Juan Rodrigo knew that the boy would not need him any longer, at least not in the same way.

"Juan Rodrigo," Santi said. "I'd like you to meet Miranda. She and I are to be married."

And Juan Rodrigo smiled, taking her hand in his, then whispering in her ear that Santi was like a son to him, and so she would be like a daughter. He held her hand in his, not wanting to let go, until, embarrassed by the wetness in his eyes, he made a joke about the emotions of old men. "They become like women," he said. "And women, they become like burros!" Then he bought not only each of them a drink, but a drink for everyone in the bar, and he and his old friend Pedro sat in the back room, as they'd done so often in the past, and talked of how life seems to pass by like a puff of air.

Time passed and Juan Rodrigo longed to leave this world and join his daughter. "I have given what I could," he said to Rosalia. "Who else would spend their lives digging graves in this tiny village in the middle of nowhere? I have told many stories, and I'm tired. Certainly, I've done my part." Rosalia grew upset whenever he talked of it, but she knew the day was coming.

"Just promise me one thing, Rosalia," he said.

"What is it, my love?"

"Promise me . . ." And here he paused, savoring the moment. "Promise me that you will not pee on my grave!"

"Juan Rodrigo!" Rosalia exclaimed, hitting him in the shoulder, as she'd grown accustomed to do. "If you die, I'll not only pee on it, but I'll shit on it as well!"

Still, he was weary—she could see it, and though he'd remained many years in the village since his daughter's death, he was ready to move on. His cough had gotten worse; blood often stained his handkerchief. And, slowly, Rosalia resigned herself to the fact that she would spend the last years of her life alone. My lot will not be so different from that of many women, she thought.

ON THE DAY JUAN RODRIGO DIED, his friend Enrique dug the grave. They placed him alongside his wife and daughter. "You would certainly come back and haunt me if I tried to tell a story like you," Enrique said as he dug into the earth. So, instead, Rosalia, Pedro, and Enrique took turns telling stories around the grave of their friend. And as the friends told stories on into the night, they half expected to see Juan Rodrigo return, walking up the path that led from his house to the cemetery in order to correct them in one aspect or other of their tale. Once, Pedro swore he saw Juan Rodrigo's crooked nose sticking out from behind the olive tree as he watched them. But the others saw nothing and joked with Pedro about his failing eyesight and poor imagination.

It was Antonio who saw the spirit of Juan Rodrigo rise into the sky like a great black bird as he watched from the balcony of his apartment in the city, where he stood smoking a cigarette and planning out how he would make his fortune. He saw the bird rising above the mountains of the Sierra de la Contraviesa, oaring the air with its immense wings. He watched as the bird circled, perhaps looking for a draft, perhaps in the end unsure about leaving the village where it had lived for so long. And he smiled as he saw the bird finally veer south, heading out over the sea.

Antonio sang the ancient song of the gypsies, slowly at first, and so quiet that not even the cats searching the garbage in the abandoned lot below could hear. But then, as he perceived the majesty of the great bird flying over him, he wailed: a cry of both astonishment and despair. And soon the ululation transformed itself into a sort of incantation. The cats turned from their garbage and gazed to the balcony above to see what sort of creature created such a sound. *The black bird has taken flight. And only the gypsies understand. The end of the world is near, for how can we exist without the other? How can we see without the invisible? Feel without the untouched? And it is only the gypsies who know this.* . . . The cats scattered at this last part, as the voice they heard was both angry and sad, and they wanted nothing of that. But though there was now no one to hear, the voice continued, *Let the beauty of the green flower unite the known and the unknown, let its fragrance surround the world and make it whole.* For though the gypsies see themselves as a doomed people, their voices are full of hope.

Acknowledgments

First of all, I would like to thank my teachers, without whom this book could not have been written.

Thank you to my parents and my sister, Julie, for their constant love and support. Thank you also to Abuelos Jesús Lopez Manrubia and María Faura Pérez, Esperanza Lopez Faura, Roger Wilson, Tito Paco, and Tita Sofia for their inspiration. Profound thanks to my agents, Ray-Güde Mertin and Nicole Witt, and to my editors, Jay Schaefer and Micaela Heekin, at Chronicle Books.

Thank you to the Clayton Brothers for art that continually moves me and to the incomparable voice of Juanito Valderrama, whose version of *La hija de Juan Simon* inspired this novel. Thanks also to all my friends in the Bennington and University of Denver writing programs.

Special thanks to C. Michael Curtis, Jill McCorkle, and Askold Melnyczuk for a faith that sustained me when I didn't believe.

Finally, my undying gratitude to Elizabeth Cox for her ability to see where others can't, Irene Vilar for her generous spirit, and my brother, Daniel Grandbois, for leading the way as always.